LOVE CROAKIES

SAM CHEEVER

ELECTRIC PROSE PUBLICATIONS

HEARTS AND HERESY

Never let it be said that I have a thing against heart-shaped stuff. Goddess knew I was currently surrounded by it.

Heart-shaped cutouts hung from nearly every surface above navel height throughout Croakies bookstore. Heart-shaped doilies dotted every flat surface.

Heart-shaped candies enclosed in heart-shaped tins and wrapped in heart-colored foil filled a heart-shaped wicker basket on the sales counter.

Heart-shaped cookies, sans frosting since I'd sworn off frosted cookies after our ill-fated Christmas fiasco, were displayed on a heart-shaped platter with a pink paper heart taped to it proclaiming, "Snarf to your heart's desire!"

And, right at that moment, a heart-shaped face, peering at me with heart-felt emotion brimming in eyes that reflected a heartbreaking level of devastation from my lack of hearty despair for her heartfelt disappointment.

"But you advertised that 'Hearts of Bomb' would be available today," The cupid's bow lips said. The heartsick client shook her head, her stick-straight mop of Valentine-colored hair swinging back and forth to reflect her disgust. "You promised."

I opened my mouth to tell Holly Heartsick that the shipment of books had been delayed, risking another accusation of bookseller heartlessness. Thankfully, the heart-rending announcement was waylaid by the arrival of my own personal Valerie Valentine.

Sebille's naturally heart-colored hair was plaited into two waist-length braids on either side of her long, freckled face. She wore a matching red dress dotted with white hearts and pink and white striped socks that covered her knees beneath the calf-length dress. Her usual Wicked Witch of the West shoes were the perfect complement to the bad dress and ugly stockings.

By contrast, I wore a plain white shirt, worn blue jeans and white sneakers. My below-shoulder-length brown hair was straight and my dark blue eyes were wary. Valentine's Day wasn't my favorite holiday. Yeah, I know what you're thinking. I don't seem to like any holidays. That wasn't true. Exactly. I just haven't found the one I like yet.

The sprite surged energetically into the bookstore, her sticklike arms wrapped around a plain brown box marked all over with heart-shaped stickers. "They're here!" Her iridescent green eyes flashing, she grinned at my excited customer, who was currently hopping around and clapping her hands with wholehearted, heartfelt glee.

My shoulders slumped with relief. I grabbed a frosting-free sugar cookie, pink sparkles glittering from its pale surface, and jammed it into my mouth, wishing I had tea to go with it. Sebille settled the box on the table and opened it, pulling out a glossy paperback whose cover was a study in...you guessed it...pinks and red hearts.

Sebille plucked a copy of 'Hearts of Bomb' from the box and offered it to my merrily cackling client.

"Yay! I can't believe it's here," Holly Heartface enthused as she did a little happy dance.

I rolled my eyes for two very good reasons.

Number one, though I loved books, and made half...okay a third...all right, a tenth...of my living with the sale of them, I couldn't imagine becoming so enamored of one that my world literally ended if I couldn't get my hands on it.

And two, unlike my heart-eyed customers, I knew the author of the book personally and was finding it exceedingly difficult picturing my Uncle Archibald Pudsnecker, a.k.a. Ben E. Nigma, as the type to write a cozy murder mystery with a cutesy name meant to bring to mind a stalky vegetable. Especially since the book that was currently all the rage with my customers was only his second. Pudsy's first food cozy, "Banana Scream Pie", had taken the mystery world by storm, selling out its first modest print run and earning two additional runs by the time the new book was released. This was no small feat for a guy whose previous works had included the riveting treatise, "Spatial Voids Around the World" and "The Argument For Embracing The Abyss".

Sebille and her new best friend shoved me out of the way and I all but ran away from the counter, leaving them to it.

In a desperate move I knew I'd regret later, I shoved another cookie into my mouth. I was going to gain ten pounds before the current Valentine's Day book massacre ended.

"Thanks so much for coming!"

I jerked around at the pleasant, happy sound of Sebille's voice and caught her waving gaily at her heart-faced bestie as the woman headed out of Croakies with a tin of candies in one hand and her new book in the other.

The door opened again and three women, all old enough to know better, bounced inside to the sound of the jangling doorbell. The oldest and tallest of the threesome set her bright, expectant gaze on me.

"Please tell me you have Hearts of Bomb in the store?"

I swung an arm toward the box. "Just came in. Help yourselves."

My dour mood didn't seem to have any effect on their excitement. The gaggle of giggling women descended on the box like a school of piranha and extracted whole handfuls of the books.

Finally, my shopkeeper mojo kicked in. "Only one per person," I told them. My Valentine's Day crankiness earned me a trio of scowls, but I yanked the box off the table and held it out for them to replace their extras.

I'd like to say that I was trying to make sure every single one of Uncle Pudsy's adoring fans got a copy of his latest book, but really, I just didn't want to face another rabid reader with the bad news that we were out of stock. Again.

Sebille happily made the three sales, doling out candy tins with every purchase, and then sighed with unnatural contentment as the three women left in a dither of excitement. She turned to me and her smile wilted like raw spinach in a hot frying pan. "What's wrong with you, Dour Dana?"

I started arranging the books atop the table in a happy display of pink and red hearts, my lips curling. "Not a thing, Valentina. Why are you so blasted happy?"

Sebille shrugged, her thin lips curving in an irrepressible smile. "Nothing. I just like Valentine's Day."

I looked agape at my usually morose and unhelpful assistant. "Why? You realize it's a totally made-up holiday, right? It's a retail holiday, created just for selling stuff."

"Apparently you haven't noticed this is a retail establishment?"

I slammed a paperback down on the table with excessive force.

Sebille came over, a half-eaten cookie in her hand and vanilla crumbs painting the corners of her lips. "Still no word from Grym, huh?"

I grimaced and didn't respond. My fight with the prickly detective was not a subject I wanted to discuss.

With anyone.

Sebille nodded. "Okay, don't tell me. I'll just guess."

Realizing that letting the sprite's imagination run wild over the bumps in the road of my love life was a recipe for disaster, I sighed. "He's about as malleable as a..." The thought slid away from my brain and turned to mist. I'd been having trouble holding a cogent thought all day. I blamed the copious amounts of sugar I'd eaten. I'd gorged on two heart-shaped jelly donuts for breakfast, a heart-shaped red velvet cupcake for lunch, two tins of heart-shaped candy, and three of the sugar cookies.

I was mood eating. And, I was in dire need of some of the stalky inspiration from Pudsy's cozy. Or anything even remotely resembling a vegetable.

"As malleable as a boulder?" Sebille finished for me, snickering. "Granite?" Her snickers turned to guffaws. "A mountain?" She bent double, happy tears pouring from her iridescent green gaze.

I was not amused. "Gargoyle humor. Har," I said, glaring.

The dividing door opened between the bookstore and the artifact library at the back of the store. A blur of pale pink and white shot into the store and skidded to a stop right in front of me. For a blip, the air around the creature looking up at me with oversized blue eyes was striped with cartoon-like contrails from his superfast arrival. Then the glowy lines on the air sifted away into nothingness.

I narrowed my gaze on Hobs, my resident hobgoblin. "Are you wearing a diaper?"

He laughed, happily bouncing on his oversized toes. "Miss Sebille made it for me. Do you like it?"

My still-narrowed gaze slid to the matching, heart-shaped spots of pale red highlighting his cheeks and then to the tiny bow in his hand. "Please tell me you're not supposed to be playing Cupid?"

Hobs cocked his head, looking confused. "I'm not supposed to be playing Cupid?" His high-pitched voice was filled with a question.

I sighed and threw a glower Sebille's way.

"What?" she objected. "Customers will love him."

My eyes went wide. "We can't..."

The dividing door slammed back on its hinges and Mr. Wicked skulked through, his dark orange gaze wide as he hit my calf with a manic, "Yeow!"

"Hey, buddy," I said, bending to scoop him into my arms. I buried my face in his fur and sucked a snout full of something small and irritating.

Sneezing violently several times, I nearly dropped my cat. I sniffled, glancing at my hands. They sparkled. "What is in your fur?" I asked him.

Wicked swished his tail. Hard. A tiny growl slid from his throat.

He was all sparkly. Pink sparkly! "Sebille!"

She rolled her eyes. "Uncoil your granny panties," she said. "He's fine."

I sneezed again, placing him on the floor. "You're killing me with this Valentine's stuff. What other surprises do you have for me?"

She flipped a dismissive hand. "I'll make tea. Maybe that will calm you down."

"Ribbit!"

I looked down at the fat, green squish on the floor by my feet.

He blinked up at me, his eyes blank pools of black, like miniature Pudsy voids.

Horror slid up my spine. "What...?"

Get it off me! screamed the irate frog in my mind. *Now!*

Enormous pink lips protruded from the frog's sparkly green face. "Oh, Slimy," I said in a commiserating tone. "I can't believe she did this to you." I crouched down and tugged at the lips, expecting them to be made of paper or wax. Instead, realistic-feeling flesh, plumped and puckered, resisted my tugging. I jerked my hand away, straightening on a squeal. "They're real!" I rounded on the Sprite, who quickly turned away from me when I tried to catch her eye. "I can't believe you gave him puckery lips! Have you lost your mind?"

She hid a grin behind her hand. "Don't you get the joke? Kiss the frog, get a prince? Come on," she said as steam wafted from my ears. "Customers are going to love it."

"Ribbit!" Slimy proclaimed indignantly.

I pointed a shaky finger toward the quivering frog. "Fix. Him."

Sebille gave me a long-suffering sigh and threw a pale green jet of magic toward the frog. The big, puckery lips disappeared with a pop.

Slimy gave the sprite one last indignant, "Ribbit!" and then hopped underneath the nearest bookshelf to work on regaining his self-respect.

"You've lost your mind, sprite," I told her, madder than I'd ever been. Well...in the last week anyway. "What's going on with you?"

Amazingly, she gave me a secret smile and headed for the door. "I'm taking my break."

I felt my eyes go wide. "What? You can't take a break. You just got here."

She shrugged and slipped through the door, leaving me with one delighted Cupid who I couldn't let anybody see, a traumatized frog, and a seriously annoyed cat.

I sagged. Could the day get any worse?

Proving that it could, the front door bell jangled and I steeled myself for more shrieking Ben E. Nigma fans. Instead, I found myself looking into a handsome, craggy face and an intense dark caramel gaze. "Oh," I said, my wit firmly intact.

"Hello, Naida," said Detective Wise Grym, a.k.a. my maybe-boyfriend.

2

PINK PUCKERY LIPS

Grym and I stared at each other for a long moment, awkwardness like a cloud between us. After several beats of taut silence, a loud crunching tugged my gaze toward the floor beside me. The pink-faced hobgoblin wearing a diaper had both long-fingered hands full of cookies, and his mouth was so full that crumbs trickled from between his lips as he chewed, forming a small pile at his feet.

Grym blinked. "Why is Hobs wearing a diaper?"

I expelled enough air to fill a dirigible and shook my head. "Ask the sprite. She seems to think we can't sell any books without putting on a Valentine's Day circus."

Grym shifted from one foot to the other, looking sheepish for unknown reasons. That was when I realized he held one hand behind his back.

"What are you holding there?" I asked, hope flaring to life in my breast. Maybe he was ready to apologize for telling me he thought we should keep our relationship a secret...just for now...with a fat bouquet of roses. Or, even better, a box of choco-lates. Anticipation put a gleam in my eye and made my mouth water. After all, I hadn't eaten anything sweet in forever. If forever could be described as "in the last three minutes."

He shuffled again and exhaled loudly, adding air to the blimp hanging metaphorically between us. He brought his hand out from behind his back, showing me its contents.

Hope crashed at my feet as I recognized the heart-drenched cover of Ben E. Nigma's over-hyped book, Hearts of Bomb. "You brought me a book? You do know I own a bookstore, right?"

He frowned. "Sebille told me Pudsy was coming to the store to sign books today. I was hoping to grab a spot at the front of the line."

I was aghast. Flummoxed. Flabbergasted. Not only did Grym finally come back without bearing apologies or gifts, but he'd come to Croakies with a book that had clearly been purchased from a competitor. "Did you buy that from Frugal Freddy's over by the mall?"

He winced. "I didn't think you'd welcome my business."

My eyes vibrated with a desire to roll. I jammed

my hands on my hips and glared at him. "But you thought I'd be happy to have you buy it at my competitor's and then use Croakies to get it signed?"

He didn't wince again, but his face flushed to a nice...yes...heart color. "I guess I didn't think."

I shook my head, fighting to regain my good humor. Even though it would be a miracle if I did since I'd lost it somewhere around a month ago and hadn't seen hide nor hair of it since.

I knew I was cranky.

Okay, I'd left cranky behind twenty-nine and a half days ago, buried so deep beneath a wave of irritation that it would take the entire crew of Raiders of the Misplaced Aardvark to find it. But I gave it the old Keeper of the Artifacts try anyway. I sighed. "Look, this is the first I've heard of a signing." It was highly possible there was one scheduled. After all, why would I, the owner of the bookstore and the niece of the author need to know such a thing? Don't be silly. It wasn't as if I had any say at all in how my store was run. I mean, my cat had sparkles, my frog had puckery lips, my hobgoblin was rocking a diaper and shooting toothpicks into the cookies on the platter with his bow.

"Hobs! Stop that. Leave the cookies alone."

He shrugged and headed into the library to see what other trouble he could get up to.

On top of everything, my almost, possibly-already-ex-boyfriend had cheated on me with Frugal Freddy.

That last part was beyond galling.

"What does Frugal Freddy have that I don't?" I blurted before I could stop myself.

Grym's heart-red cheeks flared brighter. "He's not mad at me."

That stopped me in my verbal tracks. "Oh. Okay." That made sense.

Grym looked disappointed, as if he'd expected me to deny it.

Uh, no.

"Are you ever going to forgive me?" Grym asked, his manner sliding along the scale from mortification to pique, nudging perturbed.

I thought about that for a minute. The minute stretched uncomfortably between us, turning to two and then three minutes.

Grym's broad shoulders rounded. "Got it. I'll just get out of here then."

Watching him head to the door, I chewed the inside of my cheek. I'd been waiting for Grym to apologize to me, but he clearly expected me to do the apologizing. Our fight actually had been a tiny bit my fault.

Okay, maybe ten percent my fault.

Twenty.

I'll go forty-five, but that was as far as my pride would let me go.

Dangit!

Well, that was awkward. Le sigh... "Grym, wait."

He turned back, one large, square hand clasping the doorknob. His eyes were cold, his expression stony. "Yep?"

I opened my mouth to try to break the ice between us.

A horrific jangling sound basted through Croakies. A red light of unknown origin flashed through the room, bathing everything in a Valentine-ish hue.

Trouble!

"Is that..." Grym started to ask.

"Yes." My eyes went wide, and my gaze swung to Grym. "Lock the door!" Without waiting to make sure he did as I asked, I took off running toward the artifact library.

Sebille joined me in the center aisle as I ran. I spared her a quick glance, shouting to be heard over the jangling warning bell. "What's going on?"

She shrugged. "I haven't seen anything."

Grym's heavy footsteps pounded up behind us. "Toxic Magic Vault?"

I shot him a look, frowning. "Hang back a little, in case whoever it is gets past us."

He nodded and slowed, his big body nearly blocking the aisle.

I glanced at Sebille and she nodded, popping to sprite size and buzzing higher for a bird's eye view.

Without warning, the jangling bell shut off, and the resulting silence was shocking. I skidded to a stop twenty feet away from the vault, my gaze widening at the sight.

The door was open, the light of the protective ward flashing through the space like a silent beacon. The pulsing light painted the mess inside the vault with an amber glow.

Behind me, Grym swore softly. "Can you tell what's gone?"

I grimaced, moving slowly toward the breeched vault. The secondary ward, the one that protected the vault while Sebille or I had the door open, had fallen, its remnants glowing a soft green along the floor where it was anchored.

The floor inside the vault was covered in debris, the detritus of what were powerful and dangerous magical artifacts spread across the dusty concrete floor.

The magic mirror lay on its back in front of the shelf where it had been stored, the wooden frame intact but the glass shattered into a million pieces around it. The old Black and White television stood where we'd left it, but its screen was also shattered. The theme song from the Andrew of Mayberry shows a soft echo of its death.

The other items I'd placed there had been swept off the shelves and lay in a tangled and broken pile on the floor.

I didn't go inside. The magical artifacts were no doubt leaking their poisons into the air of the vault. I'd have to get a toxic magic cleanup crew into the vault to verify its safety before we entered.

Pale green energy flashed as Sebille buzzed down to hover beside me. Her brightly hued dragonfly wings painted the air in a rainbow mix of purple and green as she hovered, the green glow of her eyes fierce as a result of what she saw in the vault. "Goddess in garters, what a mess."

I expelled air in agreement.

Grym came up beside me. "Can you tell if anything's gone?"

I shook my head. "Not until we dig around in the mess and take inventory."

"I'll help," he said, his tone deliberately upbeat, probably to offset the slow sinking of my body toward the ground.

I forced my legs and shoulders straight. "Do you know a toxic magic cleanup company we can call?"

To my surprise, he nodded. "I have people." He pulled out his phone. "I'll get them here right away."

Gratitude made me smile, despite our recent tiff. "Thanks, Grym."

He nodded, but he was already speaking into the phone, moving away from me.

Sebille was strangely silent. I glanced her way and saw that she looked more perplexed than concerned by the mess. "Can you read a magic signature?"

It took her a few beats to answer, and when she did, her tone was distracted. "I'm not sure."

"Not sure? Could the signature have been affected by the toxic magic?"

She blinked, her face clearing. "That actually would explain…"

When she didn't complete her thought, I asked, "Explain what?"

"They'll be here in twenty minutes," Grym told us, striding back down the aisle. "I told them to come around to the back. Do you want me to go meet them?"

"Yes. If you don't mind. Sebille and I need to stay here to keep an eye on things until they get here."

He nodded and spun on his heel, moving briskly away from us.

Sebille and I spent a too-long beat staring after him before we both blinked ourselves out of our perusal. We shared an embarrassed laugh.

Flushing softly, Sebille waggled her brows. "He looks as good going as he does coming."

I couldn't argue the point. So I didn't. "Finish your sentence. It would explain what?"

"It's too weird. It has to be wrong."

"But worth mentioning," I told her in a firm tone. Something very strange had happened in my artifact library, and I needed to know what.

"Aside from the usual signatures of the people who live here. There was something else." She frowned. "The best way I can describe it is Love."

I blinked in surprise. "Huh?" The sprite had definitely bought her own Valentine's Day promotions.

She popped into full size and put her hands out, palms up. "See? I told you it doesn't make sense."

Eyeing the destruction in the vault, I had to agree. "That doesn't look like love to me."

"No," Sebille agreed. "It doesn't."

After a moment of trying to come up with a reasonable explanation for that dichotomy and failing, I shook it off and tackled a different problem. "Any idea who or what could have destroyed the wards like that?"

"Not who," she responded. "But what...there is something that could have done this. Though, I thought the ogres had destroyed it."

"Ogres?" I felt my eyes go wide. "What ogres?"

Sebille grinned widely. "Oh, that's right, you haven't met the ogres." She clapped her hands. "Fun!" She spun on her heels and hurried back down the aisle, her heels smacking smartly against the concrete with every step.

"Wait! Where are you going?"

"To speak to my mother," she called over her shoulder. "She'll get us an invitation to visit King Rhorr."

My gaze narrowing on her retreating form, I

couldn't shake the feeling that I wasn't going to enjoy my visit to the ogres. I had nothing to base that feeling on, except my assistant's glee at introducing me to them.

The sprite's glee was never good for my health and happiness.

On the flip side, I doubted the ogres celebrated Valentine's Day. That meant, even if only for a brief time, I'd get a respite from the overdone and obnoxious Valentine's Day décor. I was already heartily sick of it.

G rym and I stood back and watched the two men work. I'd never formally met the Phoenix shifter who was currently performing a controlled burn to extinguish any lingering strains of toxic magic in the vault and around the open door. But he *had* saved my life once. I'd since learned his name was Brad Spence. I'd also learned the soft-spoken fireman...yeah, I see the irony of a Phoenix shifter becoming a fireman...had a soft Southern drawl, warm golden-brown eyes, fiery red hair to rival Sebille's, and a fondness for red hot candies. No surprise there.

Towering over Brad's stocky five-foot-eleven inch build was Abe something or other. I hadn't caught his name. Abe's magic was undetermined. I thought he might actually be a witch of some kind, but nobody explained it to me.

"What exactly is Abe doing?" I asked Grym.

"Reconditioning the air after the toxins are gone."

I nodded, then couldn't help asking. "Why?"

Grym gave me a smile that made the toes inside my sneakers curl. "Think of Abe as a magical crime scene cleaner. He detoxifies, cleans, brightens, and just generally refreshes and returns the scene back to normal."

I eyed the broken bits of dangerous artifacts inside the vault. My gaze narrowed as it fell on the black and white television. "Does that demon TV look less damaged to you?"

Grym nodded. "Unfortunately."

"Is Abe doing that? Because if he is, I'd like him to stop. None of the things in this vault need to be in working order. In fact, it would be best if they weren't."

"He's not doing it." Grym looked at me. "You should know by now that things always balance out in the magic world, Naida."

"I do, but when something in the library breaks, it usually stays broken unless someone repairs it."

He shook his head. "Non-toxic magic doesn't need to change form to create balance. It exists within a balanced environment that isn't affected by the form the artifacts take. If the magic escapes from a normal object, it's simply absorbed into the universe and will be used in another way."

My eyes went wide. "Are you telling me the toxic magic from these objects will be absorbed into the universe?"

"I'm telling you that's what happens with *normal* magic items. But toxic magic degrades and destroys. The natural world abhors toxic magic. It repulses and tries to expel dark magic."

"So it's not absorbed?" I asked, just to make sure I understood.

"Not absorbed. With nowhere else to go, the toxins put themselves to work rebuilding their own magical identities."

I eyed the magic mirror, which was back on its shelf and covered with the cloth again. I wondered who had put it there.

The sound of someone hurrying toward us had me turning.

Sebille nearly skipped in our direction. She wore a wide smile and held a page of some kind of paper in her hand, waving it at me. "I got it! I got our invitation."

I sighed. "I'm pretty sure I'm not going to enjoy this."

"Enjoy what?" Grym asked, his dark brows lowering with concern.

"Sebille thinks the ogres might know how the vault was opened."

He stared at me for a long moment and then his lips twitched. "Oh. Yikes. You're going to see the ogres?"

I lost control of my calm. Grabbing one of his big hands, I squeezed it hard while imploring him with my pleading gaze. "What? Tell me why everybody keeps smiling about me meeting the ogres. You're scaring me."

Grym let the smile turn into a laugh and then, leaning down, kissed me on the tip of my nose. "Give me a call when you get back. Just to...you know...let me know you're okay."

He strode down the aisle, looking like he'd just won the lottery. As he and Sebille passed in the narrow aisle, he put one blocky hand into the air and slapped her high five.

I stood there quivering in my sneakers.

They'd bonded over the horror of what was about to happen to me.

This could not be good.

3

ALL IS NOT WHAT IT SEEMS

"I really should be doing inventory on those artifacts," I said again, knowing my feeble protests were going to be ignored like a puff of powder in a wintery snowscape.

"They'll still be there when we get back," the sprite said.

"But, I'm not sure the new ward will hold."

Sebille sent me a blustery look. "I personally rebuilt the ward. Are you saying you don't think I know what I'm doing?"

Alarm swept through me. The last thing I wanted to do was hack off the sprite when she had my very life clutched in her knobby-knuckled fingers. "Of course not. I didn't say that. Did I say that?"

"Sounded like," she responded, her good mood returning.

Crickets on a crab! She was planning my demise. I just knew it. But why had Grym gone along with the outing? Yeah, we'd had a little spat. But we'd had those before. Would he really want me squashed beneath an ogre for revenge?

"...find the thief."

I realized Sebille had been blathering on while I was panicking. I'd probably missed something important. "Huh? What thief?"

Sebille rolled her iridescent green orbs at me. "You really need to learn to pay attention, Naida."

I bit down on my tongue to keep it from shooting out between my lips and branding me a five-year-old in an almost 25-year-old woman's body. Instead, I tucked a strand of my long brown hair behind one ear, fixing a hostile blue gaze on my assistant. "I have a lot on my mind."

"Mm-hm. Try to stay with me now. We need to find out who broke through the vault's wards and how they did it. This trip to the ogres is the first step in that process."

"I get that we're focusing on the *how*. But I'm just as worried about *why* they broke in."

She looked thoughtful for a moment, as if she was actually considering my argument. Then she flipped a hand in dismissal. "One thing at a time, Naida," she said, mind firmly closed.

I sighed. Sure, I could pull rank on her and return to Croakies. But part of me knew she was right. If someone had an artifact that could break into the toxic magic vault, nothing...no one...would be safe.

"Tell me what I'm about to walk into," I demanded in my most authoritative voice.

Sebille snorted. "You'll see."

Bat blisters! I was really going to regret the current excursion into ogreville. I just knew it. I tugged out my phone and hit the button to call Grym.

He answered on the second ring. "Are you there yet?"

I pulled my phone away from my ear and frowned at it. "Am I where?"

His voice wobbled suspiciously as he responded. "Did you meet the ogres?"

I never got a chance to respond. In a single beat of my heart, three things happened almost simultaneously.

One, something massive slammed into me from the right, my body sinking into it like the softest down pillow and my nose overwhelmed with the scent of flowers.

Two, my traitorous assistant popped into sprite form and shot skyward, presumably to avoid the third thing that happened.

Another pillowy attack slammed into me from the left, squishing me between the two sweet-scented bodies with only my eyes, nose, mouth, and hands free. My hands were plastered together in front of me, my cell still clutched between them.

I could hear Grym's voice like a distant life line I couldn't reach.

The dual-sided pressure smooshed my cheeks together, making my mouth pucker unattractively. The pillowy forms shook and rumbled like giant bowls of jelly in the middle of a rock slide.

"Help!" I whispered as my chest tried to expand under the onslaught.

The sprite dropped from the sky to hover in front of me, her tiny face alight with hilarity.

"Princess Sebille," the deeper voice said in a reverent tone. The mass shifted in what felt like a bow.

"Call me later," said Grym's tiny, disembodied voice. The distant sound of a call disconnecting had me fighting to pull in a breath so I could yell. "No!" But the sound puffed out like a gasp.

The mass on my right jiggled with delight. "Ah, pretty Princess. Welcome, welcome!"

Sebille didn't seem at all offended by their defer- ence. Her grin stayed locked in place on her long, freckled face. She was enjoying my dilemma way too much. "Naida, meet Rick and Maxine." Sebille lifted her gaze to a spot two feet above my head and grinned. "Kids, this is the Keeper of the Artifacts, Naida."

The jelly jiggled harder. More verbal rocks tumbled down the mountainside.

"Herro," I said through my smushed lips. I scanned my eyes from side to side, trying to see who'd made me into the squishy center of a giant s'more, but all I could see was a vibrant green mass on one side and an eye-searing pink wall on the other. "Ith nithe to meet you," I said.

The warm, soft bodies jiggled some more, the flowery scent almost overwhelming in my squashy cocoon.

I wiggled my hands, which no doubt looked like disembodied limbs sticking from the massive bellies pressed against me.

Sebille flashed to full size and grabbed the phone from my limp, benumbed fingers. She snapped a picture and quickly sent it off. I had no doubt it was going to Grym, a.k.a. The Rat.

The walls shifted slightly, releasing my arms up to the elbows, and I tried to shove away. But the ogres closed ranks again, cocooning me in pillowy claustrophobia.

"It's nice to meet you too, Keeper!" boomed the neon green mass. I was pretty sure the ground shifted under my feet from the bellowing quality of its voice.

"Charmed!" boomed the bright pink wall in a voice that had a slightly more feminine tone to it.

I tried to discreetly elbow them to gain some

breathing room. My elbows sank deep into their squidgy forms. "Do you think you could give me some...space?"

The two massive forms jerked in what I could only assume was surprise. They shifted a couple of inches away, just enough to allow feeling to return to my arms.

"Sorry, Keeper," said the ogre I assumed was Rick due to the deeper, rumbly tenor of his voice.

"So sorry," echoed Maxine.

An enormous pink hand found my head and slammed into it, shoving it forward in a painful assault. I gasped. I'd have fallen to my knees from the blow, but I was too wedged. "Umph!" I objected.

"Oh. Oh, Rick, I've broken her," lamented Maxine in supersized tones.

I shook my head, rubbing the back of my neck. "No. No, I'm fine. Just, please, step away."

The flower-scented live vise finally opened enough for me to breathe. Cooling air wafted over me. That was when I realized how hot it had been, smushed between them. My body was slick with sweat. I lifted my gaze, finally able to see my nearly lethal admirers.

The pink mass I assumed was Maxine, gave me a smile that spread across most of her face and waggled sausage-like fingers at me. Her round eyes flared slightly as I looked at her. "Sorry," she said again. "I was just trying to pet your hair. Such pretty hair."

She reached the dinner-plate-sized hand toward my head and I flinched back, holding up a hand. "No. I'm good. Thanks." My response made no sense. I knew that. But I needed to keep the enormous creature from touching me again. She clearly had no idea of her strength.

Rick, as expected, was the neon green wall. I'd say he looked a lot like Hreck of human movie fame, except he didn't have the horn-shaped ears and his face was more angular, with high, sharp cheeks and a broad chin. The bright green color of his eyes was a few shades darker than his vivid skin but not as bright as the sprite's iridescent green gaze.

Rick had a wisp of a white beard that ran from just under his wide lips to below his cleft chin and an abundance of white hair that covered his broad head. The rest of his enormous form appeared to be completely hairless. Believe me, I would know, since all he was wearing was a pair of brown shorts that tied at his waist and covered his bulging thighs to just above wide knees.

Maxine had a dense wave of golden hair on her head. The thick mane flowed to her slanted shoulders and flipped up at the ends. Her eyes were a deep purple and, unlike Rick, she had a thick forest of golden hair along her forearms and from her knees down. Her massive belly was bare and sans hair. The strategic spots in her fleshy body were covered by a short, turquoise top and a matching pair of what could only be called boy shorts that clung to her dense, muscular thighs.

Just on color spectrum alone, the female of the ogre species was a visual delight.

"How can we help the Office of the KoA today," Rick yelled with a small bow in my direction.

I wanted to shake my head and tell him there was really no office. It was actually more of a loosely formed collection of ineptitude and chaos that I stumbled through on a daily basis trying to pretend I knew what I was doing. Given that reality, the awed reverence on his broad face felt wrong.

"We thought you might know of an artifact that has the ability to break down high-level wards," Sebille told him.

Rick and Maxine shared a look. Frown lines marred Maxine's high forehead, and she nodded. "We might."

As a stubborn silence followed, I decided I'd capitalize on their obvious devotion to my title. "The Office of Keeper would greatly appreciate your help. This is a matter of great importance."

The ogres shared another look. Something non-verbal passed between them. Maxine gave Rick a tiny nod.

He motioned for us to follow and turned away, plodding heavily toward an area in the distance where columns of sharp and broken rock jutted toward the sky. The sprite and I fell in behind him. Maxine took up the rear as if expecting trouble.

The ground beneath our feet seemed to shake with every footfall the ogres made. Small animals scurried away, alarm evident in their bulgy gazes and spiked fur. The lush trees and thick green grass of the spot where they'd met us slipped away as if the world was a kaleidoscope and the verdant frame was giving way to the rock-hewn one.

In place of the grass, rocks of all shapes and sizes, most a monotone of gray or brown in dusty tones, covered the ground. Instead of trees, stalagmites of rock jutted from the ground, some the width of a medium-sized tree and some too large for me to wrap my arms around.

Cracked and broken arches of stone stood between the fractured columns, their bases thick with chunks of stone and heavy with dust.

It was a harsh landscape, reminiscent of a cave without the covering. I picked my way carefully over the rough terrain, noting that, despite their great size and awkward forms, the two ogres moved through the space with a catlike grace. They'd clearly spent a lot of time in the rocky environment.

Rick moved through a particularly large archway and his form narrowed, the air around him shimmering slightly as it folded over him until he was gone.

Sebille and I skidded to a halt, tiny pebbles skittering away from our feet as we froze in place.

The low rumble that was so like rocks sliding down a mountain had us whipping around. To my shock, Maxine was laughing. She winked at us. "All is not what it seems, small ones." She extended a hand toward the archway. "Please, continue."

I looked at Sebille.

She frowned, then finally nodded.

Reaching out, I grasped her wrist so we wouldn't be separated, and, taking a deep breath, we stepped into what was obviously a portal of some kind. The air beneath the archway was warm and wobbly. It jiggled animatedly against my skin, nonthreatening but too weird to give comfort.

The sensation didn't press *against* us so much as *around* us, like a vat of warm gelatin. We stepped out of the archway to a gentle tug of resistance and a soft burp of air, jerking to a stop at the sight before us. Unfortunately, we forgot there was an ogre coming through behind us. Maxine didn't even have time to slow before her enormous frame slammed into us from behind.

And Sebille and I were flung forward, into the hairless naked form of a gigantic ogre, who was sprawled across an enormous golden throne.

4

NAIDA ELF ON A FLESHY SHELF

"Gack! Ag!" I shoved desperately at the pale, naked thigh beneath my hands and kicked my feet, trying to extricate myself from the ogre's *au naturel* lap. Beside me, Sebille flailed manically, punching me in the side of the head in her efforts to shove free. Finally, seemingly in a blind panic, she flattened her palm over my face and shoved, hard, pressing my face into the warm, squishy flesh I was trying so frantically to escape.

Sebille shot free, landing on her knees on the dirt floor of what appeared to be a big cave. She immediately surged to her feet and shuddered, a violent, full-body affair that nearly shook her right out of her Wicked Witch of the West shoes.

One of my flailing hands found the cool smoothness of the throne and shoved. I fell forward, my sneakers finally finding purchase in the dirt. Relief shot through me like a jolt of electricity.

I was almost free.

A thick arm snaked around my waist, and I was yanked back to a thigh as wide as my entire body. It was like sitting on a warm, flesh-covered shelf.

Bright blue, bead-like eyes observed me with a definite twinkle. Above the eyes was a mop of wild, white hair. Below the eyes was a bulbous red nose. Under the nose was a wide smile framed in white hair that fell to the ogre's bare chest.

Nipples on a Nanny Goat! I needed eye bleach.

I closed my eyes, cursing Sebille for sacrificing me to get herself free.

The ogre holding me in place shook with jolly laughter. He was like an ogre-shaped Santa with a cringing, miserable tot perched on his lap.

Except that ogre Santa was sans red velvet and a reindeer short of a full ride.

Goddess in a gondola!

I was Naida Elf on a fleshy shelf.

Waving my arms and kicking my legs, I tried in vain to propel myself free. My body didn't move. Not even a little bit.

I turned to those amusement-filled eyes and glared. "Let me go!"

When he merely laughed again, I glared at the others. "Do something!" I barked out.

Sebille spun around as if she'd just remembered

I was there and held up her hands. Pale green energy spit from her palms. "Let her go," she warned the naked ogre.

Our host and hostess stopped laughing. Rick stepped forward, hands extended in supplication. "No! Don't zap The Benevolent One!"

I glared at Rick. "I'd prefer to observe his benevolence from a distance if you don't mind." Then I realized what I'd said and my face heated. "I mean. I don't want to observe his benevolence at all. Not one part of it." I flinched, my face hot enough to cook an egg. "I just want him to let me go."

"And to put on some clothes," Sebille added, her eyes lifted to the cavern ceiling high above us.

Maxine tittered. "The Benevolent One rarely wears clothes when giving audience."

I frowned, my gaze turned determinedly away as The Benevolent... Gah! His name had too many syllables. I decided to call him TBO for short. "Then wrap him in a towel or something. This is disturbing on so many levels."

"It is an *honor* to be seen by The Benevolent One," Rick said, frowning his displeasure at our reactions.

"It isn't *being* seen that's the problem," Sebille said.

"I'd prefer to see less of *him*," I snarked. "Much less."

Sebille snorted unhelpfully.

Rick continued to glare at us. Clearly, he was displeased.

"Irgh peicewa forgu," Maxine said in a growly tone. "Blawa dergh vishgu."

TBO's sparkling gaze turned my way. Whatever Maxine had said to the unwrapped ogre, he didn't seem to have taken offense. "Gerch blazu veerg," the elder responded. He gave me a gentle shove and I scrambled off his knee. Rick dropped a long red scarf of some kind over TBO's shoulders, and the elder wrapped it around his upper torso with quick, expert movements. For a guy who spent much of his time unclothed, he seemed very adept at covering the parts that didn't really need covering.

"Um," I said. Then catching Rick's glare, I swallowed the rest of my complaint.

Sebille leaned close. "Let's just get what we came for and get out of here," she murmured.

I sighed. "Benevolent One," I began.

The twinkle was dashed from the black eyes. "Gardnu freesh!" he barked angrily.

Rick bobbed frantically, his gaze locked on the dirt at his feet. "Forgitch ignu kompa."

"What's wrong?" I asked.

"You must do the supplication dance before you speak with The Benevolent One," Maxine said.

I bit back another sigh. "Okay. What's the dance?"

"You must do the Hockum Pockla."

I looked at Maxine. "I have no idea what that is."

"It is simple," she said.

"The dance is steeped in ogre history," Rick said, nodding.

"Fine," I said. "What do I need to do?"

Maxine coughed into her hand and cleared her throat, seeming to struggle to keep from coughing again. Finally, she looked up and cleared her throat one more time. "Apologies. Allergies. You understand."

I nodded.

"Okay," she said. "First, You put your right foot in."

"Then, You put your right foot out," Rick added.

"You put your right foot in," Maxine said on another cough, her shoulders shaking suspiciously.

"And then..." Rick coughed too, seeming to have to work to pull himself together. "And you shake it all about."

"You do the Hockum Pockla," Maxine said between clenched teeth.

Rick continued, "And you turn yourself around."

Maxine shrugged. "That's what it's all about."

I eyed them, starting to smell a rat.

"Have fun with that," my traitor of an assistant said.

Maxine violently cleared her throat. "Darn allergies." She smiled at us. "Both of you came before

The Benevolent One, so both must do the Hockum Pockla."

It was Sebille's turn to frown. "Goddess on a Stairmaster," she groused.

I laughed at her discomfort.

All three ogres narrowed their gazes on us.

My smile died. "Okay, Sebille. Let's just get it over with."

We put our right feet in.

We put our right feet out.

We put our right feet in.

And we shook them all about.

We did the Hockum Pockla.

And we turned ourselves around.

"And that's what it's all about," we chorused together.

My entire body was pink from embarrassment.

TBO clapped his hands, delighted. "Again!" he barked in perfect English.

Feeling like marionettes on strings, we complied. The ogres made us do it five more times before they devolved into boneless laughter and lost the ability to ask for more.

Sebille and I shared a horrified glance. Steeped in ogre history my wide white boohind.

We'd been had.

An hour later, we parked on the street and walked the two blocks toward Croakies. I stared at the object clinging to the very tips of my fingers and grimaced. "It's your turn to hold it."

I'd driven all the way back from ogreville with one hand, the other gripping the object we'd retrieved from the ogres between two fingernails.

Sebille's response was a snort of laughter. "I'm not touching that thing. I know where it's been."

Unfortunately, I knew where it had been too, and I fully intended to drop it in bleach as soon as we got home. I shoved the object I was holding toward Sebille, but she popped into her sprite form and darted several yards above my head.

"You're the worst," I groused in ill humor.

I unwound the wards and unlocked the front door of the bookstore, pushing it open. Sebille buzzed past my head, entering the store ahead of me and darting toward the dividing door. A quick flash of pale green energy opened the door that separated the artifact library from the bookstore, and she buzzed on through.

With a sigh, I started to close the front door.

A large hand slammed against the door's surface before I could close it.

I yelped in surprise and jumped, dropping the

disgusting artifact I'd been barely holding to the floor.

A tall man with lank dark hair, piercing gray eyes, and an oversized hook nose stepped through the door he'd kept me from closing.

"Oh. Can I help you?" I asked. The man in front of me oozed hostility like a baby rainbow dragon oozes happiness.

I frowned. *What had made me think about Sadie?* A beat later, my friend Rustin, the ghost witch, and his adorable amalgamate dragon came through the door behind my visitor. Ah. I must have heard the buzzing of her wings, and my subconscious added her to my metaphor.

Sadie was a rare amalgamate dragon from the rainforests of Hawaii. She'd been integral to Rustin achieving a corporeal form after his evil Uncle Jacob Quilleran put his soul form into Mr. Slimy with an experimental spell that hadn't gone as planned.

Fortunately Rustin's aunt Madeline, who was one of the most powerful witches in Enchanted and probably the world, had given him a dual form of some kind. Though, to my knowledge, none of us had seen the other side of the duo yet. Rustin might have changed magically, but at over six-feet-tall with black-as-night hair, a square chin, and wire-rimmed glasses on his classically perfect nose, he still looked like my friend.

"Rustin!" I said. Stepping past my hostile visitor, I

embraced the ghost witch. "How was your trip?" Rustin had taken Sadie to Hawaii for a couple of weeks to look for other amalgamates.

"It was good. Sadie loved being in the rain forest again." Rustin's gaze followed the little dragon as she flitted around the store, warbling softly. We watched as her slanted eyes turned turquoise, then purple, and then went black again.

"She's looking for the songbirds," Rustin said in his deep-timbered voice. His blue eyes twinkled behind his glasses.

I'd noticed his voice getting deeper lately and wondered if that was from the other half of his dual nature. I was going to have to crank up the courage to ask him about it soon. I'd been hoping he'd share. But he hadn't. And the longer he'd gone without sharing, the more I worried he had a reason to hide it.

I nodded. "Sorry, Miss Sadie. They're all gone."

Until recently, the bookstore had been overflowing with songbirds, which were the residual effect of a handheld magic vacuum we'd acquired when we'd been trapped in another dimension. Long story, don't ask. Once I'd realized that I gained several songbirds with every use, I'd declared its use off-limits to all and sundry.

But I had a resident hobgoblin at Croakies. If you know anything about hobgoblins, then you know what happened next. Yeah, telling one of the cute but naughty little creatures not to do something was like painting it in chocolate and waving it in front of their cacao-loving faces until they bit. Before I'd known it, I'd had hundreds of the birds in Croakies. I'd only recently lured the last of them outside.

Sadie warbled again, her eyes glowing with pretty aqua light. Multi-hued illumination sifted along her body, fading to white as it slid off the tip of her tail.

I gave her a smile. "Hobs, Wicked, and Slimy are in the library stalking dust bunnies. You should go surprise them."

Sadie took off toward the door with a cheerful little trill. I sent a ribbon of Keeper magic to open it long enough for her to fly through.

A cleared throat behind me made me jump, my eyes going wide. *Bat boogers*! I'd forgotten about my visitor. I spun around, praying the tall man with the mean eyes was magical. If not, he'd just gotten an eyeful of stuff he wouldn't understand and shouldn't have witnessed.

"Can I help you?" I asked again.

I sent out a wave of keeper energy, looking for a magical signature. The magic flared into the space between us and condensed again, forming a wavy gray ribbon that circled his feet and wound its way up his legs to his torso. He had a faint magical aura that was unfocused but didn't seem overtly hostile.

The man's shoulders came off straight for just a

beat, rounding slightly. "Yes. Do you by any chance have tea?"

"She does," Rustin said, grinning wickedly. "But trust me when I tell you that you don't want *her* to make it."

I bit down on my tongue to keep from sticking it out at him.

"I'll go fetch Sebille," Rustin said, sauntering toward the door through which his little dragon had disappeared.

I moved books off the small table at the front of the store and motioned toward it. "Please, sit. I think I have some..." I lowered my voice. "...brownies."

He frowned. "Why did you whisper?"

"Hobgoblin," I told him by way of explanation. If the man knew hobgoblins, he'd know that nothing made of chocolate or sugar was safe. The only way anybody else ever got a sweet treat in Croakies was to hide and sneak.

I picked up the empty cookie plate from that morning and took it along with me into the kitchen. It had still been full when Sebille and I had left to go see the ogres. Clearly, Hobs had been hungry.

"I didn't catch your name," I said as I moved some glasses in the cupboard and opened the hidden compartment in the back, expecting it to stick as it always did. But it opened smoothly, surprising a smile out of me. Sebille must have finally fixed it. We'd argued for two days over who should do the repair. She'd begrudgingly given in when I reminded her that I almost always mutilated some part of my body when I tried to work with tools.

Not that she'd jumped right on the repair. It had been a week since we'd had the argument.

I felt around until my fingers found the fat bundle I'd hidden there earlier, pulling it out. The sweet scent of chocolate assailed my nostrils and my mouth watered.

"Lovelace," the man said from just behind me.

I jumped at the sound of his voice so close. Spinning on my heel, I nearly dropped the package of brownies.

"Lovelace Cupid," the man said.

My eyes went wide. "Cupid?"

And then he shot me with a tiny bow, sending a teeny arrow into my throat before I could even think about moving.

And the world went black around me.

5

HEARTILY SICK OF PINK

I woke up in my worst nightmare.

No, not the Jurassic era again. This was arguably worse. I was also not surrounded by monsters or stuck inside a really bad black and white TV show. But it was even worse than those situations had been.

"Ugh!" I groaned, feeling the ground around me and shoving myself upright. The residual magic from the tiny arrow caused my head to pound and my stomach to roil. Or it could have been pink overload.

The entire room was pink, occasionally spotted with white hearts.

Pink shag carpet, pink walls, pink draperies, pink chairs, and a pink table. The only thing breaking up all the pink was the occasional slash of white lace and white hearts of every size. There was even a pink comforter on the pink postered bed.

"Triple ugh!" I groaned again, shoving to my feet. I grabbed a slim pink post on the bed to steady myself when the pink world went wonky around me.

When the dizziness passed, I looked for a door or a window or anything I could use to get out of there before angry Cupid returned.

There wasn't so much as a portal or a trap door.

"You can't leave," a disembodied voice said with a tinge of smugness. "Not without my help."

I jerked my gaze in the direction of the voice and found crabby Cupid draped over the pink heart-splashed bedspread. I narrowed my gaze on him. Had he been there before?

I didn't think so.

To my chagrin, he'd exchanged his nice suit for an ugly pink cardigan, matching pink slacks, and a pink bowtie with white hearts dotting its ugliness.

Goddess in a girly phase!

"You really should consider adding a few more colors to your pallet," I told him. "This 'all pink all the time' thing you've got going on is hysteria-inducing."

He glanced around in surprise, his eyebrows lifted into his hairline. "I couldn't. This is my family's signature."

If that was true, he had a strong argument for divorcing his family.

"I'd have thought red would be your color," I said. "I mean, actual hearts are red, not pink."

"Do you know that to be a fact?" His tone was smug as if he knew something I didn't.

Had somebody changed the color of real hearts without telling me? Was pink the new red in the organ world? I shrugged. It wasn't important. What *was* important was that I was stuck in heart-Hades with crotchety Cupid.

I'd prefer to deal with happy Cupid. The one wearing a diaper and sporting rosy, cherubic cheeks.

"What's going on? Why'd you kidnap me?" I demanded.

"Kidnap you? Don't be absurd."

"Absurd? Me? Don't be obtuse." I barely resisted putting my thumbs under my armpits in oversized pride. Yes, I do get a daily Word of the Day email, and I'm not afraid to use it. Color me smug.

Crusty Cupid blinked. "I simply wanted to discuss an important matter with you."

"We could have discussed it at Croakies with a lot less drama, headache, and pink." I grimaced.

"But then I couldn't have shown you this..." He performed a dramatic sweep of an arm. In the space of a single blink, we were outside the horrible room.

Standing in a wasteland of grayness and rot.

The air was moist and cold and I suddenly wished I had on more clothes. Squinting against the wind, I wrapped my arms around myself and tried to figure out where he'd taken me.

I was pretty sure I'd never seen the place before. I'd have remembered it.

We were standing in some kind of courtyard. At least that's what I assumed it had been. Once upon a time. The concrete fountain in the center was cracked and slimy with dead vegetation. The cupid in its center was missing large chunks from its cutesy form.

The bricks beneath my feet had crumbled into tiny pieces, red dust puffing up with every step. The trees that had probably once provided shade for the area were blackened, dead husks, their branches reaching to a steel-gray sky like bony limbs with clawed, gray fingers.

Small stuccoed homes surrounded the fountain square, their lines and coloration offering vague shadows of what had probably once been cute and cozy little cottages in pretty pastels. They'd sunk into broken and cracked corpses of homes, with roofs that had collapsed and windows without glass that resembled vacant, hopeless eyes staring back at me through the gloom.

"You see what we've become?"

I jerked at the sound of his voice. The place held such a note of sadness and loss, it had grabbed onto my full consciousness for a beat and I'd forgotten there was a world beyond what I was seeing. "What happened here?"

He sighed. "My brother happened."

I frowned. "Your brother?"

He nodded, motioning me toward a castle at the end of the broken brick avenue. "There were the three of us. We were all that was left to keep the family legacy alive. But he left. And now there's this."

I eyed the castle. The structure had once been white, its walls no doubt stunning under a bright sun and blue sky. But it had suffered whatever malady had taken over the rest of the little town. Though I could see that some effort had been made to keep it from falling into complete disrepair. It was likely Surly Cupid's home.

Small figures moved around and atop the huge building. I thought they might be people, but they were too far away to know for sure.

"What exactly is the family business?" I asked.

He looked astounded. "Why, love of course. We fan the flames of love in the human heart." He said it as if he was repeating something he'd once read in the company manual. Not like he even knew what it meant.

As if seeing the doubt in my eyes, he shrugged. "My sister mostly takes care of the business end of things. I take care of all of this." He waved his arms around the rotting town. I winced. If it was me, I'd never admit that any of what I was looking at was my handiwork.

He sighed. "I'm not very good at managing things. My brother used to keep the town and towns-people happy and healthy. But after he left, all the people left too. And the town fell to disrepair."

"Where'd he go?"

"I'm not sure. Maybe the earthly dimension." He shrugged again. "I think he got married."

I had so many questions I didn't know where to begin, so, I asked the most obvious question. "What do you want from me?"

He didn't hesitate. "I want you to get that serum back. He'll kill everyone with it."

I blinked at Lovelace Cupid, my thoughts a tangled mass of confusion anchored only by more questions. *Serum? Kill? He?*

And then it hit me.

The toxic magic vault! I hadn't had a chance to inventory the damages and figure out what was lost. But Peevish Cupid's words suddenly made sense. And I knew exactly what he was talking about.

"No..." I breathed.

"I'm afraid so," Cupid said. "He's gotten hold of the love serum. And he's not afraid to use it."

"But why?" I asked, horrified.

"He's bitter about the family and wants to ruin us." Lovelace's homely face turned sad. "As you can see, he's doing a good job of it."

His manner bothered me. He didn't really seem to believe what he was telling me. It was as if he were just repeating something someone else had told him. "That serum had already been misused," I said. "A previous Keeper had it locked in my vault for a reason. Even if I find your brother, you won't get the serum back."

"I am well aware. But he's using the serum to create hate and death. There will be no love left in the world when he gets done with it. That is a situation our family and this town cannot abide. We are already dying because there's not enough love in the world. The rot you see here will continue to spread until it consumes all of our world as well as all of yours. You must stop him. You must get the serum back and lock it safely away."

"I need to go home. You have to take me back!" I said, my heart racing and my mind spinning with concern over what kind of damage could be done with even a single drop of that serum in the wrong hands. I mentally berated myself. I should have been more careful. I should have known there would be magic ward-cutting tools. I should have...

"It's too late, I'm afraid."

His words ripped me from my thoughts. My gaze jerked up to his and then toward the sky, where a veritable army of little cherubs winged their way toward us, bows cocked and a nasty gleam in their eyes.

Chubby cherub cheeks! "What are those?"

Lovelace sighed. "Those are the beginning of the end." He reached for my hand and grasped it before I could pull away. "The whole world is counting on you, Naida keeper." Lovelace tugged something from behind his left ear. "You have to find that serum and stop him."

Then he stabbed me in the palm with a tiny arrow.

And the world went black. Again.

I opened my eyes to chaos.

"Watch out!" Sebille screamed just before a sizzling stream of sprite magic seared the air, mere inches from my nose.

"Hey!" I yelled, but nobody was paying any attention.

Something shot past me on the heels of that energy jolt, and the sour scent of rot, not unlike what I'd just experienced in Loveland, filled my nostrils.

I was sprawled across the rug where I'd been standing when Lovelace Cupid took me. Shoving hair out of my face, I gave a quick look around to make sure I was back in Croakies and it wasn't a dream. It was all the same, except for the battle going on right in front of my nose.

The small round table where we ate and did the

books was toppled, a form crumpled over its broken bones. Was that Grym?

"Miss!"

My gaze shot to the top of the front shelves, where Hobs and his two companions huddled behind an oversized book of spells. The hobgoblin's eyes were wide and his skin was bleached from fear. Before I could move, an acidic stream of a blood-red substance hit the front of the book and sizzled, burning through the hard cover.

With a squeal, Hobs dropped the book.

"Take Slimy and Wicked out of here!" I yelled at the hobgoblin. Hobs grabbed the frog and reached for Wicked, but my obstinate feline leaped away from his reach, sailing off the fifteen-foot high shelves.

"No!" I screamed, shoving to my feet as pictures of him broken and dying on the unforgiving carpet filled my head.

Wicked landed so softly he seemed to float the last couple of inches to the ground. Of course he did. And he ran through the melee to fling himself into my arms.

Another blast of acidic goo slashed in our direction. I jumped away from it and dove behind the sales counter.

Sebille buzzed over in her sprite form.

"What's going on?" I asked as a roar filled the air. One end of the store was shrouded in yellow fog.

The roar had come from there. "What's happening?" I repeated when Sebille didn't answer.

She shot skyward and sent a jolt of energy into the tin ceiling, leaving a large char mark along the once pristine tiles. For just a beat, her energy bolt burned away the yellow fog clinging there, and a cherubic face peered down. Then two tiny fists emerged, a small bow clutched in fat little fingers, and an arrow burst out of the acidic goo, slashing toward us.

Sebille threw up her hands, and a wall of sprite energy took the hit. "That baby thing with the scary teeth is trying to kill us. I have no idea why."

A snarky thought shot into my brain before I could stop it. Of course, it fell right out of my brain and onto my tongue. "Maybe it saw what you did to Hobs and Slimy and has a burning desire to avenge them."

"Har!" Sebille said, then shot skyward and filled the air with several bursts of energy. The fog dissipated under the assault and the cherub slammed backward, hitting the wall just beneath the ceiling and sliding bonelessly to the floor.

Another roar filled the air.

"What in the name of the goddess's favorite sushi restaurant is roaring?"

Sebille popped into full size and hurried over to the downed cherub. She tugged the bow away and flipped it over, encircling its pudgy wrists with her fingers and leaving behind a set of magical cuffs. "It's Rustin." She straightened, arching a single red brow at me. "He's..." she shook her head, seemingly without words to describe what the ghost witch was.

"He's what?"

Another roar shook the glass in the window, and another cherub flew out of the fog, slamming hard enough into the bookshelves to make them wobble. The cherub slid to the floor, eyes closed and harpy-like teeth pressed against its pink lips.

Something moved in the fog, and Sebille grabbed my arm. We forgot all about the second cherub as something huge pushed through the quickly dissipating mist and lumbered toward us on enormous, clawed paws.

"Mythical," I breathed out, answering my own question. Rustin was mythical. I turned to Sebille, a smile finding its way onto my face despite the terrifying aspect of the creature standing not twenty feet away.

"He's a Chimera?"

Sebille nodded, her grin matching mine.

I was five feet nine inches tall and the Chimera was easily twice as tall as I was. Its wings were massive, as well they'd have to be to carry the enormous creature through the air. The living myth moved closer, smoke wafting in fragrant streams from its leonine nose. The nostrils flared and a hollow chuff sounded, the thick golden mane quivering with interest. The eyes were golden too. They were intelligent eyes, but not in any way human.

The thing's leathery dragon wings had curved claws at the apex of their bony frames, and the back paws sported long, deadly-looking claws that could rip a human apart in a single slash.

His tail was thicker than a lion's but had the same general shape, with a ball of fur on the end like the big cat's.

The thing that was supposedly Rustin moved closer, his steps ponderous in the relatively small space. The glass in the big picture window rattled with every step. The nostrils flared again, the leonine head stretching closer as if to scent us. He threw back his head and roared again. Sebille and I scuttled backward with matching yelps.

"Are you sure it's Rustin?" I asked, my eyes popping wide as the enormous mouth opened and an annoyed huff escaped, along with thick coils of pale gray smoke.

"It's him. But I don't think he changed on purpose and he might not have full control over this form yet."

The Chimera lowered its head over the cuffed cherub, nostrils flaring again. Rustin bellowed, stamping an enormous paw near the fallen creature. His wings lifted, waving lazily on the air.

"What if he tries to eat them?" I asked, nodding toward the cherub.

Sebille shrugged. "It will be gross, but better them than us."

"Sebille!" My sharp tone had the Chimera whipping in our direction, wings lifting as if it was thinking about taking off. It snarled at us, spittle flying as it angrily whipped its head.

"Festering Frog freckles!" I said.

"Do something, Naida," Sebille muttered, clamping her bony fingers around my arm.

"Like what?"

"I don't know. You have about a billion artifacts in this place. Throw something at it!"

I nodded, my mind racing. Throw something...

SB! No. Rustin would never forgive himself if he ate the ancient parrot. And Blackbeard's blade, which went where the parrot went, might hurt Rustin.

I thought of the magic hand vac but decided I didn't want to see a hundred songbirds get eaten either.

Think, Naida. Think!

"Ah!" I swung a hand toward the dividing door and it flew open, a silvery ribbon of keeper energy winding its way into the artifact library.

A moment later, a single feather floated into the room, dancing its way toward me.

The Chimera's golden eyes found the feather and followed it, widening as it swirled and spun in the air between us.

The creature swiped at the feather with a thick paw and sent it flying away, only to happily return, dancing to its own music.

A beat later, the lady's hat that belonged to the feather flew into the store and joined the feather in a graceful waltz that totally captured the Chimera's attention. A moment later, the monster actually sat down, its golden gaze transfixed. Every once in a while, the creature would take a swipe at the feather with its giant paws, just like a housecat.

Hilarious.

For the first time in moments, I took an unclenched breath. "Okay, that seems to be soothing hi..."

Without warning, the Chimera hit the hat and feather with a leathery wing, and they crashed to the floor. He pounced, swallowing them in a single bite.

"Oh!" Sebille and I lamented in a mournful duet.

"Bad kitty!" I scolded. "You spit that out right now!"

The Chimera had been trying to chew but was looking a little green around the gills. Probably because the artifacts still seemed to be dancing inside its mouth. The creature's cheeks kept bulging from side to side as if being shoved around by its snack.

"Drop them, Rustin!"

To my amazement, the creature slumped dejectedly, dropping to its belly and opening its mouth to release the items.

The hat and feather flew out and surged toward the door, a bit soppy and mangled but mostly unhurt.

I breathed a sigh of relief. "Well, that was…"

The feather rushed in suddenly and bopped the Chimera on the nose, then darted away. The dividing door slammed shut behind them, followed by an angry roar that I was sure would bring the neighbors if I couldn't find a way to shut him up. "Stop that!"

The front door opened and Lea came through. "What's going on over here? I…" She stopped dead in her tracks, and her mouth slammed shut. Without another word, she turned and went back out the door.

A beat later, she seemed to have a crisis of conscience and cracked the door again, sticking her nose through. "Do you want me to zap it or something?"

A groan sounded and I turned to find Grym sitting up, holding his head. "Those little devils pack quite the punch." He gave Sebille and me a lopsided smile. "What's wrong with you two? You're looking a little pale."

In the blink of an eye, the Chimera was on Grym, standing over him with a snarl on its lips. Grym's eyes bulged. "Okay, that's a big kitty," he said, holding very still.

"That's no kitty," I said softly so as not to set it off. "It's Rustin."

Lea came into the store, her fingers dancing a spell on the air. At my announcement, she stopped spinning magic. "That's Rustin?"

Sebille and I both nodded just the tiniest bit. I couldn't shake the feeling that sudden movements might set him off. "We need to get him away from Grym."

A silvery drop of Chimera spit landed on Grym's cheek. "I couldn't agree more," the cop said.

"Meow!" Wicked rubbed against my calf as he passed by, heading toward Rustin.

I tried to grab him, but he was too fast. "Wicked, no!"

Ignoring me as only a cat can, he trotted up to Rustin and bumped against one thick leg.

The Chimera looked down and hissed, every bit an oversized cat.

"Meow!" Wicked responded, then gave the thing a hiss of his own.

The Chimera blinked in surprise.

"We need to do something," I said, my voice reaching shriek level.

Wicked rubbed his way along the creature's body, the tip of his tail sliding along the Chimera's belly.

To our collective shock, the monster backed off and lay down on the floor, resting its enormous head on its paws.

Wicked curled into a ball in the curve of the Chimera's belly and started purring.

Sebille turned on her heel and headed toward the dividing door.

"Hey! Where are you going?" I asked.

"To get your cat a can of tuna. He's more than earned it."

Yes. He certainly had. I blinked, "Wait, are you talking about Wicked or Rustin?"

Sebille snorted out a laugh.

6

LOVE. THE DEADLY PLAGUE

R ustin shivered inside the blanket I'd given him and clutched his tea cup like a life preserver in a roiling ocean. His piercing blue gaze was underscored by purple arcs and his black hair stuck up in tufts where he'd speared it multiple times with shaky fingers.

"More tea?" I asked the ghost witch.

Nodding, he scratched his classically perfect nose, which drew my attention to the fact that he wasn't wearing his wire-rimmed glasses. "And, I wouldn't turn down something to eat. Taking my other form burns a lot of energy."

Sebille quickly grabbed our cups and headed for the tea counter.

Nobody wanted *me* to make them tea. My tea was more a form of punishment than a treat.

I patted Rustin's shoulder, which, despite his

current fragile state felt muscular and strong beneath my fingers. "It *is* pretty impressive, though," I told him with a grin.

Rustin shook his head. "I'm sorry about the premature transformation. I don't have the best control these days."

I retrieved the packet of brownies I'd dropped earlier, when cranky Cupid had kidnapped me. Someone, probably Sebille, had replaced the wrapped bundle in the hidey-hole. I found a clean plate in the cupboard and arranged the brownies over it. "I'm glad to finally see it," I told him, settling the plate in front of him. "Though, for a few minutes there, I was afraid it might be the last thing I saw."

He winced. "Maddie's working with me on controlling the beast. If I'd had Sadie with me, she could have headed it off."

"Where is the little cutie?" Sebille asked, placing another steaming cup of tea in front of him.

"Birte picked her up a few minutes after Naida disappeared. They're having a girl dragon day." He smiled and sipped. "I think it involved painting each other's claws or something."

We laughed dutifully. Little Sadie looked up to Birte, who, despite her ungainly human form, transformed into the most beautiful dove-gray dragon I'd ever seen. Birte had spent too much of her life hating her dragon form, and young Sadie had been abandoned at a young and tender age and relished the sense of "family" she had with the other dragon.

They were good for each other.

"In your defense," Sebille offered, handing him another cup of tea and joining us at the table. "Those things would have startled anybody into shifting." She jerked her chin toward our two captives.

We all looked at the two cherubs, whose mouths wouldn't fully close around the terrifying rows of their lethal triangular teeth. Up close, they didn't resemble babies at all. Their features were too sharp, and their gazes much too cold. Mercifully, they were still both unconscious. Grym had lined them up near the door and was currently out on the street talking on his cell phone to his team. Grym's small team specialized in paranormal crime and criminals. Each of them had a magical form of their own.

"What are those things?" Rustin asked.

I sighed. "I'm not sure *what* they are, but I'm afraid I know *why* they are." I told them what Crotchety Cupid had told me.

Sebille shook her head. "Grym was beside himself when he came back and discovered you missing. He blamed himself."

"That's ridiculous. None of us saw it coming."

She shrugged.

I thought about what she'd said. "He came back?"

She snorted. "To apologize for not warning you about the ogres." Her eyes sparkled. Clearly, she didn't feel the need to apologize.

I narrowed my gaze on her.

The front doorbell jangled and Lea came inside, carrying a book. "I found your mean, flying babies." She indicated the thick, leather-bound tome in her hands. "They're not cupids, though they look like the cherubic version human mythology has created. They're actually demonic in nature. Their genus is Cupidea Amoris Demonica." She pointed at the long horns jutting from the blond curls in the picture. Despite the horns and the horrible maws filled with nasty teeth, the little creatures looked just like the cherubs of human myth. "They vary slightly. One thing they all have in common is a genetic makeup that's weighted more heavily toward their war god side."

I held up a hand. "Wait. I'm confused. They're not actually cupids, but they have Ares' genetics?"

She nodded. "Lots of creatures share different gods' genetics. Those guys were a randy bunch. They weren't too particular about where they passed their DNA."

"Ugh!" Sebille said, wrinkling her nose. "Okay, so they're demons. Where did they come from and why are they here?"

"Good questions," Lea said, closing the book.

"I told you I saw dozens of those things in Loveland," I reminded Sebille. "Cranky...er...Lovelace said they were the result of the missing serum. He seemed to think the end of the world was nigh if we didn't find the serum and stop them."

"Finding the serum is a given," Rustin said. "But how will that stop them?"

"No idea," I admitted. "But first things first. We have several mysteries to solve." I held up a finger. "Who took it?" A second finger joined the first. "How did they get it?" A third finger lifted. "Where did they take it, and..." I extended the last finger. "What are they planning on doing with it? Besides sending diaper-clad, flying nasties our way."

The front door opened, the bell jangling to announce Grym's entrance. Two burly men who hadn't been there before walked in behind him.

I waved at Brad Spence. "You again!" I said with a grin.

Spence shrugged. "You need to stop following me around," he teased.

The second cop was a man I'd met briefly over a magically frozen Naga. The enormous snake came straight out of the pages of mythology. Our friend Devard, who owned the vapery and apartments across the street, had been forced into the Naga form when we'd inadvertently created a leak in a magical vortex that allowed monsters into our world.

Don't ask. It was a mess.

I didn't know the second cop's name. But I remembered that he'd shifted into a demon.

I joined the three men as they stood over our two captives, discussing what to do with them. Extending my hand to the demon, I gave him a smile. "Hi. I don't think we've formally met."

Grym placed a hand on the small of my back. It was a possessive gesture, and it made me all warm and gooey inside. "Naida, this is Nick Black. Nick, this is the Keeper of the Artifacts, Naida Griffith."

Nick took my hand, giving it a firm squeeze. His black eyes were serious, but his manner was relaxed. "It's a pleasure," he told me. Nick jerked his head toward the prisoners. "These guys are from the eighth circle of Hades. If they've been let loose, something ugly's about to happen."

I grimaced. His words didn't surprise me, but they tightened the knot in my stomach. "Yeah, that's what we were just talking about."

"Does this have something to do with that guy who abducted you earlier?" Grym asked.

I realized he and I hadn't had a chance to talk about that since I'd gotten back. First the battle and Rustin's surprising magical mishap, and then Grym had been dealing with the prisoners while I'd been helping Rustin recover. "Probably," I responded. "If not him directly, then maybe someone close to him." I gave them the short version of what Lovelace had told me.

Nick nodded. "That makes sense. You know that serum is ancient, right? It's been the cause of dozens of wars and millions of deaths throughout Millennia. If it's out there in the wrong hands, we could be looking at a cataclysmic event."

"Any idea who would want to steal it?"

"Anybody who likes to create chaos," Nick answered. He studied the two prisoners. "And that includes just about anyone in the demonic realm."

Slug snot! The last thing I needed was a suspect list as long as a dimension.

"Lovelace said something about his brother," I said hopefully.

Nick made a face. "Yeah. These guys use that term kind of loosely."

"These guys?" I asked.

"Demi-gods. You are aware that many of them have roots in the demonic realm?"

I hadn't been, but it made sense after what Lea had told us. "My understanding is that the gods are kind of..." I searched for the right word. Promiscuous seemed too prim a word for what Lea had described. "Indiscriminating," I finished. The careful term earned me a grin from Nick.

"That's one way to put it." He nodded. "It's accurate, though. Many of the demis are the progeny of mixed couplings between some god and a demon. Rarely do a god and demon actually stay together as a couple though, so your Mr. Lovelace and this 'brother' are most likely half-siblings."

I didn't correct him about Lovelace's name. Whether we called him Mr. Cupid or Mr. Lovelace, he'd clued me into the real problem. I needed to get that serum back and fast.

Nothing else mattered.

I spun on my heel and headed for the library.

"Naida?" Grym called. "Where are you going?"

"To do some research." I swung a hand at the dividing door, enjoying the way it opened to my magic without my even having to touch it. Since I'd completed the pairing between us, taking up the full mantel of my role as Keeper, the artifacts and the library itself recognized my energy and responded to my every thought.

I felt pleased with myself until I remembered it had been my cat who'd clued me in to the power. Mr. Wicked had been opening doors with a thought for months before it occurred to me that he was simply channeling my Keeper energy to do it. I felt a little silly that my cat was magically smarter than I was.

But I wasn't surprised.

I pushed the feeling of inadequacy away as I swept through the door. Mr. Wicked had been trained in magic from a kitten. I'd come into my knowledge late. My New Year's resolution had been to cut myself some slack, magically speaking.

And that was exactly what I'd do.

At the top of my list was performing an inventory in the toxic magic vault before I decided how to move forward. Maybe the serum wasn't the only thing that had been taken from the vault. If something else was gone, our thief probably had a different plan in mind than Lovelace Cupid thought. Maybe he planned to sell the serum rather than use it himself, which might give me more time to find it before all Hades broke loose. Literally.

I was coming to understand what a dangerous temptation the artifacts I managed were to those with evil intentions. None more tempting than the relics in the vault.

I'd believed I had them locked down and safely under my control. The recent theft had shown me how wrong I could be.

As I passed Shakespeare's desk, I hesitated. The inventory could wait a few more minutes. I needed to learn what I was up against with the serum.

I checked the chair in front of the desk before dropping into it. My mind wrapped up in other things, I'd been caught off guard by it too many times. Casanova's perverted chair liked to slip itself under the desk and wait for a pair of unsuspecting butt cheeks to land in its molesting seat.

Fortunately, the velvet nightmare was not lying

in wait for my poor boohind, so I dropped into the chair and rested my palm in the center of the aged, tooled leather blotter. The blotter had been created to look like a book, with Shakespeare's family sigil in the center of what would be the front cover

The Shakespeare family motto was embossed in fading gold letters along the spine. *Non Sanz Droict.* Not without Right. Since I was the current KoA, I was one of the very few who had the right to utilize the desk's prodigious library. "I need information on Cupid and his Love Serum," I told the desk.

Right on cue, the tooled leather beneath my palms warmed and began to boil, like a magical curser searching for just the right volume to tell me what I needed to know.

A moment later, I was starting to worry that it wasn't going to find anything.

Light flared just above the blotter, and a slender volume popped into existence. The book was covered in a strange, pale leather that bore two words in blood red on its face. *Love. The Deadly Plague.*

Well. That wasn't terrifying at all.

I opened the book, repulsed by the cool, rubbery feel of the book's cover against my fingertips. It felt too much like human skin for my comfort.

And then I shrieked in surprise as something shiny and round popped out of the pages in front of me.

7

WRETCHED CREATURES, SLUG
MONSTERS

The disembodied head floated above the pages of the book, a hostile glower firmly fixed on the ruddy face. Doctor Mortimus Osvald was listed on the biography page of the book as a Professor of Devilry at the New York Institute of Magic. But I didn't know him as a professor. I basically just knew him as a head — a hostile head — whose essence had been infused into every one of his magical reference books like a fleshy whack-a-mole.

Osvald pursed full, dry, slightly cruel lips.

I squinted. "Are you wearing a bike helmet?"

He sniffed, the thick dark brows over his black eyes lowering like sad caterpillars. "It's a necessary precaution around you."

I just barely caught myself before I rolled my eyes. I'd definitely been hanging around Sebille too long. "Just because we slammed the book on your head that one time." Or was it two...?

The dry lips twisted. "And threatened to set me on fire. More than once."

I grimaced. Technically, it had been Sebille who'd threatened him with a book burning. But I hadn't done anything to make him think I'd save him if she tried. "Is that helmet fire proof?" I asked. A chuckle fled my chest before I could stop it.

His glower deepened. "What can I help you with, Naida keeper?" he asked in a clipped and snotty English accent.

I settled back in the chair. "So eager to be helpful," I observed, narrowing my gaze. "What are you up to?"

The head swiveled on a negative shake. "I'm simply trying to cut this as short as possible. Perhaps I might even escape with my life."

I sighed. You squash and threaten a guy one...or a few...times and you get a rep. So unfair. "I need to know everything you can tell me about the love serum and Cupid."

"Which one?" he asked unhelpfully.

"Which one what?" I responded.

It was his turn to sigh. "As would be expected for a family whose focus is on love, there have been thousands of members of the Cupid clan throughout history. To my knowledge, only two are still active.

Though 'active' is a stretch for one of them. Lovelace Cupid is a dour, unhappy traditionalist whose every thought pertains to keeping up appearances. History hasn't represented him well. He seems to be kind of a feckless creature, not good at anything he tries. While his brother, a Cupid who reportedly gave himself over to his darker, more demonic side with breathless abandon, is all about shaking up the status quo. The two brothers..."

"Half or full," I interrupted.

Doctor Osvald's full lips tightened with irritation. "Full of course."

I frowned. "But I thought demigods rarely shared both parents."

The head shifted slightly under what was presumably a shrug, though all I could see was the helmeted, disembodied head. The Cupids came from a rare pairing. Mythology is stingy on the details of Ares' pairing with Amore Cupid. I, of course, am one of the few historians who took the time to dig into the mountains of inconsequential information about the Cupids to get to the meat of it. From all accounts, Amore was a demon princess of great beauty and grace. Ares was quite smitten with the creature and stayed with her for several centuries. They were reputed to have had a dozen children together. Of that dozen, seven were daughters.

"Of the five sons, only three were interested in pursuing the Cupid family business."

"Family business?" I asked, pretty sure I knew but wanting to make sure.

"Love. You see, the Cupids have been love demons for millennia." He frowned. "Their idea of love and current day's accepted notions of it were vastly different, of course. For the demonic Cupids, love was all about control and power. Their type of love was destructive to the victim and caused great strife in the form of wars."

I nodded. "The serum was theirs?"

"Yes." He shook his head, lips tight. "Nasty stuff. It should have been destroyed Millennia ago."

"Why wasn't it?"

"Historians. Singularly short-sighted people. They refuse to see the potential for great damage inherent in some historical objects. Particularly magical ones."

"So what happened? How did Cupid begin to signify real love over the tyrannical kind."

He gave me an assessing look. "That's actually a very astute question, Naida keeper. Imagine my surprise."

I glared at him. "Ha."

Looking pleased with himself, Osvald continued with his story. "As I mentioned, Ares loved Amore to distraction. It was an all-encompassing, unselfish love which, as you can well imagine, was just as rare for Ares as it was for a demonic love princess. Fortunately for the smitten god, Amore shared his passion. The magic their shared love created sparked a new path for the Cupid dynasty."

I held up a hand. "Wait, you're telling me that, just because Amore and Ares loved each other, the entire Cupid clan gave up their cynical war for power and control?"

Osvald's laugh was bitter. "Of course not. Amore and Ares had to kill them all."

I winced. "Even their children?"

"Don't be daft," he told me. "They convinced all the daughters their destinies lay elsewhere. Most of the girls, who took after their father anyway, hadn't been huge proponents of joining the family business. They were happy to take their riches and royal titles and go out into the world in search of their own love and happiness. Two of the boys, Lovelace and Denzel, were initially on board with the change."

"And the other three sons?" I asked.

"Eaten by a giant slug monster on a hunting trip in the fifth circle. Wretched creatures slug monsters."

I swallowed hard. Alrighty then. "Fifth circle, huh?" I half thought he was pulling my leg.

Seemingly oblivious to the doubt in my voice,

Osvald nodded. "It was a huge scandal at the time. Ares and Amore went on a killing spree on the fifth, killing all the slug monsters they could find. They emerged from the deadly forests in the core of the fifth after twenty days, pale, starving, and covered in slug gore. Hideous." Osvald's disembodied head shook from side to side. "But, there you have it. The Cupid history that mythology doesn't reveal."

I nodded absently. "So tell me about the serum."

"Horrific stuff. Amore's great uncle Seymore Bastion Cupid developed it as entertainment. He enjoyed spreading it through hapless human villages and watching them tear each other part in the name of love." He shuddered.

"How did it end up in the vault at Croakies?"

"You might ask Keeper Bandy Joe Barrows about that. I believe he was the first keeper to be tasked with guardianship of the serum."

Bandy Joe had been the Keeper who gave Croakies its strange name. Along with the tatty sign depicting an ugly, spotted frog that hung outside the store, he'd created a magical entity that could not be changed by any means. Legal or magical. When I'd taken over the store, I'd tried to legally change its name and put up a new sign. My efforts had failed in the end. The legal name-change paperwork reverted the moniker to Croakies within hours every time I tried, and the new sign quickly morphed back into the ugly frog sign.

Joe loved frogs. He still had a giant aquarium of them in another dimension, where he continued to serve as KoA in that plane's own version of Croakies.

"I do know how it was taken out of circulation," Osvald continued, seemingly oblivious to my distracted thoughts. "Interestingly enough, it was one of Ares and Amore's daughters who removed it from her uncle's evil clutches. Mythology says she was Bastion's favorite niece. She's reputed to have used her wiles to convince him she wanted the serum to make a human male love her. Bastion didn't see through her lies because there was too much truth in her story. Young Desiree had a soft spot for earthly creatures and, apparently, had fallen in love with a human male. However, she had no intention of using the foul serum on him. She did it to show him the strength of her love. They eventually married, and Desiree greatly mourned him when he died." Osvald tsked. "Humans have such short lifespans. Even with the princess's magical interference, the poor sod only lived a mere four hundred years."

"One last question," I said, my mind spinning with all the information he'd given me. "How is the serum spread? And what's with the mean cherub things?"

He arched a dark brow at me. "I see you're no better at math than you are as Keeper. That was two questions."

I narrowed my eyes on him. "And here I thought we were getting along."

"Surprisingly, the serum is not generally spread via an arrow shot from a magical bow, although it certainly could be. However, the action would be redundant. The magic that is spread from the arrows those chubby little flying demons shoot is spelled there. No serum is involved. The spelled arrows were the inspiration for Bastion's creation of the serum."

"And the serum?" I asked, hiding my astonishment at his answer.

Osvald shrugged. "It is as you would expect. Ingested or absorbed through the skin. Unfortunately, It is very easy to infect someone with the serum. However, both methods, the spelled arrow and the serum provide the same result. Toxic, overbearing love."

"Then the person sending those cherubs out doesn't necessarily have the serum?" I asked.

"No." He frowned. "As to your second question, I'm afraid your guess is as good as mine on the cherubs. Both Lovelace and Denzel have cherub armies." His eyes widened. "There is something you need to know, and you're not going to like it. Whatever you've heard from human history, know this. Those cherubs are demonic. They are neither all good nor all evil. Their intent is driven solely by the objective of their master's desire. Either brother could have taken the serum. Both men are extremely cunning and both are capable of great artifice to get what they want. Take nothing at face value and believe nothing they tell you. Either one could be your culprit." He frowned thoughtfully. "Though I have to tell you, Denzel hasn't been seen in centuries. Speculation is that he fled to the human realm to remove himself from Loveland's corruption and his own weakness in the face of it. I've heard rumors he married a human girl, but there's no proof of that."

Well, wasn't that just the bat's boogers?

I thought about his warning for a long moment. He was right. I didn't like it. Not one bit. Finally, I asked, "What about the others?"

"Others?"

"The sisters. Desiree."

"Unclear. Amore moved back to the demonic dimension a thousand years ago, declaring herself done with men and love. I fear Ares wasn't able to stay as true to her as she might have hoped. The last known accounting of Desiree was that she'd walled herself up in the family castle in Loveland. The place is called Broken Heart Castle, renamed by the princess when she was mourning the loss of her human. But that was centuries ago, and there's been nothing said about her since. I doubt she's still residing in the castle. The girls..." He shook his head, the helmet bobbing from the force the movement and dislodging a lank string of dark brown hair to hang limply down his ruddy cheek. "The other girls fell from the pages of mythology long ago. Their exploits weren't interesting enough to earn them a spot on the pages of history."

"So, technically, any one of them could be behind the missing serum," I said in a voice that clearly reflected my despair.

Osvald agreed with a sharp nod. "Yes. Though, if you're interested in my opinion on the matter..."

"I am," I responded, showing how truly desperate I was.

"Aside from Desiree, the girls were a fluffy bunch. All of their brains and gumption added together amounted to nothing. Amore doesn't care enough about humans to even enjoy toying with them. If any of the group has even the most remote chance of being your culprit, it would be Desiree. The girl's sharp as a tack and bitter about the loss of her human love."

"Do you know where she is now?"

"I'm sorry. I do not." Osvald gave a sharp nod. "Well then. Good luck, Keeper. You're certainly going to need it." He dipped his nose toward the pages of the book and dove into them, sending the aged yellow paper fluttering as the leather cover snapped shut behind him.

I sighed. I was tons of information richer and still had more questions than answers.

Story of my life.

I shoved to my feet and headed toward the vault. I had an inventory to complete, and then I'd need to contact Bandy Joe. Maybe he could give me better information about the serum. It was the only thing I could think of to try.

8

YOUR EYES ARE POOLS OF
LIQUID...URP!

I sat in the middle of the vault, several piles of broken debris around me. I'd managed to identify the remains of the Grimm Brothers' monster clock I'd confiscated from my friend Theo, a giant who owned the local pawn shop in Enchanted. I'd carefully bagged the melted remains of a light-sucking candle. The malformed wax had still given off a stinging energy as I'd shoved it into the magic-quelling containment bag, but it didn't plunge me into darkness from the permanent removal of the light behind my eyes, so I called it good. Next went the killer shoes Grym and I had captured the first time we'd worked together. They still had enough juice in them to morph into patent leather tap shoes before I got them contained. I had no idea what they'd been trying to do with that particular form. They generally tried to entice the wearer into slipping them on by selecting a form with specific appeal to the target. I really had no hidden desire to tap dance. Though, I had enjoyed watching old Shirley Temple movies with Grandma Neely. Thinking of her wiped the smile caused by the memory right off my face. I'd recently learned that Grandma Neely hadn't really been my grandma. She'd been a nanny, hired by my mother to keep me safe while Narina ran all over the universe doing goddess knew what.

Narina's activities might have been important. I didn't have any way of knowing because she'd shoved me out of her life, leaving me with a troll for a nanny and effectively depriving me of my magic in the process.

Bitter? Not me.

I shoved the thoughts away for another time when the world wasn't in danger of ending at the hands of a bunch of cranky cherubs armed with killer serum.

It seemed a reasonable excuse for putting off thinking about my dysfunctional family.

The magic mirror had partially rebuilt itself, which told me the attack hadn't completely neutered it either. The myriad pieces of glass, like a fragile, glistening jigsaw puzzle, were mostly reassembled. A few pieces still lay at its base, glowing softly as if being reenergized for the trip to the mirror's face. And the cracks between the pieces still showed.

I figured that, given time, the mirror would completely rebuild itself. As would all the artifacts locked in the vault.

The coin purse that created golden coins and spurred killer greed in its owners was unchanged from the attack. One of the cleaners had already shoved it into a magic quelling pouch and put it on the shelf.

By the time I finished, it was clear to me that everything on my list was accounted for—except for the serum.

I climbed wearily to my feet an hour later. All of the items had been contained and returned to their assigned spots. I sent an extra wave of my Keeper magics over the shelves, giving them an additional layer of resistance from outside interference.

Then I closed and locked the vault, adding a ward to the one Sebille had created that would require both of us together to open it.

It was all I could do until I spoke to Madeline Quilleran about adding further protections. I couldn't allow the vault to be breached again. It was bad enough that the love serum had been taken. But if any of the other deadly artifacts had been taken with it, we'd be looking at an array of possible disasters that could have risen to biblical proportions.

Stretching my back and legs, I headed wearily toward the communicating mirror at the front of the library. If I was lucky, I could catch Bandy Joe in his other-dimensional Croakies before he left for the day.

I wasn't lucky. He didn't answer my call.

As I disconnected and threw the cloaking shroud back over the mirror, the connecting door opened, and Sebille stuck her head through. Her fire-engine-red braids snapped around her narrow face with the abrupt movement. "We have a problem."

I bit back a sigh. "Just one?"

"Come on. Grym's already on the way."

"On the way where?" I asked, grabbing a sweater off the back of the desk chair as I hurried toward the door.

"I'll explain it while you drive."

The sprite did a poor job of explaining anything during the short drive to the local mall. Her cell and mine kept ringing with frantic calls that were short on real information and long on shrieks and calls for the goddess.

By the time we screeched into the parking lot and squealed to a messy stop in the nearest spot we could find, people were running shrieking from the glass doors along the front of the building. Some of the runners appeared terrified, and some had decidedly predatory expressions on their faces.

"What in the name of the goddesses favorite bowl cleaner is going on?" I asked, my eyes widening as a terrified elderly woman threw herself into my arms, sobbing.

"Please, help me!"

Distinctly uncomfortable with the unexpected full-body contact with a complete stranger, I lamely patted her back, meeting Sebille's startled gaze over the woman's shoulder.

Sebille shook her head, as flummoxed as I was.

"Help!" screamed a twenty-something woman with wild eyes and spittle dotting her chin. She threw herself toward Sebille, only to meet empty air as Sebille neatly sidestepped her. The woman barely blinked before turning and flinging herself at the sprite again.

She got a face full of magic dust and blinding pale green light as Sebille popped into sprite form and shot skyward.

Blinking in confusion...and probably from the sprite dust in her eyes...the young woman turned to me. "What just happened?"

I was still ineffectually patting the elderly woman. I shrugged, my teeth grinding together. "Some people are just really bad with human inter-action." My tone clearly stated my disgust for the cowardly sprite hovering somewhere high over our heads.

Her response was to sprinkle me with magic dust.

I sneezed.

Heavy footsteps pounded toward me, and I looked up just in time to see a wild-eyed man, probably in his mid-forties if I had to guess, barreling toward the woman in my arms.

A burly biker chick lumbered toward Sebille's abandoned charge, a hungry glint in her narrowed eye. "There you are, my pretty. Now stop flirting with that bunion on a frog's butt and come with me. We're meant to be together."

"Hey!" I objected. "I'm no bunion. Besides, frogs don't have butt bunions. Toads do have bumps, which are generally mistaken for warts, but they're not really war..."

A massive, tattooed hand snapped out and punched me in the face. Agony razored through me and my vision went wonky. I stumbled sideways. The sobbing woman who'd been clutching me as if I were a lifeboat on storm-tossed seas quickly released me rather than follow me to the ground.

I landed on my hip, pain radiating up my body and into my jaw. Or maybe it was the other way around since my jaw felt crooked on my face. "Hehya! Daltpt hurbpt!"

I clasped my estranged jaw and felt my eyes go wide. It wasn't where it was supposed to be. "Dyoupt pbrokt bmy djaw!"

The forty-something man reached the sobbing elderly woman and wrapped her into his arms, cooing softly as she tried to extricate herself from his determined clutches. "My love," he said, "Your eyes are pools of liquid...urp!"

The woman kneed him in the family vault, and he turned green as she smacked him on the head with her purse. "Hands off, Romeo. I ain't your Juliet. Now off with ya, son." She stuck a gnarled hand into her oversized purse and pulled out a gun. "Or I'll finish the job I started with my knee in a more permanent way."

Keening like a newborn, the unfortunate lothario shuffled away, one hand up to hold off her hostile response, and his body doubled protectively around his injured stick and pebbles.

A shrill scream rent the air. I turned to find Sebille's abandoned charge kicking and shrieking her outrage from her spot on the biker chick's broad shoulder.

Sebille buzzed down and popped back to full size. "You just going to stand here and watch that happen?" she demanded.

My hands clenched into fists. "Ibpt tabpts dnervbe!" Agony speared my face from trying to speak and I groaned, clutching my jaw.

She rolled her eyes. "You sound like an idiot." She touched my jaw and heat flared through the fractured bone and bruised tissue. Painful heat. Pits of Hades-type heat. I'd have screamed from the feeling of being boiled alive, but my entire face was locked into Sebille's healing magic. I couldn't so much as blink.

A few frantic beats of my heart later, the sprite

lowered her hand and the heat sifted away, leaving me pain-free and able to talk again. "You're lucky I need to deal with this mess, or you and I would be having a *discussion*."

Her iridescent green eyes mock-widened. "Oooo! *Not* a discussion." She clutched herself, fake shaking. "Not that!"

"Shut it!" I growled, stomping after the still-shrieking woman. "If you hadn't flown off like a scared little girl, that poor woman wouldn't be in the clutches of a maniac right now."

Sebille caught up with me. "What can I say? I panicked. I don't people well."

"You don't people at all," I corrected. "But Grym asked for our help for...whatever this is. So try to be more helpful next time."

"Whatever." The sprite flashed forward and smacked the biker chick on top of the head. Green light spurted from her palm as her hand connected to the woman's dark, closely-shorn skull. The over-sized woman jerked to a stop and slowly folded toward the ground—sleeping like a giant tattooed baby.

Apparently, I just needed to point Sebille at the right kind of problem, and she was happy to step in. Violence seemed to be the key ingredient necessary for her "help".

I stuck that one in the memory banks and grabbed the biker chick's almost-prisoner, easing her to her feet. "Are you all right?" I asked the wet-faced woman. She sniffled noisily, dragging a hand underneath her glossy nose. "I think so."

I grimaced at the slime on her hand. "Uh, okay. You should get out of here then."

But she didn't immediately leave. She glanced at the fallen biker chick. "What happened to her?"

"She fainted," Sebille offered, shrugging for effect.

"Oh." The woman frowned. She didn't look convinced.

Behind me, the mall doors opened again and a chorus of screams filled the parking lot until they were sliced off by the closing doors. "We need to get in there," I told Sebille.

She nodded and fell in beside me as I hurried toward the mall.

"Wait!" the young woman behind us called out. "We can't just leave her here."

Since that was exactly what we were going to do, I lifted a hand and waved her off, calling over my shoulder. "Go home. We'll send her some help as soon as we can."

"But..."

Her worried protestations faded to the background as I caught a glimpse of the chaos inside the mall.

Actually, chaos was too moderate a word for it.

Sebille and I shared a look as our determination

wavered. Did we really want to insert ourselves into that?

With a sigh, I grabbed the door handle. "This is going to be okay," I told my assistant, not even convincing myself.

"Yeah? Then why is returning to the Jurassic era starting to look like a better option?" Sebille asked. "I could definitely use me some T-Rex about now."

I sighed. She wasn't wrong.

9

GET YOUR HAND OFF MY BOOB, LADY!

I'd never seen the mall in such an uproar before. And I'd been there for the big Black Friday electronics sale. Two times. Once, they'd had fifty-inch TVs on sale for two hundred dollars. That had been a zoo.

But this...

This...

A slender form flew through the air and smacked into me, knocking me into Sebille and sending all three of us to the ground. The woman on top of us groaned and tried to shove herself free of the tangle.

A strangled squeak told me she'd shoved against something belonging to my assistant that wasn't public touch approved.

"Get your hand off my boob, lady!" Sebille shrieked.

I'd never heard the sprite sound quite so outraged.

The woman gave a little yelp and yanked her hand back, rubbing it against her jeans as if trying to wipe off the boob cooties.

The three of us took a moment to disentangle ourselves from the messy pile. It wasn't easy to do without inadvertently molesting each other.

Finally, we stood fairly upright. In my case, even my hair was upright. I reached up to shove the messy strands relatively flat. "What happened? Why were you flying through the air?"

The woman harumphed, crossing slender arms over an abundant chest. "It wasn't my fault."

I dug deep for patience. Sebille, who wouldn't know patience if it gave her boob cooties...heh... rolled her eyes. "We know it wasn't your fault. That isn't what she asked. What's happening here?"

Okay, that wasn't what I'd asked either, but it was a better question. I nodded, feeling stupid.

The woman's lip curled. "I have no idea. I was running away from those things..." She threw a hand in the direction of the central mall area and shuddered. "The next thing I knew, somebody gave me a shove and I went flying." She absently rubbed her hip. "I don't know who thought those cherub things were a good PR stunt for Valentine's Day, but they've backfired in a spectacular way. Somebody's going to get sued."

At her mention of cherubs, Sebille and I shared a look.

I started running toward the center of the mall, where the screams and explosions had reached a crescendo. Sebille flashed past me in her sprite form.

Buzzard blisters! "Sebille!" I yelled after her. "Not in front of the non-magics."

I couldn't see her tiny green eyes roll, but I knew they were arollin'. "She's gone," she yelled back. "Give me some credit, Naida."

We hit the end of the short spoke of stores on the first level and emerged into a large, open area with picnic tables and the sweet-spicy mix of smells that told me we'd stumbled into the food court. Even as I had the thought, something warm and meaty splatted me on the side of the face.

Sebille flashed back to human size. "What a mess."

She wasn't wrong. The place looked like someone had emptied the entire contents of the food court into the middle of the mall. And what was there had been smashed and ground under a hundred panicked feet.

The scent of catsup hit my nostrils as the hotdog I'd been attacked with slid slowly down my cheek on a condiment track and plopped onto the food-littered floor.

"Heads up!" somebody screamed. Sebille and I

ducked just in time to miss being hit in the face with a fried rice plate.

My stomach growled at the smell of crisp and tangy egg rolls.

"When did they add Chinese food to the court?" Sebille asked, spinning to avoid a paper cup filled with liquid. The cup hit the ground with a wet splat just behind us, the liquid splashing the back of my calves. "Ew! What is happening?"

We ducked behind an overturned picnic table and looked around. Several people were hightailing it to the exit at the end of the wide hall. The escaping customers were battered and blotched with food, and a couple of them were limping. As I watched, one young woman went down, shrieking. She covered her head with her arms as a plate of nachos hit her square in the back. I couldn't tell where the cheesy projectile had come from. It had seemed to come out of thin air.

All over the messy marble floor, people lay in messy piles, limbs at awkward angles and eyes wide and glassy.

"Are they...dead?" I asked in a horrified whisper.

Sebille merely frowned.

The air above us spun and thickened. A terrifying cherubic face appeared. Sharp metallic-looking teeth gnashed too close to my nose, and a slender arrow pierced the space between Sebille and me.

Sebille shot energy at the nasty thing, but the cherub disappeared with a pop of displaced air.

"Why are these things here?" I asked. "And where's Grym?"

Across the court, a man stumbled out from behind a post, arms frantically flailing against the air. He jerked suddenly, yelping, and slumped toward the ground, a tiny metal shaft protruding from his throat.

The air above the man thickened and a cherub seemed to buzz into view from nothing. The creature hovered about head-height, its tiny wings moving at hummingbird speed to keep it aloft. It held an empty bow in its chubby fist. Sebille's fingers spit with energy. "Keep it busy," she barked out. Then she popped into a dragon-fly-sized sprite and buzzed away, leaving a sparkling trail of pale green magic in her wake.

The cherub's gaze slid in her direction. I grabbed the hot dog that had painted my face and surged to my feet. "Hey, ugly!" The creature jerked around to face me, a horrifying smile spreading on its chubby face.

An arrow appeared in one pudgy hand and the thing nocked it, a gleam in its black eyes.

I wound up and, using my best pitcher-on-the-mound technique, threw the dog at the cherub.

It splatted the spot just between its eyes.

The thing jerked, buzzed skyward in a panicked

movement, and then growled before swiveling the bow in my direction.

Sebille suddenly appeared, hovering on the air behind it. A fully-formed web of magic flared from her fingers and dropped over the nasty critter.

Unfortunately, the arrow the cherub had nocked flew free, heading right for me.

Something big slammed into me, sending me flying just as the arrow hit the space where I'd been. The figure that had hit me grunted softly as we landed, and we skidded several feet through the slippery food debris before we came up hard against another large post.

I'd ducked and covered my head, expecting impact, but it never happened.

As we came to an abrupt stop, I looked up to see a muscular arm stretching toward the column. The hand attached to the arm had kept me from crashing into the big post.

Grym's dark-caramel gaze looked slightly feverish in the harsh light. "Are you okay?"

I nodded, my gaze locked on his. "Fine. Thanks for saving me. You got here just in time."

His yummy lips curved slowly upward, the sight making me feel warm and tingly in all the right places. "Nice pitch."

Heat flared in my cheeks. "Um, yeah, thanks. I played a little softball back in the day." I shifted uncomfortably, hoping the movement would inspire him to move. His nearness was making me a little dizzy.

His gaze heated. "Well, you throw a mean hotdog."

My mouth became a desert, my tongue a dehydrated husk in my mouth. "I..." I cleared my throat, trying to find some moisture to rehydrate my mouth.

A large bug buzzed overhead. Sebille hovered on the air a foot from our heads, arms crossed and a judgy look on her tiny face. "Are you two done congratulating each other? Because these things won't capture themselves."

Grym and I glanced up at the cranky sprite. Her fire-red brows lifted into her hairline.

Grym blinked as if suddenly remembering where he was. "Oh. Yeah. Sorry." He shoved himself off me and climbed quickly to his feet, reaching down to give me a hand up. "You're sure you're okay?" His tone was tender, his gaze skimming quickly over me to check for damage.

Words wouldn't come. I swallowed hard and nodded.

Then I saw the speck of blood on his shoulder. "You're bleeding."

He glanced at the small slice through his denim shirt, his mouth curving up on the corners. "It's just a flesh wound." He laughed. "I've always wanted to say that."

I rubbed my gritty hands on my jeans. "What's going on here?"

Grym looked around, his expression turning dire. "The cherubs seem to have adjusted their attack to stealth mode."

"They're invisible?" The shriekish quality of my voice was embarrassing. I worked to tone it down. "The one that attacked us just kind of popped out of thin air." My stomach twisted into a painful knot. The only thing worse than shark-toothed cherubs shooting people with poison arrows was not being able to see those cherubs coming.

But Grym shook his head. "Not invisible. I mean, for all practical purposes they are invisible to the naked eye. But it's more like they're using voids or something."

I thought about what I'd seen and realized it was exactly like that. Archie was a void sorcerer, and he'd stepped out of voids in thin air just as the cherub had. "Is that possible?" I asked Sebille and Grym. Though we were all magic-users, they'd been part of the magic world all their lives, where my magic had been ignored and hidden from me until it was impossible to ignore any longer. I knew next to nothing about the magical world compared to them.

Though, my job was proving to be an adept teacher on the subject, if a little death by fire-squadish in the delivery.

"I haven't seen anybody who could use a void like Uncle Pudsy," I said

Grym nodded thoughtfully. "Yes. But the thing is, demons aren't generally able to use voids that way."

"Spatially restricted invisibility magic?" Sebille offered.

Grym thought about her question for a beat and then shrugged. "Could be. I've heard of demons who were able to utilize that type of magic in controlled situations." He looked around, frowning. "But this whole place would have to be spelled for it to work."

"That would be a humdinger of a spell," Sebille said, sharing his frown.

"Like something a demi-god might be able to use?" I said, reminding them what...or who...we were dealing with.

"Hello?"

We all turned at the sound of an uncertain male voice. A short, portly man was waddling in our direction, his sparse combover flopping in his eyes before he shoved it off his forehead. The air behind him shimmered and I glanced at Sebille. She buzzed away, using the small trees adorning the central mall space to keep out of sight of the approaching human.

A beat later, a wash of green energy lit up the space behind him and he jumped, rubbing the back of his neck as he turned to look.

Seeing nothing, he ambled in our direction

again. "I'm evacuating the mall, folks. Some kind of flash mob has taken over and people are acting crazy. It's not safe here."

Grym showed the man his badge. "Detective Wise Grym of the Enchanted Police Department. And you are?"

The man examined Grym's badge, his expression relaxing. "Thank goodness you're here. I don't know what's going on." He seemed to realize Grym was still waiting for him to identify himself and nodded. "Name's Pinch. Ralph Pinch. I'm the manager of this mall." His gaze slid toward the pile of ostensibly sleeping people. "Are they okay?"

Grym nodded. "They passed out."

The manager's eyes went wide. "Oh my! You mean all this is because of a bunch of people who drank too much?"

Grym opened his mouth and stopped, seeming to rethink whatever he'd been about to say. Finally, he nodded. "I'm afraid so."

The man nodded. "Well, in all my years managing this place, I'd have to say this is a first." He crossed pudgy arms over his well-padded chest and shook his head. "What will we do with them?"

"I've called for backup," Grym told him. "We'll get this cleaned up in no time, sir."

The man nodded. "Good. What do you want me to do?"

"Getting people out of here is a good idea. Then lock the doors and watch for my people to arrive."

The manager nodded. "I have a few staff left in the building. I'll see if I can roust them to help."

"I can help," I told the man. I shared a look with Grym and he frowned. "I'll back you up," I told the manager in a firm tone that was meant to remind Grym the human manager was in danger from the cherubs. He probably wouldn't even see them coming and, if he did, he wouldn't know what to do about them.

Not that I was a super hero in the defensive magics myself. But in a pinch, I could zap the little monsters with my Keeper energy. It was enough to curl their hair or make them pee into their diapers.

Grym got a constipated look on his handsome face. "I don't want you to go with him." He blinked even as the words came out.

We stared at each other for a beat, then both of our gazes slid to the small wound on his shoulder.

"Oh, oh," Sebille said, coming up behind the manager.

Grym's lips compressed. "I can handle it," he finally said.

"Handle what?" the manager asked.

"Coordination of the cleanup," Grym said, his hostile gaze sliding to the man. "You can evacuate anyone who isn't passed out?"

"Yeah," the man said, his expression turning

leery in the face of Grym's inexplicable hostility. "I can do that." He turned to me. "I'd love your help, young lady."

A growl throbbed in the air. We all looked at Grym. He made a point of looking over his shoulder. "Is there a dog in here?"

Sebille snorted out a laugh. "There's definitely something feral."

Grym glowered at her.

"Shall we go?" the manager asked me.

I nodded.

He reached out and placed a hand on my arm to guide me toward a sign that said 'Elevator'. It was just to one side of the doors Sebille and I had entered through. "Let's start there...oh!"

Grym was suddenly chest to chest with the manager, his big form shoving the smaller man backward and away from me. "Don't...touch...her!" he growled out.

"Grym, back up," I commanded.

The big cop ignored me, his gaze locked on the other man in a threatening way.

"Grym?"

Nothing. He appeared to be lost to the Cupid's poisonous spell.

I swallowed hard, my gaze sliding pleadingly toward Sebille. She took a step closer to Grym and casually placed a hand on his shoulder. Pale green light flared from beneath her palm and Grym twitched as if shocked by a bug zapper.

Grym's eyes rolled back in his head, and Sebille tucked herself quickly beneath his arm, keeping him from falling. She jerked her head toward our destination. "Go. Hurry. He's heavy."

"Is he..." the worried manager asked.

I grabbed the man's arm and gave him a tug. "He'll be fine. He's...erm...epileptic. It'll pass."

The man let me drag him away but kept glancing back toward Grym. "Are you sure he's okay? Maybe we should call an ambulance."

"No. He's fine. That's his assistant there with him. She knows what to do."

I turned back just in time to catch Sebille smacking Grym on the forehead. He snapped right out of whatever she'd done to him.

I grinned. Good thing he had a hard head—a rock-like one, to be precise.

10

GOOD GODDESS ON A ROWING MACHINE!

"Hurry," I told the manager.

"Why? Is there something you're not telling me?"

Yeah, I thought. *Lots of things.* "I just have a bad feeling. We need to get the people out of here."

He nodded, pointing toward a short hallway with restrooms on one side and an elevator at the end. "Our offices are on the third floor."

The elevator door seemed to take forever to open. Behind us in the mall, I heard the heavy pounding of hurried footsteps.

I eyed the elevator. "How much longer...?"

The doors dinged and opened. I all but shoved the manager into the elevator and pushed him back while I punched the *close* button a dozen times.

"You know that won't make it close any faster," the man said, frowning.

"I know." The words came out angry. I closed my eyes and took a deep breath. "Sorry. This whole thing has me stressed out."

He nodded. "I understand. Believe me."

Thank the goddess, the door finally slid closed. I punched the button for the third floor. "How many employees are up there?"

He shrugged. "Generally, we have a dozen people here during the day. I'm pretty sure I saw five of them slide out the doors with customers. Two people are sick today, so that leaves four, plus me."

I nodded. "Is anybody armed?"

He paled, his eyes turning to golf balls in his face. "Armed? Like with weapons?"

I barely resisted the urge to roll my eyes. "Yes."

"I don't think so. The Armitage Group forbids any kind of firearm."

The bell dinged and the doors slid open. We were in another short hallway, the restrooms along the side just like the ones on the first floor. In fact, the whole setup was so similar, I glanced at the number above the elevator door just to make sure we'd changed floors.

"Where's the office?" I asked.

He pointed toward the mall. "Out there."

"Lead the way."

Something felt off about the place when we stepped from the hallway into the wide aisle where the stores were. Like just about every other mall I'd ever visited, the center space was open to the floors below, with a wide, horizontal walkway in the center that crossed from one side to the other.

The floor was tile, the surface glossy and with pale veining like marble. Large pots held small trees or an abundance of tropical-looking plants and flowers. The ends were anchored by large department stores, and the walkways on either side were lined by smaller shops.

It should have been pretty. A soothing oasis from work and life where people could happily spend all their hard-earned money in a stress free environment.

Instead, the place was a mess.

Torn paper, discarded bags, and trampled sale items lay strewn over the slick floor. A woman's brown leather purse lay in front of us as we emerged from the hall, its contents strewn over a six-foot-wide space.

The owner of the purse was nowhere to be seen. Somewhere down the mall a distance, someone was sobbing.

I reached out and grabbed my companion's arm, stopping him. "Something's happening near that central walkway."

He nodded, stepping close and lowering his voice. "How do you want to play this?"

I nearly grinned at his thriller movie dialogue.

My gaze slid to the floor. To the oversized purse. It wasn't exactly a weapon, but it was something.

I quickly scooped up the purse. It was sewn from heavy leather, but it wasn't heavy enough to hurt anybody. I scanned the area, finding a store down the way that had what I needed. I put a finger over my lips and pointed to the store.

Very carefully, I removed my shoes and pointed to the manager's shoes. Once we were both in stocking feet, we padded silently along the wall toward the workout wear store I'd spotted.

We ducked inside the store and eyed the carnage. It looked like every pair of running shoes and every spandex top and running bra had been ripped from shelves and racks and flung around.

We were dealing with some really angry cherubs.

"Are we going to spandex them into submission?" the manager asked, his expression dubious.

"Hopefully not," I said, kicking clothing aside in search of my goal.

I found it a few minutes later, the hard way. My toe smashed into something hard and heavy near a toppled dummy.

"Ouch, ouch, ouch, ouch, goddess! That hurt." I glanced at my tender toe and found blood seeping through my sock. *Sizzling bat scat*!

My companion crouched down and uncovered my attacker. A small stainless steel weight. Probably about three pounds. "Is this what you're looking for?"

I nodded, releasing my bleeding foot and taking it from him. I dropped it into the purse and swung it to test its heft. "That's better."

"How'd you know..." he started to ask.

The sobbing in the mall turned more desperate. A woman's tearful voice added pleading to the mix. "Let's just go home, honey. Those things are going to come back."

That didn't sound good.

A curtain shifted behind the checkout counter, and a big woman with dark red hair teased up into a peacock thing on the back of her head stepped from what was probably the office slash inventory room.

Her flat, bulldog face turned belligerent when she spotted us. "What are you doing in here?"

"It's okay, Daisy," the manager said. "She's helping."

The woman had smallish, deep-set eyes in a wide face. When she slid her focus from me to the man with me, the gaze softened and her small mouth curved. "Ralph. You came to see me." Her muscular body softened along with the smile. "I knew you'd come."

She moved toward us on enormous cat feet, light and agile despite her bulk.

Ralph Pinch swallowed hard and took a step back. His hands came up as if to ward her off. "Now

Daisy, we've had this conversation. I told you, I'm a married ma..."

Daisy, a more misnamed wretch I'd never seen, reached toward him with long muscular arms and smashed him up against her massive breasts. The man's feet literally dangled above the floor. She rubbed her face against his as if scent-marking him. "I knew you loved me."

Ralph's bulging gaze slid to me, filled with pleading.

Beyond the open shop door, the sobs had reached a fever pitch and shouting had joined the crying.

"Please help," said a pleading voice.

I blinked, realizing the plea had been delivered in a man's voice and was much nearer than before.

It was Ralph.

I smiled at the woman. "Daisy, is it? Hi. I'm Naida. It's nice to meet you."

The woman's lips curled on a silent snarl.

Aardvark cankles! I was going to be eaten.

I forced my lips to curve into a smile, lifting my hands to show how harmless I was. The weight-laden purse slipped into the inside curve of my bent arm and swung against my hip. "We're just trying to help that woman out there. Can you help too? She sounds really scared."

Daisy's bulldog face turned purple. "You can't have him. He's mine."

Too late, I noticed the slender shaft of a Cupid arrow jutting from the side of her thick throat.

"I promise I don't want him..."

Her glower deepened and a growl rumbled in her throat. "Are you saying Ralph's not good enough for you?"

Good goddess on a rowing machine!

"No, Ralph's very nice."

"Nice!" she roared. "He's perfection! Do you think you can come in here and insult my man like that?" She shoved Ralph aside, sending him crashing against a shoe display, where he tumbled to the floor with a neon green running shoe in one hand.

With a bellow of pure rage, Daisy threw herself at me, teeth bared and fingers curved into deadly-looking claws.

I gave up trying to talk sense and gathered the straps of the purse in one hand. Weight on my toes so I could dance out of her way, I spun the weighted purse in one hand, like Wonder Woman with her lasso. As Daisy moved closer, I braced to jump away. She made a grab for my arm, snarling wetly, and I sent the heavy projectile flying toward her head.

It hit her right between the eyes.

Daisy went down like a ton of bricks.

"Oh," said Ralph.

I turned to find the mall manager looking flushed and confused, the running shoe perched on his palms as if he were a salesman giving a hot prospect the big pitch.

I grinned. "Do you have that in my size?"

Ralph blinked in confusion. "Huh?"

Apparently, he'd hit his head on the shelves.

I walked over and offered him my hand.

Ralph shoved the shoe in it.

Hm. Lightweight, gel insoles. Nice shoe. I shook out of my shoe coma and threw the runner to the floor. "Come on, let's get out of here before she wakes up."

Behind me, Daisy groaned and shifted, her fingers twitching.

I grabbed Ralph's clammy hand and yanked. He came to his feet but was a bit wobbly.

"Let me see your head," I told him, turning him around to examine his scalp for a goose egg or worse.

Nothing.

"You're okay. Come on." I turned and started toward the door.

Ralph didn't move.

I stopped and frowned at him. "We need to go."

Ralph nodded, blinked, and then slid into a boneless pile on the floor.

Badger bunions!

I stood there for a beat, unsure what to do. If I left him behind, Daisy might hurt him. But what if I couldn't wake him up in time and Daisy got us both?

Another sob sounded in the eerily silent mall.

My head whipped back and forth between the woman in the mall and Ralph.

Daisy flopped like a landed fish. She was waking up.

I hurried over to Ralph, bent over him, and slapped him hard on the face.

He came awake with a surprised, "Ungh!" His soft, white fists popped up, and he turned an angry gaze my way.

"It's me!" I told him. "Daisy's waking up, so if you don't want to be her little play thing, you need to snap out of it and get moving!"

Ralph's gaze slid to the enormous woman and widened. It was all the warning I had that she was on the move.

I ducked as a shadow swept over me and twisted, whipping the purse into her belly as I spun away from her attack.

Daisy bent double, pale and wheezing like a wounded buffalo.

Ralph shoved to his feet and ran. Daisy was already straightening as I cleared the door. But Ralph was messing with something on the edge of the opening.

"What are you doing?"

"Closing her in."

Daisy's eyes found me and locked on. With one arm still wrapped protectively around her middle, she stumbled forward, growling. Her fingers curved into claws. "I'll kill you, you little pipsqueak."

"Ralph?" I braced my feet wide, twirling the purse as she lumbered closer.

"Almost..." There was a clanking sound and then the sound of metal unrolling as Ralph tugged the security door across the wide opening.

Daisy was so focused on me that it took her a moment to realize what he was doing. When it finally sank in, her head shot in his direction and she howled. "No, Ralph! Don't leave with her."

He slammed the door home just as she reached it. For a terrifying moment, she fought him for control of the unlocked door.

I could do nothing. My weapon of choice wouldn't work through the heavy metal mesh. I threw myself at the door and held it closed while Ralph dug in his pocket.

"What are you doing?" I shrieked.

"The key!" he yelled back.

Daisy was probably a lot stronger than I was normally. But under the influence of the Cupid's poisonous magic, she was a beast. I'd wrapped my fingers around the mesh and was leaning back, putting all my weight behind holding it closed, and still she was managing to wrench it open by inches.

Ralph had found the key. "You need to keep it closed so I can lock it!" he yelled.

Red-faced and sweating, I threw him a look. "I'm open to suggestions!"

He threw his weight into getting it closed, but when he released it with one hand, Daisy yanked it open again. She got it far enough open to snake one thick hand through to claw at me. Her fingernails were short but sharp, and she clawed bloody tracks in the soft skin of my wrist before I could yank my hand away.

As soon as I let go, she roared and yanked the door open another foot.

It was enough for her to wedge herself into the breach.

She got hold of Ralph's shirt front and slammed him into the mesh.

I panicked and did the only thing I could think of to do.

I hit her with a blast of my Keeper energy.

She jerked to a stop, Ralph droopy and bleeding in her hand, and her eyes went wide. All the hair on her head rolled up into Shirley Temple curls, and she released Ralph to clutch herself. "I have to pee!"

Without another glance, the big woman spun on her heel and crab-walked as fast as she could toward the back room.

Ralph shoved the door closed and fumbled with the key for a moment, his fingers shaking so badly he could barely insert it into the lock.

"Won't she have a key too?" I asked, panting.

He shook his head. "New security measures in the mall. Only management and security have keys to the security doors."

"Thank the goddess," I said, slumping against the wall. "That's one strong woman."

Ralph shook his head. "She's always been really gentle and kind."

"She's not herself," I said.

"Why?" he asked. His expression was a mix of confused and sad. "What's going on in my mall?"

A blood-curdling scream pierced the silence.

Thank the goddess I didn't have to answer his question. I took off running toward the sound.

11

JUST ANOTHER UGLY DIRIGIBLE

The screaming turned shrill as Ralph and I ran toward the center of the floor. A large tree dominated the area in front of the crosswalk, blocking the view of what was happening until we were almost on top of it.

As we reached the tree, a man jumped out at us, an enormous knife clutched in one strong hand and a feral look in his eyes. His short, straight brown hair stuck up in clumps all over his head as if he'd been continually running his fingers through it, and blood painted the front of his hooded sweatshirt in large drops.

My eyes went wide at the sight of the blood.

Ralph lifted his hands when he spotted the knife. To his credit, he tried to block me with his own, quivering form. "Now, let's just calm down, okay?" He nodded toward the woman cringing behind a bench along the railing. "Is she hurt? Do we need to call an ambulance?"

The man with the knife lunged forward, causing us to backtrack quickly to avoid being jabbed. "She's not going anywhere without me."

Dang those cherubs and their arrows!

I took a careful step to the side, the purse clutched in my left hand. It wasn't optimal since I was right-handed. But if I tried to shift it to the other side, Ralph would be in the way.

I realized in a moment of pure terror that I'd brought a purse to a knife fight. The one benefit of my weapon was that nobody looked twice at it. Everyone just thought it was my purse.

The man's hostile glare spun my way. "You stay back now. I don't want to hurt anybody."

I nodded toward his sweatshirt. "Too late for that, eh?"

He blinked, looking down at himself in surprise. The man shook his head. "That's my blood. I've just been trying to protect her." His tone was angry, determined. "I can't believe this. I must be paying for the sins of my youth."

"Please help," the woman said, her face a pale oval from the shadows behind the bench.

The knife-wielding man whipped around as he shushed her. "I need to think, honey. They're going to be back."

She nodded, her pretty face stark with fear. The woman was clutching the side of the bench with one hand, and I took note of the deep scratches in her flesh.

I jerked my head toward her. "How did she get those scratches?"

The man straightened his shoulders in a jerky motion. Then he ran a hand over his face, wiping a gloss of sweat away as his eyes jerked around the space. "I told you. It was those demons."

"Where'd they go?" I asked. When his gaze wrenched to mine, I clarified. "The demons?"

He swung the arm with the knife around the space, his eyes wide. "They're everywhere. They tried to take Nina. I can't let them take her."

The woman sobbed again, shifting around behind the bench until I saw her belly. "She's pregnant?" I exclaimed without thinking.

The man tensed, his gaze turning shrewd. "You're not touching that baby."

I held the purse in front of me because it was all I had. "No. I..."

"We came to help," Ralph squeaked out. "I'm the manager, and she's..." He frowned. "She's with the police."

The man's expression cleared. "Police?"

Nina's head slid out of the shadows. "Honey, maybe she knows Grym."

Well, I'll be a slug's auntie.

"You know Grym?" I said, stepping closer before I realized what I was doing.

The man's knife hand lowered a few inches. "I work for him."

"You're one of Grym's guys?" I smiled, lowering the purse with relief. My arm had been shaking from the effort of holding it up.

"Detective Devin Sampson. That's my wife, Nina."

Behind him, Nina nodded enthusiastically. "Are you a cop too?"

"No." I hesitated, then asked. "Are you part of Grym's *special* squad?"

Devin's eyes turned gold, and the hand he held at his side grew pale gray fur and black claws.

That would be a yes. If I had to guess from the shape of the transformed hand...er...paw...Devin Sampson was a Wolf shifter.

Standing on the cop's other side, Ralph was oblivious to the change. "What's a special squad?"

Devin let the illusion fall. He relaxed visibly. "We handle the weird stuff."

It was as good an explanation as any. The truth of the matter was that all of Grym's special squad guys were supernormals. I'd met a few of them but had never met Devin. I offered him my hand. "Naida Griffith."

I let him roll my name over in his mind a

moment, watching the moment he recognized it. "Ah. It's nice to meet you, Keeper."

I nodded.

"Keeper?" Ralph asked, growing increasingly confused. "Keeper of what?"

I shrugged. "Think of me as a mini-museum. I store and protect rare artifacts."

Ralph nodded. "Cool."

"Have you tried using your..." He glanced at Ralph and frowned. "Look, Keeper, there's no way we can hide all this from the norms. We'll need to bring in help afterward to clean this up."

He meant that Grym would need to bring in some witches to wipe everybody's memories.

I grimaced. I knew he was right. But I just hated the thought of messing with people's minds. "I know. In answer to your question, I haven't. Not yet. I wasn't sure what we were dealing with." That was a lie—a small one. I knew what we were dealing with, but it hadn't occurred to me that there might be magical artifacts in a place like a mall. However, just like the weight I'd found in an athletic clothing store, people used lots of different items for display purposes. "I'll do that now." I looked around, noticing that all of the closest shops already had their security doors closed. "Why haven't you moved to a more protected spot?"

Devin tensed for a moment, a frown finding his face. "Every time we try to move, they attack. We actually started way down on that end of the mall. It's taken us over an hour to get here."

We all looked toward the hallway where Ralph and I had just been. "You need to get to the elevator."

He nodded. "If you can provide any kind of cover, I'd appreciate it." He glanced at Nina and stepped closer, lowering his voice. "I know what these things are. They want the baby. They're not getting her or that baby as long as I'm breathing."

I thought about the story Osvald had told me and couldn't help wondering if Desiree might be playing a special kind of game. "Let me do my thing." I jerked my head toward Ralph. "Keep an eye on him for a minute?"

Devin nodded.

I moved away from the group, tucking myself into an alcove between two stores, and pulled as much energy as I could muster into my fingertips. I sent the magic into the universe, giving it an extra boost that I hoped would find any artifacts available in the enormous mall.

Maybe even something useful.

There was a distant ping. And then another. And another.

My eyes went wide. I would never have guessed there could be three magical artifacts inside the mall. The air above us thickened and roiled. I felt the sting of deadly magic a beat before the cherubs emerged from thin air.

Four of them.

All armed with jagged teeth and poisonous arrows.

Devin dove toward Ralph as the first nasty cherub nocked an arrow and aimed. He shoved the man behind a large potted palm, leaping into the air and punching the cupid in the face before it could fire the arrow. The thing tumbled tail over teakettle and slammed into the wall above my head.

"Oy!" I screamed as the demon slid down the bricks and slammed into me.

A whistling sound had me flinging up a hand just in time to catch an ancient-looking metal lantern. As my fingers touched it, flame flared to life inside the scratched and cloudy glass. The demon on my back had drawn back its chubby arm and was ready to stick me with a poisoned arrow. The lantern light flared brightly, transposing a squat skeleton over the fleshy demon before my eyes.

The cherub screamed, a terrified, high-pitched shriek of fear and pain that made my teeth hurt. It flew backward off me in an attempt to escape the illumination and slammed into the ground, writhing in agony as the light turned the spectral vision of a skeleton into reality.

Within the space of three screams, the cherub had been reduced to nothing but ash.

The fire in the lantern went out.

Ralph screamed as another cherub dove from the sky and landed on top of him behind the big pot.

Nina had somehow gotten her hands on my weighted purse and was pummeling another cherub with the fashionable leather weapon.

Devin had a big hand around the throat of one cherub and was stabbing the knife at the other, continually missing as the thing dodged easily from side to side.

As I shoved to my feet, my horrified gaze spotted another cherub speeding through the air in Devin's direction.

I threw up my right hand, my brain automatically registering the soughing sound of air being displaced by a flying artifact. A stiff width of felt met my palm, and I looked down at a wide-brimmed felt hat with a hard brim.

Devin went down under three cupids, his husky cries turning my blood cold. His form became indistinct, wavering in the light, and started to grow. Dense gray fur sprouted along his arms.

He was shifting.

The cop dropped the knife and punched a suddenly massive fist into one of the cherub's faces. The nasty demon flew backward directly at me. I yelped and flung my hands up, not even thinking about the hat I was still clutching. To my surprise, the brim of the hat made a deep slice across the creature's back.

The cherub screamed and hit the floor near my feet. It promptly turned black and disappeared in a burst of gray dust.

I sneezed as the dust assailed my nostrils.

Devin's hands had turned to paws and he swung a thick, furred arm at another cherub, raking the nasty bug in four, deep furrows across its chest.

The cherub shot skyward, shrieking in pain, and then plummeted toward the half-shifted cop again. Acting on pure instinct, I threw the hat at the thing like a frisbee. The brim caught the cherub in its middle and the creature slammed into a thick pillar near the stairs and popped into dust.

The hat flew back my way. I threw up a hand and caught it, running at the cupid that was still attacking Nina. It had managed to yank her from behind the bench and was lifting her off the ground, its tiny wings moving as fast as a hummingbird's. Before I could reach her, a second demon had joined the first and they'd managed to get her a few inches off the floor.

I flew at them, smashing the brim into the first one and then, without thinking, slamming the hat down over the second cherub's head.

It disintegrated in a puff of dust.

Sebille buzzed past me, and green light filled the air above our heads. When I glanced up, I saw with horror that the air was thick with the ugly little things.

Heavy footsteps announced Grym's arrival, probably in gargoyle form by the sound of the footfalls.

My left hand shot into the air. A bottle slammed into my palm.

I threw the hat at two cupids diving toward Ralph, hitting first one and then the other. They disintegrated with a satisfying pop.

The hat came soaring back, and I caught it again.

I glanced at the bottle in my hand. "Super Pop. A sugary delight!" the label read.

"Great," I mumbled. "Soda pop. Not very useful."

"Behind you!" Nina yelled.

I reacted without thinking, swinging the hat at the demons. Before the artifact could connect, another cherub slammed into me and the hat hit the floor. I fell on top of it, and the cherub attacked, wings humming as its razor-sharp teeth snapped at my throat.

All I had left to fight with was the sugary pop.

I jammed the bottle between the deadly teeth and it broke, spilling the sugary liquid into the cupid's snapping jaws.

The demon went very still, its black eyes going wide, and with a sound like a balloon inflating, it suddenly expanded and started to float away. It was as if somebody had put an air hose into the thing's mouth and blown it up.

The cherub floated out of my grip and, tiny arms and legs flailing, sailed away like an ugly dirigible.

"Awesome sauce!" I said.

Another scream pierced the air. My shoulders sagged. I looked around for the culprit and found Nina fighting off three cherubs. With a sigh, I stood, one hand clutching the hat and the other holding the bottom of the broken soda bottle.

With a weary sigh, I trudged toward the battling woman with my strange weapons.

12

SPOTS TO BE A-VOIDED

Nina, Sebille, and I sat on the dust-covered bench where Nina had been hiding. The dusty remains of the cupids would have been off-putting, except that I couldn't find any part of my person that wasn't already covered in the stuff. What was a little more cherub dust on my weary butt?

Nina's hair stood straight up at the top, the fine strands glued together with battle gore. Her eyes were white spheres in a sea of gray grime. She stared straight ahead, one hand rubbing her copious baby bump, and said nothing for long moments.

Devin had been over several times to make sure she was okay. She'd nod each time, give him a weary smile, and then insist she was fine and that he should go back to work.

I wasn't sure if she was a strong woman or just so

freaked out by what had happened to her that she'd gone to that special place in her mind.

Beside me, the sprite looked fairly unaffected by the great battle of the demonic cherubs. She was inspecting the split hairs on the end of one of her long, red braids when I glanced her way. "What took you guys so long?" I asked, flinching at the accusatory tone of my question.

Sebille fixed me with a haughty look.

"Sorry," I said. "I'm a little grumpy."

Sebille rolled her eyes. "It wasn't a walk in the mall down there, you know. We kicked some serious cherub butt before we came up here." She grimaced. "Grym's cleaners are going to need a lot of vacuum bags."

I nodded. "It could be worse. At least the little guys pouffed into dust instead of entrails."

Sebille's gaze rose slowly upward to the glass dome at the center of the mall. "Except for those guys."

Half a dozen cherub balloons were stuck to the glass of the ceiling, tiny arms and legs flailing. I grinned. "As Lea would say, blizzardy!"

My friend Lea was a great BFF and a talented witch. But her grasp of modern slang left something to be desired.

Sebille snorted out a laugh. "I'm not sure how they're going to get them down."

"Pop them," said a soft voice beside me. Sebille

and I turned to find Nina grinning. "That's what I'd suggest."

We all laughed, the sound turning slightly hysterical before we managed to rein it in.

"Unh," said Ralph, who'd placed himself on the bench across from us and was looking a little green around the gills. Nobody had asked the mall manager how he felt because we were afraid he'd tell us.

He was a non-magic human. He'd watched what had to have been close to a hundred demonic cupids try to kill or abduct a bunch of his customers. He'd seen one man turn into a wolf. Yeah, Devin had finally gone all the way to furry. It had been stupendous.

Plus, Ralph had seen a dragonfly-sized Sebille shoot green energy at the nasty cherubs. He'd watched Grym pound them into literal dust with his rock hands. And he'd witnessed me slicing them with a sombrero and inflating them with sugar.

Busy day.

It was no wonder the man was currently mumbling to himself and twitching as if he'd swallowed a live wire.

I jerked my chin in his direction. "Should somebody go and...I don't know...hold his hand or something?"

Grym came up the stairs from the first floor, his

human form firmly back in place. His gaze searched the area until it found me. He smiled.

My tummy warmed from that smile, and my world stopped threatening to topple.

I stood as he headed our way and met him at the end of the crosswalk. "How's it going down there?"

He rubbed a hand over his weary face, the day's whiskers making a crackling sound against his hand. "The witches are here. They've managed to remove the poison from most of the affected and are working on wiping everybody's memories."

I nodded, rubbing my hands over my arms. "Ralph needs some attention." I gave Grym a meaningful look. "I'm starting to worry he'll never recover."

We both glanced toward the bedazzled manager. The man was smacking the air in front of his face as if he was being attacked by gnats.

Grym winced. "I'll have someone come up and take care of him."

A long, feral shriek sounded from the other end of the mall. I jumped and bumped into Grym. He steadied me, pulling me into his warmth. I wanted to pull away. To show him I could stand on my own two feet, but his warmth felt way too good to push away.

I sighed. "That will be Daisy. We locked her into the athletic attire store so she wouldn't kill me for looking at Ralph."

Grym made a non-committal grunting sound.

"I'll send the witches there after they finish with Ralph. Did you ever locate the rest of his staff?"

I shook my head. "I checked after the worst was over. The office was empty. They must have flown the coup."

He held me for a long moment, until I found the strength to pull away. We stood in awkward silence for a beat.

Then Grym pointed toward the domed ceiling. "Is that your handiwork?"

I looked up and barked out a laugh. "Guilty."

He shook his head. "It's never boring around you."

"I do try." I gave him a narrow-eyed look. "Are you over the whole caveman thing?"

He frowned. "Caveman thing?"

I formed my voice into what I assumed a caveman might sound like, though I had no way to know for sure since we hadn't run into any when we'd visited the Jurassic era. I wish we had. It would have been icy. "I man. You woman. I kill any man who touches woman."

Grym winced. "Yeah. Sorry about that. I kicked that off pretty quickly after you left. I'm surprised it even affected me. Poison usually doesn't."

"Maybe because you were still in your human form?" Grym's gargoyle form was, not too surprisingly, hard and impermeable. Not much got through it. And his system was attuned to that form. But although most poisonous things didn't have their full effect on him, occasionally something slipped past his defenses. "I'm glad it's gone. I kind of like you the way you are."

His eyes sparkled. "Ditto."

We stared at the flailing beachballs for a minute. Then I couldn't help myself. I had to ask. "How are you going to get them down?"

Grym's lips curved in a slow smile. "Well, there's only one way to get a balloon to descend."

I grinned too. I couldn't help it. "Pop them?"

He nodded. Light filled his gaze as he refocused it on the inflated cherubs.

"How are you going to do it?"

He bent down and pulled something shiny off the floor, holding a tiny arrow up for me to see. "It just so happens I have access to a whole bunch of sharp projectiles. I'm guessing there are a few discarded bows around here somewhere."

The inherent justice in using the cupid's bows against them was almost too much. I dissolved into laughter again. And was happy when Grym's deep chuckles joined with mine.

We were all sitting around the table at Croakies. Grym, me, Sebille, and Archie, trying to come up with a plan for finding the serum and stopping the cherubs.

Archie sipped the tea Sebille had given him. "I've been giving it a lot of thought, and I keep coming back to the missing serum."

I nodded because I agreed. "Whoever was behind the theft has to be the same one sending the evil cherubs around."

"Did the ogres admit to selling a ward-busting tool like the one they gave you to anyone else?"

"They denied it. But I couldn't help feeling like they weren't telling the whole truth." I glanced at Sebille.

She nodded. "I agree. They're a slippery bunch."

I barked out a laugh. "That's certainly one way to put it."

"Feel like giving them another visit?" Grym asked, a sparkle in his eye.

"Do I have to?" The fact that I sounded like a pouty seven-year-old trying to get out of eating her spinach did not escape me.

"We need to find Lovelace," Sebille said. "I think we should talk to this sister of his. Maybe she knows where the missing brother is. We'd probably have more luck talking to her than those big, naked guys."

Grym and Archie's eyes went wide. "Naked?" Archie asked.

Sebille's gaze slid away from his. I fidgeted for a moment before I glanced up at the big clock on the wall. "Will you look at the time. I need to...um...go... see somebody about something."

Grym grabbed my arm before I could escape. "You get a temporary pass on that story, but I'll expect a full accounting when this is over."

I flushed. "Yeah, we'll see."

Archie had a thoughtful look on his face. "What are you thinking about?" Sebille asked him.

The void sorcerer blinked. "Huh? Oh." He shook his head. "Something's niggling. I'll remember it, given enough time." He turned to me. "What type of artifact did the ogres give you?"

"It looks like a bottle opener. They insist it can pierce any ward."

One of Archie's shaggy brown brows lifted. "Have you tested it?" he asked.

"I haven't had time." I frowned. "I just don't know what good it will do us. It won't find the serum or the person who took it."

"I'm not so sure about that," Archie said. "As luck would have it, I'm familiar with that device. It's called a Toll Token, one of a family of single-use artifacts that can be rented for a limited time. After the token is used for the pre-specified task, it automatically returns to the person who rented it out so it can be loaned again."

My eyes went wide. "Really? I've never heard of such a thing."

Grym looked, well grim. "They're not exactly legal. I'd like to see the device," he told me.

Archie held up a hand. "You didn't pay the ogres anything for it, did you?"

Sebille and I shared a look.

"What?" Grym asked.

"We didn't pay them," Sebille said. "But we did sign a contract."

Archie paled. "What kind of contract?"

Sebille looked at me. I grimaced. "Something about guaranteeing the item's safety and...a bunch of other junk. It'll be fine." The airy quality I tried to insert into my voice sounded more panicked than lighthearted.

"I can't believe you signed a contract with the ogres you didn't read."

"Of course we didn't read it all," Sebille exclaimed. "The tricky parts ended on his backside."

Grym and Archie stared at her.

Finally, Grym said, "Please explain."

Sebille rolled her eyes, which was less than helpful, so I jumped in.

"The contract was written on the big naked guy's hairy back. Unfortunately, it was really wordy, so it kind of trailed down into other areas. I wasn't looking at that any more than I had to. They were lucky I put my signature at the bottom." My body convulsed in a violent shiver. "It was beyond disgusting."

"How did you affix your signature?" Archie asked.

The sprite and I gave him a look.

He waved it away. "Ink? Energy transfer? What? It's important."

"Energy transfer," Sebille said. "He gave us a choice, but that one didn't require any touching."

"Dastardly buggers," Archie exclaimed. He scrubbed a hand over his face and glanced at Grym. "It'll take the two of us to handle this, I'm afraid. You as the law of Enchanted and me as a representative of the Société."

Uncle Pudsy was a Void Sorcerer with the Société of Dire Magic, the ruling magical body for the Earthly dimension.

"So Sebille and I don't need to go?"

Archie glowered at us. "No. You've done quite enough damage."

My assistant and I bumped knuckles.

"Don't be so happy," Grym said, narrowing his dark-caramel gaze on us. "You'll have to decipher the log on the artifact. And believe me, as bad as our task is, yours is going to be ten times worse."

Despite his words, I couldn't wipe the smile off

my face at getting out of another visit to the ogres. I nodded. "Just tell me how to do it."

Archie sighed. "You must find a spot that is completely free of conflicting magical energy. There must be no interference of any kind, or the log won't open."

"Okay. Where would that be?"

Sebille shrugged. "No idea. As far as I know, magic exists everywhere."

"Not quite true," Archie said, standing up and brushing his hands over his robes. "There is one place that provides the neutrality you require."

"Where?" I asked.

In answer to my question, Uncle Pudsy smiled.

It wasn't a nice smile.

13

TO GRANDMOTHER'S HOUSE WE GO

I'd never seen so many glowy numbers, words, and icons. My eyes were slowly going crossed as I tried to make sense of them.

The infernal crunching sound behind me wasn't helping.

"Will you please stop eating those cheesy crunchies and help me here?" I barked at the sprite.

"I'm not done yet."

I made a grab for the bag, but she ducked out of the way, spilling cheesy crunchies onto the black, rubbery floor of our cozy little void. I shrugged. I was pretty sure the five-second rule didn't apply in a magical void. I grabbed the fallen soldiers and crammed them into my mouth.

Sebille leaned over my shoulder, her cheese breath wafting over me. "Maybe the columns are horizontal instead of vertical."

I peered at the wall-sized mess of indecipherable symbols and stuff and slowly tilted my head.

Nothing.

I squinted. The symbols wavered and then settled right back into their unintelligible order again.

Sighing, I flung myself backward, startling Sebille into jerking away from me. "Watchit!" she yelled as two cheesy crunchies fell from her bag and onto the blackness beneath us. I plucked them up and shoved them into my mouth. "We're never going to figure this out," I mumbled around the savory treat.

Sebille dropped down next to me with a sigh. "That hairy naked guy's starting to look better and better."

I thought about it for a beat and then shook my head. "Nah. I'd still rather be in here trying to decipher the log."

We lay there, staring at the iridescent green figures hanging on the air in front of us. At first glance, they seemed to be a bunch of nonsense. Like somebody sneezed out a random mix of numbers, letters and symbols and they stuck to the wall.

I frowned at the thought. "Do you think this was a trick?"

Sebille crunched. "What do you mean?" she asked, a bright orange crumb shooting from her mouth and sticking to the wall of symbols.

I stretched my sock-covered toe toward the crumb and flicked it off, so it didn't confuse us even more than we already were. "I mean, maybe this isn't supposed to be legible. Maybe Grym and Archie just put us in here to punish us because they had to go read a hairy naked guy's backside to find out what you and I promised in return for that artifact."

She shrugged. "It's what I'd do."

"Yeah," I said on a breath. "Me too."

We lay there a long time, only the sound of mutual crunching breaking the silence. Then Sebille said. "What if they forget to get us out of here?"

"Grym wouldn't forget us."

"Not on purpose. But the ogres might capture them or something. What if they can't come back for days? Or weeks?"

I frowned into the darkness. "How many bags of cheesy crunchies did you bring in here?"

"Just one. But I have one of Lea's apples and a dozen cookies too."

I sat up, leaning on my elbows. "You have cookies and you didn't tell me?"

"You'd have eaten them all by now."

I collapsed back onto the nothingness that formed the floor of the void. What could I say? She was right. "I'm thirsty."

Silence met my statement, and horror filled me. "You didn't bring any drinks, did you?"

"Why was it my job to think of everything?" she objected. "You could have brought drinks."

"You said you'd get us snacks. I just assumed."

"You know what they say about assuming, don't you?"

I flapped a hand at her, annoyed.

We lay there a few more minutes, and another problem asserted itself. "I have to pee."

Sebille's only response was to scoot further away from me.

I sighed, squiggling uncomfortably. My bladder became more insistent by the moment. My foot bumped the artifact that was lying on the ground beneath the wall of figures.

The columns of nonsense words and numbers shimmied and changed as the artifact moved.

I blinked as one column of figures came into focus, and I was actually able to understand what it said. I sat up, using my finger as a pointer while I read. "Pascal Ormond, December 3rd, 2014, Warg spell. One use. Returned December 5th, 2014."

An indecipherable jumble of numbers and words followed that information. I figured it was an address because it ended with the name of an alternate dimension. "They rent inter-dimensionally too?"

Sebille dropped her bag of crunchies as she sat up. "Makes sense. That portal they took us through probably feeds a bunch of pathways." She glanced at me. "How'd you make that change?"

"I bumped the artifact with my toe."

Sebille lay down on her belly and shimmied to the artifact, taking care to stay beneath the wall of shimmering symbols. She changed the orientation of the artifact slightly. "What did that do?"

I squinted but saw no change. "Nothing."

She tried again and again, but nothing changed. All we had was Pascal the Warg.

Sebille flopped back down beside me. "Another dead end."

"I really have to pee," I whined. Sebille probably rolled her eyes, but I couldn't see them rolling in the dark.

We lay there another few minutes. Then an idea occurred, and I slapped my head. "Of course!" I sat up and threw myself to my belly.

"What are you doing?" Sebille asked, sounding bored.

"I'm an artifact Keeper," I declared, reaching for the artifact.

"Well, duh," she responded in a dull voice.

"No. I mean, it won't respond to you because you don't have Keeper energy. I do." I moved the artifact slightly and Sebille surged upright, her green eyes glowing in the cast-off light from the log. "Yes! Keep moving it. Slowly. It's changing."

Ten minutes of subtle turns and shifts of the artifact finally landed us on the information we needed.

I held the pointy end of the opener off the ground an inch and shifted it sideways a centimeter, stopping as Sebille gave a whoop of joy! "That's it! There she is!"

I couldn't let go of the artifact to read it. "Memorize it and read it to me, so I can memorize it too. We don't want to go through this again to find it."

Silence met my instruction. "Sebille?" Nothing. Dread started to dance along my spine in spiked heels. "Um, Sebille, my finger's getting tired here."

The sprite sighed. "We don't need to memorize it. We've been there before."

I hesitated another minute. "You're sure?"

To my surprise, the sprite flopped onto her back again. "Unfortunately."

Still, I was reluctant to let the artifact go. "Where is she? Where's the princess?"

Sebille scrubbed a hand over her long, freckled face. Dread's stilettos dug more deeply into my spine. "You're freaking me out here, sprite."

"Good. You should be freaked out. Princess Desiree listed her address in The Enchanted Forest."

I swallowed. I hated that place. The last time we'd been there, I'd almost been eaten by a two-headed snake, killed by wraiths, burned alive in the clutches of a mad and powerful sorceress, and watched everyone I cared about nearly die.

Fun times.

"Okay. Well, that's bad. But it can't be as bad as last time, right?"

Sebille made a losing buzzer noise. "Wrong again for a thousand. It's exactly as bad as last time. The Princess's address is the black castle. We need to go back to Dacara's castle again."

Sizzling slug snot!

14

SHORTCUT TO THE SORCERESS'S LAIR

"But we didn't see her the last time we were there," I argued. Aside from a quick pee break, we'd been arguing about the sprite's bad news since Archie sprang us from the void. "This has to be a mistake."

Sebille stuffed the depleted bag of cheesie crunchies into the cabinet and gave me a look. "You saw the address on the log. It's no mistake. If you want to talk to Princess Desiree, you need to do this."

I sighed. I knew I was being difficult about the whole "visit the evil sorceress in The Enchanted Forest" thing. But who could blame me? Dacara was about as evil as they came. She and her wraiths had nearly killed all of us the last time we'd gone there.

Dacara was called the dual sorceress because she was one of a rare few sorcerers who wielded more than one kind of magic energy. In her case, death magic, represented by her ability to call and direct wraiths, as well as a deadly fire energy. She'd been banished to her ugly black castle in The Enchanted Forest by the Magical Universe, whose bidding had been done by the Société of Dire Magic.

Dacara wasn't supposed to be able to leave the forest. But she'd recently found a loophole in the form of a sweet time-and-space-traveling tortoise named Tildy.

My friends and I had nearly died keeping her from tortoise-napping the sweet magical dinosaur to escape her prison.

The demonic Desiree deciding to pay the dual sorceress a visit was a bad thing. A really bad thing. If the two of them escaped into the world and combined their magics...well...the word apocalypse came to mind.

I blinked. "Wait a minute. Dacara's castle is spelled so she can't leave it. Are you telling me Desiree just popped into that castle to see her?"

"*We* did," Grym reminded me. I glanced his way. He and Archie had been bent over some star-chart type maps they'd spread over the table—the table that had been in three broken pieces when Sebille and I went into the void. Either Hobs had gotten good with tools, or I had a fairy godmother in the store.

I was guessing the former.

When Grym wasn't correcting me, he and Archie had their heads down and were murmuring softly in between pointing at several black circle things dotting the map.

"We did get in," I agreed. "After fighting our way through an army of wraiths," I complained.

Archie's head came up. His eyes, the same shade of blue as mine, were underscored by purple arcs of weariness. "We might be able to skip the wraiths this time," he said, his brows lowering into an expression filled with concern.

I perked up. "How?"

Archie poked a long finger at one of the black circles on the map. "Altas Magnanimus. Alt-Mag for short."

"Altas Whatsus?" I asked.

"It's a rare kind of void," Grym told us, looking excited. "Archie says it comes around once in a millennium."

Archie nodded. "Yes. Rare indeed. And as unpredictably dangerous as a female bear with young ones." The twin lines between his brows deepened. "But, if I can control it, we can bypass the trek to the castle, the deadlier aspects of the forest, and the wraiths."

"If?" Sebille asked, arcing a red brow.

He nodded thoughtfully. "Alt-Mag is a scientific oddity. There are no other voids like it in the

Universe. In fact, some in the void scientific community have argued that it's not really a void."

"There's a void scientific community?" I asked, totally missing the larger point as I had a tendency to do.

Archie ignored my question, proving it wasn't important.

I did a mental shrug. "What is it then?"

"If you buy into the train of thought that it's not genus voidis, then the logical conclusion is that it's an anomaly." When he saw the dual blank looks Sebille and I were sending him, he shook his head. "The Universe is constantly shifting and twisting. The action pinches some things and expands others, creating an area that's prone to gathering magical detritus, if you will."

Our blank expressions deepened.

He sighed. "Think of it as a magical gas bubble."

I blinked. "The Universe has gas?"

"Once in a millennia, yes," Archie agreed.

"But does that mean it's in danger of popping?" Sebille asked.

Archie sighed. "Ay, there's the rub."

Aaaannnnnddd he was quoting Shakespeare.

It was as if England was reaching out through one of his voids and sucking him back.

"Stay with us, professor," I teased. "Tell us why this Alt-gasbag does us any good."

He blinked. "Oh, yes. Well, it can carry us right to the castle like a taxi, can't it?"

"I don't know. Can it?" Sebille asked.

"It can." With the affirmation, Archie seemed resolved. "I can do this. It should be just like driving any void."

I hated to pop his proverbial confidence bubble, but... "I seem to remember, when we were in the age of dinosaurs, that 'driving' the voids home was going to take years or more."

"Well, yes, Naida," he said, clearly offended. "But that was through thousands of years. This is a simple spatial shift. And the bubble should be some-where in the forest already."

"Piece of cake then," I said.

Sebille rolled her eyes.

Grym's phone rang. "I need to get this," he told us after glancing at the ID. He wandered away from us talking on his cell.

"Okay," I said. "We just need to go to the forest, find this gas bubble, and ride it to the castle?"

"Praying it doesn't pop," Sebille added with a grimace.

Archie bobbed his head back and forth. "Yes, and no. That's far too simplistic a portrayal of what needs to happen."

"Then 'splain it to us," I said. "I have a feeling we're running out of time."

For the first time since I'd known him, my uncle

seemed short on words. His lips moved a few times and then slammed together, his gaze lowering to the small circle on the map.

"Spill it, Pudsy," Sebille demanded.

Archie shook his head. "I need to speak with Professor Osvald."

Sebille and I shared a surprised look. Neither of us had apparently seen that one coming. "The book head?" Sebille asked. "Why?"

Archie tipped his head. "Did Osvald ever explain to you how he got locked inside his books?"

"Mostly he just ducks and runs when he sees us," Sebille said.

I winced. She wasn't wrong. "He might have mentioned a curse or something."

"Osvald was 'riding' Alt-Mag as you so crudely put it..."

"Hey. Don't go full British snotty on me, Pudsy. That wasn't crude. It was succinct."

He flapped a pale hand. "Whatever. The last time the anomaly showed up, a sorcerer dared Osvald to try to control it. He managed it quite well for a while, steering it from London to Dublin, Ireland without much trouble at all."

"But," I urged, watching Grym head back our way.

"But, the Universe with its infinitely restless nature decided to twist just as he was crossing Dublin Bay. The bubble went off level, started spinning out of control, and Osvald was magically incised."

My brows lifted into my hairline. "Incised?"

"Luckily...or unluckily for him depending on your viewpoint...he was able to fling his essence into the book he was using to drive the anomaly and preserve himself in the way you see today. It was quite brilliant, actually. Osvald has always been magically talented. He was intricately connected to his books...supernormally speaking. The result was that he succeeded in spreading his essence across every volume he'd ever written." Archie frowned thoughtfully for a moment as if trying to understand the magic involved in making that happen. Finally, he shook his head to dismiss his thoughts. "The connection was weak at best, but Osvald knew a sorcerer with talents in the area of anchoring. He underwent a magical procedure that anchored him firmly to the volumes. Quite the feat, actually. Though Osvald would later come to think of it as more of a curse than a blessing."

I frowned. "This happened a Millennia ago?" I was pretty sure I remembered seeing a picture of the professor in fairly modern clothes in one of his books.

"Actually, it was only about fifty years ago."

"But you said these bubbles only come around once in a Millennia," I argued.

"Yes, yes, generally. The law of averages puts

them into existence about every thousand years. But once in a while one appears outside of that time-frame. It's been hypothesized that those interim anomalies are less stable. Which might explain why Osvald ended up implanted inside his books."

"We have a problem," Grym said as he joined us.

"What's wrong?" I asked, noting the tightness around his eyes and lips.

"Those cherub things are back. They're attacking all around the city, and my people are having trouble containing them." He sighed. "I have to go. Will you wait until I get back before going into the forest?"

I shook my head. "I don't think we can. The only way to stop these cherub things is to get to Desiree." Which was an overly optimistic statement since our success hinged on her being cooperative. Even if she was willing, there was no guarantee she'd be any more helpful than Lovelace had been. And he'd been motivated.

Grym held my gaze for a long moment and then sighed. He tapped a finger gently against my chin. "Take care of yourself. Okay?"

"I'm the queen of taking care of myself," I told him.

Sebille snorted.

I glared at her.

Grym looked at Archie. "Who else can you take?"

"I've got someone in mind. Don't worry. Go do what you need to do."

Grym nodded and left.

Watching him go, I remembered their visit to the ogres. We'd been so distracted by the location of the demon princess, we hadn't talked about it. "How'd it go with the ogres?" I asked my uncle. "Did Sebille and I sign away our firstborn children or anything?"

She snorted out a laugh. "As if. I'm never having kids. I have my hands full with the hobgoblin, the frog, and the cat."

"Worse," Archie said. "But let's not focus on that right now. We have bigger fish to fry."

I didn't like the sound of that, but the dividing door slammed open before I could ask him what he meant. Hobs flashed across the room. The diaper from earlier was gone. In its place was an adorable tuxedo, complete with a polka-dotted bow tie and a matching cummerbund. He'd even combed the light brown thatch of hair between his big ears to one side. The hair made him look like a cute little nerd. He fixed his enormous, light blue eyes on me. "Have you seen her, Miss?"

"Seen who?" I asked, frowning.

"My date, Miss. She should be here." He cast his gaze around the room. "Where are the cookies?" He stomped an oversized bare foot on the carpet, making the long hairs that decorated his big toe dance. "We need sweets, Miss!"

I held up a hand. I'd never seen him so agitated.

"Okay, okay. I might have something upstairs. Don't get your bowtie in a twist."

Hobs tucked in his chin and tried to see his bow tie. "It's twisted?" With a wail, he spun around and retreated back through the dividing door. Presumably to fix his tie.

I cast Sebille a glare.

She threw up her hands. "It's not me. That hysteria is all his."

"This stupid holiday is infecting everyone. Is he even old enough to date?" I asked the others.

"He is," Archie said, typing with his thumbs on his phone. "In hobgoblin years, he's in his late teens. But there aren't many hobgoblins around. I'd be surprised if he'd found a girl hobby his own age."

I shrugged it off. As Archie said, I had bigger fish to fry. But I made a mental note to go get the stash of heart cookies out of my room before we left for the forest. If Hobs was in love, I certainly didn't want to get in his way.

Lea opened the front door and stuck her head inside. "Hey, Naida. Did you know you had a line of customers out here?"

"I do?" I had a moment of sheer panic. I'd had the store closed all day, and I just realized I'd totally forgotten about the Hearts of Bomb signing. I turned a panicked look on my assistant. "Sebille?"

She accurately read the rattled look in my expression. "I've got this." Hurrying to the tea area, she opened the closet beside the counter and pulled out something that was pink and red and covered in stupid frilly hearts. She handed it to Archie. "Here, go into the bathroom and put this on."

I watched in awe as Archie did as he was told. Sebille jerked her chin toward the sales counter. "Grab him some pens and a bunch of those Hearts of Bomb bookmarks we had printed."

I did as I was told too. It was better than standing helpless and alarmed as my business took a nosedive before my very eyes.

By the time I'd gathered up the stuff she'd told me to get, Sebille was filling the empty cookie tray with a fresh display of heart cookies. Lea wandered over and took one. "Can I have some of this punch?"

"Punch?" I asked, my eyes bulging.

"Sure," Sebille said. "Would you pour for the customers too?"

"You got it," Lea said.

"Where'd you get all this?" I asked, flabbergasted.

"My secret," Sebille said. She lowered her head to hide her grin, but I spotted it. She and I were going to have a talk later.

Archie emerged from the bathroom in the Valentine's Day decorated robes and headed toward the table where he'd be signing books. I dropped the pens and bookmarks on the table.

The dividing door slammed open again, and I

expected Hobs to barge back in. It wasn't him. My cat sauntered into the store, wearing a tiny pink vest covered in hearts and roses. He was also wearing a red bow tie.

Movement at the edge of my vision had me turning in time to see Sebille jerking the blanket off the top of Mr. Slimy's terrarium. She reached down behind the table holding his glassy home and grabbed a large piece of white cardboard with the words, "Kiss a Frog. Meet Your Prince." written in tidy block letters.

I glanced in horror at the pudgy green squish. He was staring at me with his bulgy black eyes, his throat working in agitation. Slimy had the kissy lips again.

I'm going to give her so many warts when this is over! sayeth the frog.

I gasped. "Sebille!"

She blew me off with a raspberry and went back to the tea counter, where she grabbed a large bag of chalky candy hearts that said stupid things on them like, "Be my Valentine". Or, "Pucker up, there's a frog in your near future". Okay, maybe that last one was mine, but you get the idea.

"Has the world gone totally mad?" I asked no one in particular.

"Meow!" Wicked said before brushing up against my calf.

Sebille hurried to the front door and turned to me. "Ready?"

I wanted to scream *No!* and stamp my feet. But I sighed. "Where do you want me?" And more importantly, when had I completely lost control?

"Behind the counter. We're gonna sell some books!"

15

DING DONG, THE WITCH IS DECIDEDLY
LESS DEAD THAN WE'D HOPED

Osvald's ruddy face was angry, the thick veins on his neck bulging with pique. "Have you lost your mind, man?"

Archie looked completely at ease in the old wooden chair at Shakespeare's desk. His smile was slightly condescending, which I didn't think was going to go over well with the irate...er...head. "Don't throw a wobbly, Morty..."

I snorted. *Morty*.

"We need your expertise," Archie told him with a frown. "You're the only person who's survived navigating one of these things. Your practical knowledge is invaluable."

A dark, bushy brow lowered over a menacing black eye. "Yes, and it worked out so well for me, didn't it?"

Archie shrugged as if the loss of a body was a trivial issue. "You had a spot of bad luck."

Osvald's dark, scraggly head tipped backward on a bark of laughter. "Yes. You could call it that."

Archie's manner softened. He leaned forward. "Look, Morty, this is important. I wouldn't ask you if it weren't."

Archie's change in manner seemed to reach Osvald where his previous arrogance hadn't. "How far would we need to travel?"

Archie grinned, clapping his hands and rubbing them together. "A mere mile or two. Hardly long enough to matter."

When Osvald didn't immediately refuse, Archie's face lit with excitement. "Brilliant! This will be one for the books." Judging by his wide grin, I was starting to worry he was more interested in piloting an anomaly through The Enchanted Forest for the scientific chops it would give him, rather than to help me.

But, if it got us out of dealing with those wraiths, I was all for it. I'd just try not to focus on the whole, losing my body thing.

Ogre boogers!

The bell on the front door jangled, and I jumped. Sebille had already locked up and set the ward. I touched Archie on the shoulder and mouthed, "I'm going to see who's here."

He nodded and turned back to Osvald. The two

of them were lost in plotting our adventure through The Enchanted Forest.

I opened the dividing door and stepped through, looking at the door. If I squinted, I could still see the glow of the special ward we used to keep magical trouble out. The regular deadbolt was still in place too.

Despite the jangle, the door didn't appear to have been opened.

Hm.

The store was empty and quiet.

I caught movement out of the corner of my eye and swung around.

There was nothing there.

Ice formed on my spine as I pulled Keeper magic into my hands. It flared silver and bright, spitting into the silence of the store. My magic might be defensively limited beyond Croakies' walls, but it was a force to be reckoned with inside them. "Whoever's here, show yourself."

The atmosphere thickened and swirled in creams and browns near the door and something twirled away, leaving a high-pitched giggle in its wake.

I frowned. "I said, show yourself!" Putting magic into my voice to lock the intruder into place with my command, I sent a cloud of silver energy rolling through the area where I'd seen the movement. The illuminating energy caught on something, or someone, who stood about two-feet-tall and had shiny brown hair. The creature blinking down at me from the top of one of the bookshelves had enormous dark eyes. It grinned widely before spreading its dainty hands on the air and making rolling motions, like waves on an ocean. Several books on the shelves below straightened up and one that had been left out of its slot slipped back with a hearty snick.

"Who are you?" I asked.

The creature giggled again, its long, brown hair swaying as it threw its arms into the air and, with a saucy wink, disappeared on a soft gasp of displaced air.

"What in the world?"

I turned and looked at the door. Had whatever... whoever that was, just broken through my ward again? I rubbed the gooseflesh on my arms as dread slipped through me. I'd enjoyed the feeling of safety my security measures had given me. But, suddenly that feeling of safety was gone.

The dividing door opened behind me. I turned to look at Sebille. She was dressed for bed in a red onesie with white horizontal stripes. Her fire-engine red hair was pulled back from her face, no doubt woven into a single thick braid that trailed down her back. Her expression was filled with concern.

Adrenaline pumped instantly through my veins. "What's wrong?"

She sighed. "Don't go all drama llama on me. I just thought you should know."

"Know what?" I asked, closing the distance between us.

"It's Hobs." Despite her impatience with my reaction, I couldn't miss the lines between her red brows that highlighted her own worry.

I grabbed her hand. "Is he hurt? Sick?" My chest tightened. I tried to remember the last time I'd seen him. It had been a couple of hours. Just before the book signing. "Where is he?"

"He's upstairs. Sitting on your couch." The worry lines deepened. "He doesn't look good, Naida. I..." She clamped her lips closed and frowned.

"What?" I asked, clutching her bony arm with both hands. "Tell me, Sebille. You're scaring me."

"I think he took some of the love serum."

Oh, goddess, no!

I dodged past the sprite and flew up the stairs, taking them two at a time. My toe caught on the last step and I started to fall, only managing to stay on my feet by fast-stepping and windmilling my arms.

I slapped a hand against the unlatched door and all but fell over the wooden threshold, stumbling awkwardly through the door.

I caught myself on the back of my couch and stopped, panting like a puppy.

I really needed to get in better shape.

Hobs was sitting in the middle of my couch, his

short legs sticking straight out from the cushion and his spidery fingers wrapped around a heart-shaped box of candy in his lap. His head drooped on his tiny chest, his pale blue eyes closed.

He was still wearing the tuxedo from that morning and looked adorable.

I hurried around the couch. "Hey, buddy. What's going on? Who's the present for?"

He didn't respond.

"He won't talk. I've been trying for a while." Sebille was leaning against the doorframe, her bony arms crossed over her flat chest. From her negligent posture, someone who didn't know her might think she was bored. But, I knew better. I saw the worry darkening her green eyes. They didn't even have their usual sheen that made them seem to glow.

I sat down next to Hobs, lowering my head to look into his face. "What's wrong, Hobs? Do you feel sick?"

He didn't say anything. He didn't even blink. I wasn't sure he could even hear me. I glanced at Sebille. "This is bad."

She nodded, her lips tightened. "We need to get Doctor Whom."

I reached out and wrapped my fingers around one of Hobs' little hands. They felt like ice. "What makes you think he took some of that serum?" I asked, giving his hands a squeeze.

She shrugged. "I told you this morning that

drama was his." She motioned to his clothing. "That getup was his idea. I helped him find it, but it was all him."

I gave her a disbelieving look.

She held up a hand. "Okay, I was guilty about the puckery lips." She giggled. "You have to admit the customers thought it was a hoot."

I narrowed my eyes to slits.

"Okay, you don't have to admit it. I can see it in your eyes. You loved it."

"Sebille." My voice was a growled warning.

"I put the bow tie and vest on the cat too. But this..." She waved a hand at Hobs. "This is all him. He's in love."

"He doesn't seem very happy about it. Are you sure?"

"One hundred percent sure. I've seen this kind of thing before. Hobgoblins don't respond to strong emotions like the rest of us. They live life in over-drive. They do everything at five hundred percent, going five thousand miles per hour. So, when they love, they love completely, to the point of making themselves sick."

I frowned. "Which means that, yes, he might be in love. But it doesn't necessarily mean he took the serum, right?"

"Wrong. The other thing about hobgoblins is that, because it affects them so deeply, they're slow to embrace emotions. Think of it as a biological safety valve. If Hobs fell naturally into love, we'd have seen or heard it building for months. Maybe years. But there've been no signs. None."

She was right. I'd been caught totally off guard that morning when Hobs had declared he had a date. I winced. "You think he broke the ward and took the serum?" I didn't want to believe it. I'd gone against all the advice of my friends to let him live at Croakies. Even though several people had warned me it would be dangerous. Hobgoblins were tricksters. And having a trickster living in a place with tens of thousands of magical artifacts was risky.

I sighed, my own heart breaking. It might be hard for hobgoblins to embrace emotion, but it wasn't hard for me. I loved the little guy. And he was in serious trouble.

"I don't think he stole it," Sebille said, chewing her lip.

I wanted to believe her, but Sebille loved the little guy too. We could both be fooling ourselves because we didn't want to consider the alternative.

"If he did, he'd have hidden it here at Croakies," I said.

She frowned but nodded. "Unfortunately, Hobs is a master at hiding stuff."

He was. He'd once hidden a stash of frosted chocolate brownies in a wrinkle to another dimension. The thought made my stomach twist in alarm.

"He could have even opened up one of those doors to another plane and hidden it there."

We'd never find that serum.

"I just don't think he'd take it, Naida."

Sebille's voice was firmer than before. She meant what she said.

I expelled air. "Okay. Let's go with that for now. If he didn't take the serum, how did he get exposed?"

"Someone deliberately gave it to him."

"Why would someone do that?"

"Because he snuck up on them and caught them stealing it," Sebille said, shrugging.

Okay, that made sense. I nodded. "It's definitely plausible."

Hobs' little body convulsed suddenly, the shudders violent enough to have pitched him off my couch if I hadn't been holding onto him.

I wrapped myself around him and held on, tears rolling down my cheeks. "What can I do!" I yelled at Sebille, my heart breaking.

She held up a finger and ran out of the room. A second later, I saw a burst of green energy on the landing and heard the buzz of her wings as she flew away.

"Wicked!" I screamed, wondering where my wayward feline had gotten to.

Sebille ran back into the room, holding a gooey square of chocolate pastry in her hand.

A frosted chocolate brownie! Hobs was crazy for

them. It was as close to an addiction for the little hobgoblin as anything we had.

"Hold this under his nose."

I grabbed the delectable treat, the intoxicating scent of rich chocolate wafting to my nose as I took it, and shoved the brownie in front of Hobs' little button nose.

Nothing happened for several minutes. I'd just about given up on it working when his long-fingered hand snaked up and grabbed the brownie from me. He pressed it against his lips, not biting but just inhaling the treat. Ever so slowly, Hobs' muscles slowly relaxed until he sagged against me, giving a long sigh as he fell into a restless sleep. His breathing was still much too fast, and his chest heaved as if he struggled to get enough air into his lungs.

I sagged too, completely wrung out. "That was horrible."

Sebille slid her arms under Hobs and moved him to my bed, covering him with the blanket. She stood looking down on him for a beat, her brow furrowed with concern. I'd never seen her so pale. "We need to get Doctor Whom."

I nodded.

"Meow!"

I turned to find Mr. Wicked trotting into the apartment, tail high and whipping. He was naked again, having somehow ditched his little bow tie and vest.

"Where have you been?" I scolded my cat, earning a hostile glare from his flashing orange eyes. The message couldn't have been clearer if he'd spoken the words. "I'm a busy cat. Cut me some slack."

Though I had no idea exactly what kept my magical cat busy all day and night, having first-hand knowledge of his whereabouts pretty much only when he was asleep on my pillow or sitting on the windowsill in the sun with Mr. Slimy at his side, I sensed that he used his magical connection to me to keep Croakies running smoothly and limit magical explosions of the kind we'd been suffering since the toxic magic vault had been breached.

Mostly he was successful. Occasionally, things got past him.

I'd long ago admitted to myself that, of the two of us, Wicked was easily the most magically astute.

Mr. Wicked jumped up onto the bed and draped himself alongside Hobs, placing a tiny gray paw in the center of the hobgoblin's heaving chest. A faint charcoal glow appeared beneath Wicked's paw, and I gasped as I felt the tug of his magic use in my belly.

Hobs' chest stopped heaving and his breathing slowed. Finally, he sighed and melted into a much more restful sleep.

Wicked folded himself into a tidy coil next to his friend and proceeded to join him in a nap.

"Okay," Sebille said. "Let's get the Doc here before Wicked's magic wears off."

I eyed Hobs. "You think he's going to get worse again?"

She stood and nodded, her manner totally free of her usual judgmental disdain. "Yes. His problem isn't gone. He's just oblivious to it while he sleeps. But the cat's spell won't last forever. It's just given us some time to get help." Sebille fixed my cat with a rare look of respect.

As if he could see her through his lids, Wicked's eyes flashed open, the orange flaring with hostility. He hissed at the sprite, his claws flexing free before he sheathed them again.

Sebille hissed back at him. Then she turned on her heel and strode determinedly from the room. "Come on, Naida. We don't have much time."

I glanced at my cat, arching a brow in question. He softened his gaze, a soft rumble vibrating in his throat.

I shook my head. "You two. I'll never understand your relationship."

Wicked bathed a perfectly clean paw, ignoring me completely.

16

WHOOO?

I felt like an idiot.

"Try again, Naida. We need him."

I glared at Sebille, certain she was playing games but unable to deny her for fear that Hobs really would die without help. I expelled a breath and tried again. "Paging Doctor Whooooo!"

"More uplift on the Whooooo," she said, her lips twitching. "Like an owl."

I stamped my foot, then jumped and yelped as a bright light flashed in the middle of the library, and an enormous birdhouse appeared.

Light flared around the structure for a moment, blinking like silent, golden emergency lights on an ambulance. And then the lights cut off and the door in the center of the small structure opened on silent hinges.

A creature straight out of the pages of a Grimms fairy tale stood blinking owlishly at us.

He was approximately five feet tall. Several inches shorter than my own five-feet-nine-inch height. His form was pear-shaped, with a sloping aspect, as if he was made of wax and had spent too much time in the sun, partially melting. Doctor Whom wore a cloak of feathers that fluttered from his narrow shoulders to his much wider hips, dropping just past his knobby knees to brush the calves of his short, skinny legs. Just like the last time he'd been summoned, the Doctor's bowed calves were covered in fitted, yellow socks that stopped at his ankles. They looked like support hose for birds. His feet were bare, the toes long and curved downward like claws.

The doc blinked slowly at me through enormous eyes, which were set close together on either side of a sharp, beaklike nose. "Whooo?"

I was briefly distracted as several tiny gray and white mice skittered past his long feet from the interior of the traveling birdhouse and disappeared beneath the bookshelves.

I sighed. Visits from the good doctor always required rodent poop cleanup on aisle five.

"Whooo?" the good doctor repeated, his lips pursed with pique.

"Um, my friend, Hobs." I pointed toward the steps. "He's upstairs."

Whom didn't turn his body to look at the second floor landing. He only turned his head, rotating it nearly a full three-hundred-sixty degrees without difficulty.

I grimaced, my hand going to my throat in sympathetic pain.

Without another word, Doctor Whom spun around and returned to his birdhouse, closing the door behind him.

"Um," I said.

The golden lights began to flash again and I took a step toward the birdhouse. "Wait, don't leave!" I threw myself toward the house, determined to hold him there by sheer will if I had to.

The house disappeared in a burst of eyeball-searing light and I stumbled forward, slamming up against the stair railing. Pain radiated through my shins, where they met the immovable edge of the steps.

Before I could straighten, light flared through the open door to the apartment upstairs.

Sebille and I shared a surprised glance and then hightailed it up the stairs.

Wicked hissed at the magical birdhouse, all the hair on his back standing on end. A constant yowl emerged from his throat, and the whipping of his tail could have turned eggs into meringue.

Still, there was a hungry glint in his eyes as he watched Doctor Whom waddle across the room. I caught Wicked licking his lips when the birdman came close.

Talk about punching above your weight class.

I hurried over to the bed so I could watch the doctor work. "We think he might have inadvertently gotten some love serum, and it made him love crazed," I told Whom. "Then he went into some kind of fugue state and finally convulsions."

Whom tugged his stethoscope from under his feathery cloak. He pressed it against the little hobgoblin's chest and listened for a moment, frowning.

I threw Sebille a worried glance.

She shook her head in a quick jerk.

Whom replaced the stethoscope beneath the cloak and lifted a strange, gnarled hand that had feathers springing from the knuckles instead of hair. A curved claw emerged from the yellow flesh.

I'd seen his method of assessment before, so I was ready. Or I thought I was. But I still grimaced as he sliced the claw along the inside of Hobs' skinny arm. Blood rose from the gouge and beaded there. It was a sickly pink rather than the vibrant red I'd expected. "Does that blood look right to you?"

Doctor Whom grunted in response.

Sebille shrugged.

The birdman sniffed his bloody claw and jerked away, making a birdlike sound of alarm.

Wicked spit at Whom, crouching lower on the bed as if preparing to attack.

Doctor Whom turned his enormous eyes on me. "What did you say he was poisoned with?"

"We think love serum," I told him.

He shook his head. "I'm not familiar with the pathology of this poison." He turned his head and coughed, bringing up a lumpy dark gray ball that was slashed through with the stark white of tiny bones.

I gagged, covering my mouth with my hand to keep my last meal...or cookies...from making an uncomfortable return.

Doctor Whom pressed the slimy ball of bird barf onto the bloody scratch. He rested back on his bent legs, squatting rather than actually sitting, and closed his eyes. He began to whistle.

We watched him in what appeared to be a meditative state for fifteen minutes before I lost patience and spoke up. "Doctor?"

He opened one eye, narrowing it at me. "Have

patience, young lady. The process must complete itself."

"Yes. But...is anything happening?" The last time I'd seen him do the puke poultice method, the poison rose up from the cut and into the poultice. I didn't see anything coming out of Hobs' arm.

He glanced down at the poultice, his thick black brows dipping toward his beaky nose. "We'll give it more time." And then he closed his eyes and started whistling again.

I sighed. "How about some tea?" I suggested to Sebille. She and I both knew I was asking her to make it since she was tea-talented and I was...not.

She threw Hobs a last, worried glance and nodded, heading toward my little kitchen. I spun on my heel. "I think I have some pie..." I jerked to a halt, my gaze caught on the scene playing out on the floor in front of me.

Unnoticed by me, my cat had jumped down from the bed and gone exploring. Clearly, the giant bird-house invading our home was the logical place to start his exploration.

Wicked was crouched, tail barely moving, and eyes fixed on the tiny white creature squatting near Whom's door. The mouse's cute little pink nose twitched with alarm, its long whiskers quivering.

I watched in horror as Wicked licked his chops.

He'd apparently realized a giant bird was beyond

even his formidable hunting skills. Not so a tiny mouse.

"Wicked," I warned in a soft voice. At that moment, I really wished my cat was a dog, so I'd have a snowball's chance in Hades of getting him to listen.

But he wasn't a dog.

And he'd caught the scent.

And if I didn't do something fast, that cute little rodent was going down.

Wicked's backend tensed. The mouse twitched in alarm. And I started to leap, knowing I'd be too late.

Wicked pounced. The mouse squeaked and flew into the air.

I threw myself at Wicked and hit the carpet hard, skidding along the rough surface on my elbow. Fire burned along my arm, the pain exquisite. "Ayee!" I yelled in pain and frustration.

The room exploded in a burst of yellow light. Sounds were muffled and everything turned weightless.

I floated above the floor in a formless bubble, even the pain in my elbow dulling beneath the magic that held me in thrall.

Wicked floated past, legs flailing in a useless attempt to control his movement. His mouth was open and he was giving the Universe a feline-shaped talking to. I'd have smiled at the sight, but I became distracted by the little mouse. It was floating past on its back looking completely relaxed. The rodent's little button eyes fixed on me, and its nose twitched adorably.

I grinned.

An angry claw slashed toward the mouse, missing it by a mile.

Somewhere Sebille was talking, but she sounded far away. The noise of my cat yowling with temper and frustration came to me through a thick layer of cotton wool. My ears felt like they had the time I'd followed a fainting goat up a mountain looking for a demon's lair. I moved my jaw around, but they refused to pop.

A gnarled, yellow hand with curved claws appeared and the tiny mouse floated into it, settling down with a twitch of its whiskers.

And then suddenly, the weightlessness stopped and I slammed to the ground.

Wicked managed to land on his feet, of course, but I landed on my back, the impact knocking the air out of my lungs.

Whom stood looking down at me, his beakish nose twitching like the mouse's whiskers. "The poultice is not working, young lady," he said. "You must collect the serum that has poisoned him. I will create an antidote from that. Be quick now. The lad is in dire straits. Call me when you have the serum." He tucked the mouse into an invisible pocket in his feathery cloak and ambled toward his house.

Wicked spat at him as he waddled by. "Mind your Ps and Qs, young man. It is not copacetic to take someone else's medicine." With that odd statement, he disappeared into his birdhouse with his mouse. Golden light exploded into the room and, a blink later, the birdhouse and the good doctor were gone.

And I had one heck of a backache.

17

INTO THE GREAT UNKNOWN
TOGETHER

We stood in a flat area at the bottom of a tall, spiky peak. Around us, the sweet smell of pine needles softened the cloying stink of dark magic permeating The Enchanted Forest. I looked around the place, my skin crawling as I remembered the last time I'd been there. The area where we stood, surrounded by oversized trees of both the evergreen and deciduous varieties, reminded me too much of the spot where the two-headed snake had tried to make me its dinner.

I shuddered, drawing Sebille's curious glance.

"According to my calculations, we should be just about on top of it," Archie said. He was carrying the book on magical anomalies he'd gotten from Shakespeare's desk in the artifact library. The author of the reference book was none other than Doctor Mortimus Osvald.

I glanced nervously at my phone. "Maybe I should check in with Lea again."

Sebille shook her head. "You checked in two minutes ago and three minutes before that. The little runt is fine. We're going to get the serum back to him in time."

I frowned. "Who are you, and what have you done with Sebille?"

She rolled her eyes.

"Oh, there you are." I sighed. "Don't act like I'm the only one who's worried about Hobs. I've seen you texting Lea like five times since we left."

She shrugged. "I was just telling her where the brownie stash was. In case."

"You old softie, you."

"Shut it," she snarled.

I chuckled.

Archie set the book down on the ground and pulled a contraption out of his pocket. It looked like a sundial, but I was pretty sure it wasn't. Holding the metal dial flat in one palm, he carefully turned the pointy part on top. A yellow glow emerged from the triangular metal piece at the top of the dial, bathing the ground in light.

Archie stretched his arm out, and the dial floated away. It hovered over the ground, the light it emitted seeming to shift and lengthen as if searching for something. "There." He shoved the sleeve of his robe back and glanced at his watch. "We should have a firm location in five minutes." He glanced around, frowning slightly.

"Are you expecting someone?" I asked. He'd been doing that since we'd arrived in the forest several minutes earlier.

Skimming me a quick look, Archie slid his gaze back to the dial without responding.

We watched the dial move a few feet farther away, painting the ground beneath it in an ever-widening arc of light. The golden glow on the ground stretched and spread, moving in a slow, counter-clockwise arc.

The motion reminded me of the moon going rapidly through its phases — waxing crescent, first quarter, waxing gibbous, full, waning gibbous, last quarter, waning crescent. The cycle repeated itself several times as it moved slowly over the ground.

The leaves on the trees behind us rustled as two people moved into the clearing.

My eyes went wide, all the blood leaving my face. "You!"

Archie threw me a guilty look. "Yes, well, Naida, I did tell you I knew of someone who could help."

I turned a glare on him. "A little warning would have been nice."

Archie busied himself making a minute adjustment to the dial.

That left me to address the newcomers. I hadn't expected to see them again. At least not so soon. I inclined my chin in greeting. "Narina. What a surprise."

My mother's smile faded at my cool greeting. Really though, I didn't know what she expected. I barely knew the woman. And that was entirely her fault.

My gaze slid to the man with her. It was my brother. "Edric." I slid a searching gaze over him. The last time I'd seen Ed, he'd looked weak and tired. He'd been kept prisoner for goddess knew how long, his jailer the very woman we were going to visit. Dacara had kept him inside a prison cell made of magical flame, sleeping on a platform like a male version of Sleeping Beauty. When we'd broken him out of the cell, he'd revived, but he'd looked like he'd run thirty miles with wraiths licking at his heels.

Maybe he had.

"You look better than last time," I told him, smiling.

His answering smile was like a knife in my chest, ripping loose a forgotten memory of a man long dead. Healed and hearty, Edric was the spitting image of our father. Though he had blond hair like Narina's, his locks curled softly around his handsome face where hers was straight, and his eyes were the same deep blue as mine. Our father's eyes. He'd been thin and pale the last time I'd seen him, with lines around his mouth and in the corners of his startling eyes. But he'd put on weight since then, and the lines were gone. He was no longer pale, and, even without the lines of strain on his face, he looked more mature than I remembered.

Our mother, Narina, was a powerful wind sorceress. She was my height, around five-nine, with long, straight blonde hair and hazel eyes that I knew would glow with silver energy if she had to use her magic. I'd been told my eyes glowed silver when I was threatened too. Though I'd never, of course, seen it myself. I generally didn't think about looking in a mirror when I was under attack. Pity. Having glowing eyes was pretty kick-butt, and I'd have enjoyed seeing it.

Unlike the last time when she'd been dressed in soft, feminine clothes, Narina was wearing form-fitting black leather pants and ankle boots, with a white tee and a matching leather jacket over it.

My mother caught me checking out her outfit and smiled. "Wraith resistant." She jerked her head toward my own jeans, tee, and sneakers. My usual uniform. "They can claw right through that."

I grimaced, my experience with the wraiths' deadly claws and acidic spit one I'd hoped never to repeat. "Good to know."

Next to me, Sebille eyed my erstwhile family with a grim expression. Though she and Narina had both been poisoned by the wraiths the last time we'd visited Dacara, the sprite didn't seem inclined to indulge in small talk or niceties with the sorceress.

I wondered what had her most-likely striped panties in a twist. However, with Sebille, being cranky was more the usual state of affairs than an oddity.

"I believe that will do," Archie announced. We turned to look at him.

The dial had dropped to the ground and a solid circle of yellow light pulsed on the dusty ground around it.

Archie picked up the book and tucked it under his arm, turning to us. "Ready?"

No! I'd probably never be ready to face off with Dacara again. But Hobs would die if we didn't get hold of that serum. So I nodded.

Narina looped her arm through Eddie's and moved toward Archie. I would have never anticipated the twist of real pain the sight caused in my chest. They were my family. Though I hadn't known them for most of my life. And it hurt to feel like an outsider when I saw them together. Something must have shown on my face because Narina smiled at me. It was a genuine smile, her eyes warm with emotion, and I blinked back my tears of hurt and turned toward Archie, terrified of her rejection.

Archie stepped into the sphere of light and disappeared.

I jolted to a stop, eyeing the empty air where he'd been. "Um. Archie?"

An arm slipped through mine. My gaze jerked

toward Narina's. She met my gaze with her own and gave my arm a squeeze. "It looks like we're going on another adventure," she said. "A family affair."

Sebille bumped into me on her way by. "Not if we don't stop dawdling and get our butts in gear." Sebille stepped into the yellow glow and popped out of sight.

Narina lifted her brows over Sebille's rudeness.

I shrugged. "She got a gooey center. She just hides it well."

Eddie chuckled. "I kind of like her. She's...feisty."

"Yeah," I said, feeling a little gooey in the center myself when Eddie took my other arm. "That she is."

A bony hand snaked out of thin air and grabbed my wrist, giving me a muscular yank.

And the three of us stumbled into the great unknown together.

18

GODDESS IN A WET SUIT. IT'S GOING TO BE CHAOS!

At first, I thought we'd somehow missed the anomaly. Then I saw Archie and Sebille and realized we couldn't have. I looked around at the clearing where we'd been, clearly seeing the trees, the sky, and the ground, minus the yellow glow. It looked the same. Though, if I turned my head, the view seemed slightly glossy in my peripheral vision. Like we were in a clear bubble. "Shouldn't this be dark and black and...spongy?" I asked Archie.

He had Osvald's book in his hands and was reaching for the edge of the dark brown leather cover. "This isn't a void, Naida," he said in a distracted voice. "It's an anomaly. Abnormal by its very nature."

Eddie and Narina dropped my arms, and I instantly felt the loss. I fidgeted, not knowing what to do with myself.

Sebille was tapping the edge of the bubble with her fingertips, mumbling quietly.

Archie opened the book and Osvald's dark, ugly head rose into view. The professor spun slowly to fix his black gaze on each of us in turn. He raised his brows. "So many people willing to be sucked up into the twisting magic?"

Sebille reached out and flicked him on the ear. "Shut it, Mr. Happy. Your gloom isn't helpful."

Eddie cleared his throat, his lips twitching, and slid Sebille an assessing glance.

The sprite gave him an innocent look.

"Ow!" Osvald complained. His gaze spun to Archie. "I say, Pudsnecker if you can't control the peanut gallery..."

Archie shook his head. "Let's focus on the job at hand, shall we? The girl is right. One of our friends is in danger. We need to do this as quickly as possible."

Osvald grimaced. "The hobgoblin? Nasty creatures. Not worth dying over," he murmured.

Sebille's fingers came up, and he flinched sideways. "Bloody hellcat! There's no need to be violent."

Archie lifted the book. "Osvald, if you please?"

Sighing, the professor settled his attention on the pages below him and they started to flicker. Osvald's black eyes were cast downward. His lips moved as he read the words printed on the quickly turning pages.

Without warning, the ground beneath our feet

jolted. I yelped softly, stretching my arms as if to brace myself, and was surprised to find a firm surface beneath my fingers.

The anomaly rose laboriously into the air, seeming to struggle with our weight, and then wrenched so quickly into a spin that we were all thrown against the opalescent walls.

Still spinning, the anomaly shot forward and we suddenly found ourselves high above the trees in The Enchanted Forest, flying at a dizzying speed.

My stomach roiled at the unaccustomed movement and the height. I dropped to my knees as dizziness threatened to topple me, placing my palms against the bubble's walls.

Being a creature that spends a large portion of her time flying, Sebille was unaffected by the height, but I noticed with some satisfaction that she turned a little green when the orb occasionally kicked into a rapid rotation.

After the fourth time it started to spin, I figured out that the nausea-inducing movement was caused by Osvald's instruction to change direction.

The trees flying past beneath our feet, I lifted my gaze toward the blue atmosphere high above. I imagined stretching a hand up to touch the fat, fluffy clouds floating through the gorgeous sky.

A wide-eyed bird that had been perched in a dead tree startled skyward. Wings akimbo and feathers flying, the owl screamed a question in our direction as we rushed past.

"Whoooo?"

Something thick and muscular rose from the trunk of a particularly big tree and snapped at the anomaly. The snake looked to be upwards of thirty feet long, with jaws that spread wide enough to swallow a small human whole. I shuddered at the sight, sighing in relief as it missed us and slammed back into the tree.

"Ooh," Sebille said. "That had to hurt."

I giggled, my heart and head suddenly feeling light.

Sebille and I shared a grin. "We're flying!" I told her and she rolled her eyes.

Osvald's gaze swung my way. "Beware the euphoria," he told us sternly. "It is the beginning of the end."

Sebille and I both snorted at his overly-dramatic warning.

"Stop being such a putz," Eddie said, surprising us both into turning in his direction.

Eddie made a crabby face and Sebille devolved into helpless laughter.

"What's that up there?" Narina asked. She didn't seem in danger of succumbing to excess euphoria. Her attractive face was serious as she pointed toward a black shape in the sky ahead of us.

I squinted at it. "Some kind of big bird."

"It looks like a raven," Sebille said, stressing the words.

My gaze swiveled to hers and we both spoke at once.

"Rasputin!"

"Morty!" I yelled. "Bump the bird!"

Osvald's dark gaze narrowed on me. "Archie, I believe we have a problem."

Archie flapped his hand dismissively. "Let them have their fun. Don't you remember the exhilaration of your first flight?"

"I do remember it," Osvald said, his tone dark, "and then I was banished into the pages of my tomes for all time. I'm telling you, this is not good."

Archie sighed. "The girls are right, Old Man. You're about as much fun as a snake's ankles."

Sebille and I slapped Archie five.

We were gaining on Rasputin fast, but it looked as if we might miss him by a smidge. Sebille and I started throwing ourselves at the wall, trying to change our flight path so we'd bump him. After a moment, Eddie joined us.

Watching us all play and giggle finally teased a smile from Narina.

Osvald's dark eyes were filled with worry, and I noticed he'd started reading faster.

When we were five feet away from the big raven, Rasputin turned and looked over his wing, his entire body twitching when he saw what was riding up on him.

The big raven's feathers flared like the hair on the back of a cat, and he lost altitude for a beat before he managed to reorganize his plumage. His head on a constant swivel to keep an eye on us, Rasputin's wings pounded the air harder and faster. He appeared to be trying to outrun us.

A moment later, we were even with the wide-eyed bird, the bubble's walls mere inches from his pounding wings.

Sebille, Eddie, and I were sweaty and panting from trying to move the anomaly toward Rasputin. But we couldn't move it even a fraction of an inch.

"Ssssizzling sssnake ssspit!" Sebille complained, flinging Eddie and me into helpless hilarity.

"Bump the bird," we all started to chant. Only Narina and Osvald resisted joining.

Finally, as we seemed in danger of passing the big raven without so much as touching his tail feathers, Narina gave in.

"Okay, just a little bump," she said, and she sent a gust of wind into the air around us. The anomaly shot sideways and banged into the bird. Rasputin's eyes and beak flared wide, and his clawed feet grabbed at the air in desperation. But there was nothing to grab. He started to roll across the sky in a comedy of flailing wings and grappling claws.

We laughed hysterically.

Just as he began to right himself, the anomaly gave a little lurch. We screamed happily.

The next lurch was harder, throwing us to the ground. Our laughter eased away.

"Oh no!" Osvald yelled. "You've done it now."

The anomaly gave a violent jerk, flinging us around the space. We crashed into each other and fell in a tangle of limbs in the center.

Osvald read frantically from the book. But it was too late. The anomaly gave one last, jerking hiccup, and then started to spin so hard and fast it pinned us to its sides and locked us there. Even our cheeks blew back from the resulting force.

Osvald and his book slammed to a stop, hovering above the direct center of the rotational sphere. With a twisting, wrenching sensation, we all fell to the floor, and the incredible force started to drag us slowly but inexorably toward the magical book.

With a jolt of pure horror, I realized we were all going to be joining Osvald in his book.

Not one, but six heads floating above every page. *Goddess in a wet suit.* It would be chaos!

Then I had a worse thought. Sebille and Osvald would kill each other.

"Narina!" Archie screamed, his knuckles white from clawing at the ground.

The circular vortex dragged me another inch closer to the perfectly still book at its center. Osvald hovered above the pages, his black eyes wide with panic as he watched the five of us being helplessly and unavoidably pulled in his direction.

Against my will, my arms were pulled straight, fingers scrabbling uselessly against the smooth surface of the anomaly in an attempt to stop my forward progress.

Beyond the bubble of the abnormal void, chunky flares of green, blue, and white flashed past, the colors of the sky and trees merging into one dizzying kaleidoscope that hurt the eyes and threatened to seduce me into a catatonic state if I stared at it for too long.

"Narina!" Archie screamed again. "Counter vortex...now!"

Beside me, the wind sorceress turned a confused hazel gaze to her brother-in-law, her brow furrowed. "I don't understa..."

A shrill scream tore through the heavy sound of the whirlwind. My head whipped around in time to see Sebille's fingers, elongated beyond reality and twisting like fleshy pretzels before our very eyes. The whirlwind's core had grabbed her, and it was trying to twist her into its grip.

Panic tearing away any small semblance of calm I still retained, I turned to Narina and screamed, "Do it, mom! Whatever Archie's talking about, do it now. Before this thing takes Sebille."

Narina's beautiful face stilled for a beat, her eyes finding mine and softening, and then she nodded. Without hesitation, she lifted her hands, sending a silver wash of energy into the anomaly. Her body jerked forward and her eyes went wide. What little resistance she'd managed to create was gone, and she was immediately sucked toward the core.

Narina plunged into the core with both arms, the anomaly's magic twisting her limbs in a tortuous and no-doubt excruciating grip. She threw back her head and screamed, the sound sending ice along my spine.

Gritting my teeth, I jerked one hand from the ground and clamped it around her arm. On my other side, Archie was trying to hold onto Sebille the same way. I gritted my teeth against the whirlwind's insistent pull, screaming in frustration as it continued to drag me closer.

With the first dregs of true fear, I felt the core get hold of the tips of my fingers, a yanking, twisting, burning sensation that brought a scream immediately to my lips.

A big, warm hand found my wrist and yanked, wrenching my fingertips free of the violently coiling magic. I looked into Eddie's eyes. What I saw there made my mouth go dry and my pulse spike.

His dark blue gaze was fractured, pixilated with roiling, animated shapes that reflected color and movement in a vertiginous medley of chaotic movements. Energy built in the chaos, power that swelled his skin, enlarging his form in short, dense effusions of power.

"Calm down, son," Archie warned in a gruff rumble of a voice. "It's working, Eddie. You'll only make things worse."

Working? I tore my gaze from my brother's and glanced frantically around at the slightly slower flash of exterior shapes and color. The vortex was slowing. Sebille's screaming had stopped, and she was slumped on the ground, Archie's hand still pressing her skin white where he gripped it.

A sudden whip of power shot from Eddie to me where he had hold of my wrist. It tore at my insides, ripping and scalding. My back bowed on the front edge of that phenomenal power and my lips and eyes went wide. But the scream shredding the back of my throat never emerged. It was weighted down by his power, snagged on the sharp edge of the energy passing through me and emerging from my palm. It was as if Eddie had used me like an electric cable, sending energy to his mother through me.

I felt as if I'd had ten thousand volts of energy ripping through my flesh.

The power shooting from my palm bowed Narina's back as it had mine, but her screams tore free in the face of it.

With a pop of displaced air, Narina's arms came free of the twisting core, and she shot backward, slamming into the anomaly's clear wall.

She ripped me away with her. For a beat, my arms were nearly yanked from their sockets as Eddie held onto me.

Then, with a tight jaw and gritted teeth, Eddie forced his fingers apart and I hit the ground, skidding toward Narina.

The anomaly's rotational pull fell away with a sigh. The world outside its walls stilled.

Osvald's book slammed to the floor with a decisive thump.

The buffer between us and the world disappeared, leaving behind the rich scent of earth and the sweet smell of broken vegetation. My flesh felt the cool softness of grass beneath it, and the tension in the air disappeared.

We all lay perfectly still for a beat, panting and wide-eyed. My limbs were so heavy I didn't think I'd ever be able to move them again.

"Well then," Osvald said in his snotty, English professor voice. "That's better."

Something sounded different about the good professor. But I was too weary to look at him. "No giggling in the anomaly," I murmured. "Got it."

A deep, rumbly sound thrummed the air.

Laughter?

I dragged my head off the ground to find the source of the rumble and felt my eyes go wide. "Professor Osvald?"

The man standing a dozen feet away from me

laughed joyfully, his black eyes alight with happiness. "In the flesh."

That he was, I realized with a start. All six and a half feet of him.

Professor Osvald had regained his body.

Well, I'll be a trail of slug snot.

19

THAR SHE BE

I was so surprised it took me a beat to realize there was an enormous black castle behind Osvald. The circular peaks of Dacara's ugly castle rose high into the gray sky, disappearing into the low clouds that were a regular feature of the place.

The previous time we'd been there, Archie had speculated that the stormy aspect of the sky above the castle was caused by residual energy from Dacara's magic.

A daunting thought. It would take some serious magic to create storms in that large an area around the magic-user.

Someone groaned behind me. I turned to find Sebille wrenching herself off the ground. "How could I have been hit by a train in The Enchanted Forest?" she asked, holding her head. "There are no trains here, right?"

"The Hagwarts Express?" I asked, earning myself a glare from the sprite.

Archie appeared at my shoulder, his face filled with awe. "Osvald, you're whole."

The professor's grin spread across his homely face, Making him look almost not hideous. "It's a miracle."

"Yes, it certainly is," agreed Narina, joining Archie and me.

Osvald placed his palms together in front of his face, pressing the tips of his fingers against his mouth. His black eyes glittered with tears.

I blinked. I'd never seen the man as anything but angry.

"Bless you, Wind Sorceress. You've returned my life to me."

Narina looked uncomfortable under his declaration. "Uh..."

Eddie wrapped an arm around his...our...mom's shoulders. "You saved us all, Mums." He kissed her temple.

I looked on, feeling like an outsider again.

"I hate to break up the celebration," Sebille said. "But I suggest we get into the castle before *those* things decide to attack." She pointed toward the sky and the gray, tattered forms riding the air currents high above our heads.

Wraiths.

I glanced quickly around and realized we'd

landed on the back side of the castle. At least, I assumed it was the back side since there was no sign of the cliff face we'd had to climb to get to the castle the first time.

That was probably why the wraiths hadn't immediately attacked. I doubted most visitors came over the mountain to the castle. Most would come from the forest side.

But as I watched the terrifying dark forms dip and circle above us like large, ugly black birds, I realized their movements were becoming more frenzied.

Had some of them dropped lower in the sky?

"We need to go," Archie said. "Now!"

We started to run, just as a strident scream tore the sky above us.

I shot past Osvald, who was paging quickly through an enormous red-leather book with a golden lock engraved in the dust cover.

He walked quickly rather than running, fingers flicking through the pages in a way that reminded me of the Book of Pages. The screams in the dark sky had multiplied. They also sounded closer. Without looking up, I knew the wraiths were descending on us. And coming fast.

A gust of wind spun the leaves on the nearby trees and sent the branches to waving.

The screams of the wraiths turned more shrill.

I looked up in time to see them rolling away from

us in the sky, some of them slamming into the rocky face of the mountain behind the castle.

I panicked, remembering how the wraiths consumed any magic used against them and became stronger from it.

I opened my mouth to warn Narina, but she'd turned and was running toward the castle again. The wraiths regathered, some of them slower to rise, and I realized they hadn't consumed her magic.

Maybe earth energies didn't affect them the same way. Wind magic was one of the four core elementals: Air, fire, water, and earth. That made sense.

We headed for the nearest door. Eddie reached it first and tried the knob.

It wouldn't open.

"It's warded," my brother told us, running his open palm over the lock to assess its components. "Blast! All four magical elements were used." He looked over our small group. "We don't have the energy needed."

A wraith screamed and dove from the sky, its horrible claws raking the air near Narina. I shoved her sideways and punched the thing as hard as I could in the area covered by its hood. As soon as my skin touched the shroud-like cloth, ice flared over it, burning and digging beneath my skin to freeze my bones.

Narina whipped a hand out and blew the wraith

back. It hit the ground several yards away and rolled, tattered shroud whipping in the residual drafts.

Another wraith dove toward Sebille. She popped out, turning into her sprite form and evading the raking claws with a quick burst of movement.

Eddie's hand came up and a blob of something flared from his fingertips. It was an unruly mass of energy that absorbed whatever it touched and kept on rolling. The chaotic energy caught the attacking wraith and two more that were dropping down from the sky in a giant splotch of roiling shapes and colors. As it carried them away, the magic fractured the wraiths into a Picasso-like mix that left them screaming silently from mouths that were in the wrong place and trying to claw free with limbs that faced the wrong direction. It was nightmare-inducing.

And it couldn't have happened to more deserving creatures.

I watched in delight as the bubble captured more and more wraiths and then frowned as it interned a huge tree, decomposing it immediately into the fractured shapes inside the bubble. "Will that thing just keep going?" I asked him, starting to worry. I didn't want helpless people and animals to get caught up in the magic. Though that two-headed snake was on its own.

"No." He responded.

I relaxed.

"It'll eventually blow up," he said.

Oh. Gulp.

"Step aside," Osvald told Eddie, flicking his long fingers in my brother's direction. "I've got this."

Eddie did as he was told, watching his fractured blob consume more and more wraiths as it moved toward the mountain top. The wraiths seemed unable to avoid the thing as it pulled them into its orbit and sucked them up.

My eyes widened. I couldn't tear my gaze away from the train wreck of a magic bubble. It had grown as big as my car and was still growing. "When will it explode?"

Eddie shrugged. "Pretty soon, I think. That mountain's going to be too much for it to consume."

My lips flapped like a fish's. "It's going to eat the mountain?"

"It'll try," he responded, watching his handiwork with as much fascination as I was.

A loud click preceded a gasp of sulfurous air. The ward was broken. "There!" Osvald said, his tone self-satisfied. He turned the knob and pushed the door open, stepping back and giving a bow and a flourish. "After you," he told Archie.

Archie squeezed Osvald's shoulder. "It's good to have you back, old friend."

A happy light came into the ugly professor's eyes. "It's good to be back, old friend."

With an impatient sigh, Sebille pushed past the two men. "Join a knitting circle, you two. Geesh."

I laughed softly at the looks on their faces and followed the sprite inside.

Eddie was on my heels, followed by Narina, who was chuckling, and then Archie and Osvald.

Our smiles didn't last long. In fact, they dropped dead as we stepped into a large, well-apportioned kitchen. Killed by the scary-looking woman wearing the scarlet robes covered in pink hearts.

"Thar she be," I said, channeling my favorite deceased pirate parrot. I'd know that clothing color scheme anywhere.

The demon princess, Desiree.

IS THERE A BOOK FOR THAT?

"Well, well, well," the princess said in a condescending tone. "What have we here? An assembly from that busybody Lovelace, I presume?" Her smile was mean. "Or simply a group of the love-less?" Her laughter was husky, the sentiment behind it mean.

Archie stepped up behind me, Osvald loitering near the door.

Marina and Eddie took up places at each of my shoulders. Their presence felt like a buffer against the evil I could feel coiling around our hostess. Or, should I say, Dacara's visitor. Taking strength from my family surrounding me, I notched my chin upward. "Where's Dacara?"

Desiree's head tilted slightly, reminding me of a curious bird. Her waist-length, mahogany hair hung in glossy waves around her face, slipping past her plump shoulders to curl around her waist. She wasn't slender by any stretch of the imagination. In another time she would have been called Rubenesque. The demon princess set her pale, beautiful features into a pleasant mask. Her skin was flawless, her cupid's bow lips red, and the purple of her eyes was so dark they looked black when the light wasn't hitting them.

I could feel the rage and malevolence pulsing on the air around her, along with a phenomenal magical energy. She was a very powerful creature.

In that moment, I wished I'd left the only artifacts I'd found in that castle intact. The Ferryman of Hades' scythes, used to ferry the dead across the River Styx, would have come in handy about then.

"The dual sorceress is...resting. She wasn't in the mood to be helpful so I've given her some time to think about it."

"Helpful?" Narina asked. "With what?"

The princess looked down her nose at my mother, her lip curling just the tiniest bit. "That's my business." Her gaze slid to Eddie and she smiled. The sight of that smile made my bowels twitch with fear. "But since the inspiration for that business is standing right there..." She licked her lush lips.

Archie, Narina, and I all moved closer to Eddie.

Energy flooded from my brother at the feral look on Desiree's face, biting at my skin.

I rubbed my arm and forced myself to hold my

ground. If Desiree wanted to hurt Ed, she'd be going through me, my uncle, and my mom. And judging from the page flipping sounds behind us, Osvald too.

"Stand down, peasants." Desiree laughed. "I have no desire to dominate the handsome sorcerer, though I would enjoy playing with his scrumptious magic."

Eddie tensed, his power level rising until my hands were rubbing frantically against my arms.

He glanced at me, frowned, and said, "Sorry. I'm a bit tense."

Fortunately, he tamped his energy down a few ticks.

"I merely wanted to question the Dual Sorceress about the devotion magic she's been working on. I understand it's quite powerful. Not as good as love, of course, but good for a start."

I frowned. "Devotion? Why would a demon love princess need that kind of spell?" Unfortunately, I knew why *Dacara* thought she needed it. She'd likely been creating it to use against my brother. Dacara had always wanted Eddie for her own. Or at least she'd wanted his magic. After experiencing even a small amount of that magic, I could understand why.

"That, also is no concern of yours. A much better question is, why are you here?" Desiree demanded, her dark-purple eyes narrowed in obvious anger.

"We've come to take back the serum," I said, fighting to keep the wobble out of my voice.

"Serum?" Two lines dented the pale flesh between Desiree's slender, arched brows. "What serum?"

A soft, derisive snort sounded somewhere above me.

I stilled, hoping Desiree hadn't heard the sprite. As before, Sebille had come into the castle incognito and in sprite form, so she could be our backup plan in case things went mammaries up, as they tended to do when Sebille and I went on an adventure together.

Desiree's gaze narrowed, lifting toward the sound, and I spoke quickly to distract her. "The love serum. It belongs in the vault at the artifact library. As Keeper of the Artifacts, it was under my protection. You removed it from the library. I've come to get it back."

Desiree's expression turned mulish. "That serum belongs to my people. We created it. We've used it at our wish and will for millennia. You have much nerve coming here and demanding my own property from me!"

Energy thickened on the air, biting against my skin. Around me, my companions shifted and twitched, rubbing at their skin as the magic feasted on it. The disgusting stench of rotten eggs pulsed within the magic.

Sulfuric, dark, demonic magic.

My own energy burst to the fore without my even calling it, a primal directive fed by my survival instinct. A sultry, lazy wind floated around our small group to form a protective, living wall, its gentle force making Desiree's scarlet robes dance around her ankles. Near the door at our backs, I could hear the sound of pages flipping, as Osvald no doubt used his power over the written word to search for a way to neuter the demon.

The air behind the demoness thickened slightly, a thin black line dividing it at its center like a metaphorical zipper. Archie was creating a void.

Next to me, Eddie's body had gone very still. I risked a glance toward my brother and gasped. His blue gaze had fractured. Random shapes and colors flared and roiled and shifted within his eyes like shattered glass filtering a kaleidoscope of light in a thousand different directions.

A thin sheen of multi-hued energy slipped over him, snugging itself to his skin like a micro-thin wetsuit. Chaotic waves of energy roiled and spun away from him like starbursts, alternately shifting space and then sucking it back only to turn it upside down with a soft moan of air bumping up against unnatural energy. I'd never seen magic like Eddie's. It was powerful and disordered and it had me fascinated.

What exactly was my brother?

Standing next to him felt like snuggling up to the front edge of unbridled nuclear power just before it blows. To say that it was discomfiting would be an unsatisfying description.

It was life-changing.

Desiree's energy sharpened, its stench thickening as it pulsed against the wind barrier my mother had thrown. A roiling red miasma poured from her spread fingers and pooled near her feet. I watched it form a misty river of power and flow toward us, the energy creating ice along the floor before it bumped up against our protective energy.

Eddie's unruly magic thrummed on the air. It pulsed around him, throbbing painfully against my skin. I turned to Narina. "Is that going to be all right?"

My mother looked past me to her son and winced. "Probably not. It might be best if we..."

She never finished that statement.

A hollow, echoing boom imploded on the air, the power so impossible in the restrained space that it sucked back into itself, forming a spinning globe of barely-restrained power in the center of the room. The magic globe began to spin, whirling faster and faster and pulling the demon's sulfurous black energy toward it in a glittering black stream. When it could hold no more of the ugly energy, it gave a final throb, like the last beat of a dying heart, and then popped. Chaos exploded outward in a wash that would have blown us out of the room if it weren't for a thick, purple wall that had somehow popped into place at the last moment.

Desiree was blown out of the room, her lush form crashing through the wall behind her and skidding across the shiny dark floor of the room beyond. She crashed against the wall and went slack and unmoving.

The silence that followed was startling. We all stared at the pretty purple wall and blinked. Then, as if we all reached the same conclusion at once, we slowly turned our stunned glances to the tall man standing by the door.

Osvald's black eyes were wide. His ruddy cheeks paled as we turned our questioning gazes his way, and then he slowly grinned. "Well then. That worked out quite nicely," Osvald said. He released the slender tome with a sparkly purple cover and snapped his fingers. The book disappeared into thin air before it hit the ground.

The dense purple wall disappeared with it.

We stared at the motionless demon across the room for a long moment, nobody speaking. When she didn't move, I looked at Archie. "What do you think?"

He shrugged. "The boy's chaos magic is powerful. It's possible she's incapacitated."

I turned to my brother and found him leaning against the wall next to the door, looking pale and slightly dazed.

"He'll be okay," Narina said softly to me. "He's created a lot of focused magic since we arrived here. It just takes him a moment to regain his strength."

Focused chaos magic? I thought. *Hm.*

"Where do you suppose her evil hostess is?" Osvald asked, his hands shoved into the pockets of his dowdy gray slacks. The gray-blue sweater he wore was tatty looking, with moth holes peppering the wool, and his slacks were an inch too short over scuffed black loafers. With the jaunty red bowtie and wrinkled blue button-down shirt, he looked the epitome of a bookish professor.

"That's what I'm worried about," Sebille said, buzzing down to our level. She had a cobweb running from one wing to a pointed ear. Apparently, she'd been skulking about near the ceiling. "I'll go do a quick reconnoiter. See if I can locate Dacara."

I nodded. "Be careful."

She buzzed off, disappearing around the door

leading into the main house from the kitchen. I noticed she gave the sleeping princess in front of the fireplace a wide berth.

I looked at my companions. "Ready?"

To their credit, they all nodded.

I looked at Osvald. "Do you have a book that tells you how to do a binding spell?"

His black eyes narrowed in thought. He nodded, snapped his fingers, and a dusty book covered in some kind of brown paper with bent and tattered edges appeared in his hands. He looked at the book, and pages started flipping.

I left him to do his thing and forced my feet to move forward.

At the door, I stopped and stuck my head through, looking around the room before stepping inside. Aside from the seemingly unconscious Desiree, the big room was empty. It was quiet too. Unnaturally so. With only the sound of the fire in the enormous fireplace crackling and spitting as I moved slowly toward the perfectly still princess.

We spread out around her, approaching from all angles. The sound of flipping pages followed us from the kitchen.

Desiree lay with her hands crossed over her chest, her beautiful face serene and the thick arcs of her eyelashes resting on her flawless cheeks.

"She looks like Sleeping Beauty," Eddie said, a shadow in his eyes.

I wondered if he was thinking of his own imprisonment in that castle. He'd been lying on a raised platform in much the same way when we'd found him there. His prison walls had crackled with magical fire rather than the old-fashioned wood kind that bathed Desiree in a golden glow. But the parallels were creepy.

He shuddered slightly, confirming my suspicions. "Do you want to wait in the kitchen?" I asked him softly.

He shook his head. "I'm okay. It's just weird being back here."

That was an understatement of massive proportions.

A phone rang into the silence and we all jumped. I looked around the big room. "Do you see a phone?"

Everyone glanced around as the phone continued to ring.

Eddie frowned. "It's coming from you?"

I blinked and then felt my pocket, embarrassed color heating my cheeks. "Oh. Ha." I tugged my phone out of my jeans and answered it. "Lea? Is he okay?"

There was a loud crackling noise and, somewhere in the background, something crashed. Panic crawled over me with sharp, feline claws. "Lea? What's going on?"

"Naida!" Her voice was harsh and panicked.

"They're here. Hurry!" The call disconnected and I looked at Archie. "Croakies is being attacked."

Archie frowned. "Did she say by whom?"

I shook my head. "No. It sounded chaotic there. But I'm betting it's the cherubs."

"Cherubs?" Narina asked, frowning. "Why...?"

"Because I sent them," the demon behind me said.

My gaze whipped around to Desiree. She was standing in front of the crackling fire, her expression petulant. "You've been so tedious. I was really hoping we could do this without violence." She sighed, so disgusted with us.

"Do what?" I asked, backing away.

Desiree's false smile slid away. "I want that serum."

I blinked. "Huh?"

"We thought you had it," Archie said. "We came to get it from you."

Desiree stamped her foot. "Don't be tiresome. I want my serum!" She threw her hands into the air and something burst from them. Lots of somethings, actually. And the floating things slashed at my skin as they glided past.

"Ouch!" I smacked at the heart-shaped magic saturating the air, earning a new set of bloody wounds for my trouble. In desperation, I flung my energy at the thickening mist of heart-shaped blades, managing to barely knock the nearest ones away.

Around me, people were yelping and screeching in pain. Only Archie seemed adequately covered to keep most of the damage at bay. He'd pulled his sleeves down over his hands and pulled the collar up around his face. The bell-shaped sleeves of his robe were quivering at the ends as if his fingers were moving inside.

I hoped he was trying to open a void.

A stiff wind slashed through the room, blowing some of the little blades away from us. They hit the wall with a thwuck, and many of them stuck there.

All around us, things began to lift off tables and other surfaces, dancing on the air in a wide vortex of erratic movement. A pair of candlesticks jerked skyward and slashed toward my head. I dove just in time to keep from getting clipped and they sailed past me, crashing through a window across the room. The mantel clock rose up and shot toward Desiree. She flipped her fingers, and it transformed into rose petals as it hit her skin.

The sweet scent of roses filled the room.

A blanket flew into the air, dancing with the throw pillows from the same couch. The blanket collided with a small table, whose contents swirled around it as it pranced across the room.

The fireplace poker spun away from the hearth and nearly impaled Osvald. He dove beneath a dainty chair. The small chair lifted away from him and smacked into the fireplace, falling in pieces into the flames.

A cloud of hearts flashed toward a giant mirror that suddenly flew to cover Eddie. The blades sank into the mirror's wooden frame and stuck there.

But there were too many of them to avoid completely. The razor-like hearts slashed and ripped, scraped, and sliced everything they encountered.

I huddled behind a couch and eyed the action, my eyes going crossed from the activity. It was magic mania.

Narina's wind magic was rocking the room. Lashing the window curtains and blowing some of the heavier furnishings toward the demon princess in front of the fire.

Eddie stood in the center of his own type of whirlwind. Arms up and eyes closed. Chaos surrounded him.

Desiree stood fearlessly in the same spot, never dodging, never moving, and yet somehow never taking a hit.

Archie had dropped to a crouch, but his fingers still worked inside his robe.

Behind Desiree, the air thickened and roiled. His void slowly opening.

Pain slashed along my arm. I looked down, horror turning my blood to ice. All along the scratches caused by Desiree's heart-shaped weapons, something sprouted from my skin. Something green and leafy with...

All the color fled my face.

"Roses!" I yelled. "The cuts sprout roses." A thorn ripped through my skin and pain sliced through me in a jagged tear. I screamed as warm blood gushed from the wound.

No one seemed to hear me because the wind drowned out my voice. Eddie was lost in his own little world. Behind me, poor Osvald was shrieking in pain.

Green energy flashed through the room.

Sprite energy.

I lifted my head to look for Sebille. A bladed heart slashed across my cheek, barely missing my eye. I yelped and dropped back down but spotted Sebille as she fired another blast of magic toward Desiree.

A slash appeared in the air behind the demon. A narrow black opening split the air. Desiree didn't seem to notice. "Give me the serum!" she screamed to the room at large.

Sebille hit her with another blast of energy. It smacked the air in front of Desiree and bounced off in a wash of crimson energy that crashed into Sebille and sent her flying to smash against a wall.

Desiree swung an arm at Sebille, and a dense stream of the deadly hearts shot toward the sprite.

Shaking off a daze, Sebille flashed out of the way. But Desiree's swinging arm made something hanging from her neck flash in the light. A thick silver chord hung around the princess's neck. A small vial hung from that chain. It was about two inches long, slender, and made of silver. Ornate silver vining and leaves wound around the small vial and culminated in a rosebud at the top. Inside the vining, something red glistened in the light.

I recognized that liquid. I'd seen it before. In the vault at Croakies.

It looked like love serum!

I needed to get hold of that vial. But the void behind Desiree was open and, as I glanced in her direction, Desiree was slowly turning as if sensing the abyss behind her.

Narina swung her arm in a fast circle, wind whipping the space around it. I realized she was going to send Desiree into the void with a brutal gust of wind.

If she did, I'd lose my chance at that vial. "Narina, wait!"

Too late, Narina released the burst of air and it slammed into Desiree.

The princess stumbled, her arms flailing and her hair whipping around her face, blinding her. She tried to lean into the squall, pushing back against it, but one of her stumbling feet hit a flying stool and she started to fall toward the void.

Sebille buzzed past and I screamed. "Sebille! The vial!"

She glanced my way. I pointed toward Desiree. The princess stumbled back into the void, and, in the blink of an eye, it started to close.

Sebille shot toward it, but she was going to be too late.

Or worse. She flew into the void with the demon, just as it started to close.

21

KEGEL, KEGEL, KEGEL

Sebille shot through the narrow slit of the void, and there was a burst of green before the opening snapped shut like one of those old-fashioned spring-loaded coin purses.

The screaming behind me stopped.

The wind died on a final, whisper-like sigh.

And everything that had been floating through the air slammed to the floor.

Silence pulsed. I ran toward the spot where the void had been and slid my hands frantically through the spot. There was nothing. It was as if Sebille and Desiree had never been there. I spun around, fixing Archie with a panicked look. "Can you open the void again?"

"I can, but Desiree will be waiting for it. She knows we'll want Sebille back."

I paced, my fingers twisting. "We can't just leave her in there."

Archie sighed, looking at Narina and Eddie. "Be ready." He lifted his hands and...

Bzzzz

An insistent dragonfly buzzed my head, sifting green dust onto my face. I fought a sneeze as relief spilled through me.

With a final, whirring loop de loop near my left ear, Sebille popped into full size. She stood in front of me, grinning. The chain with the vial dangled from her fingers. "Looking for this?"

I gave a happy little scream and, before I thought about what I was doing, grabbed the sprite in a relieved hug. "How'd you get out?"

She shoved me away, a look of pure disgust on her narrow, freckled face. "No full-body touching." She shuddered. Then she shrugged. "I have mad skills."

"What's that?" Osvald asked.

When we turned in his direction, we found him climbing slowly to his feet. He was covered in bleeding slices and his dark, greasy-looking hair was a jumble on his head. Like me, he was sprouting green and thorny things from the slices in his flesh. I shuddered, beyond disgusted. Osvald caught us all looking at him and pointed to a spot somewhere in front of where he stood. "That. There. What is it?"

I squinted at the spot, seeing nothing. "I don't see

anything. With Sebille and the vial back, I turned my thoughts to the next problem. "We need to get back to Croakies, like yesterday." My hopeful glance at Archie earned me a negative shake of the head. "The anomaly is defunct. We won't be taking it back to the edge of the forest."

I groaned, my stomach twisting with alarm. "It will take us days to walk back."

"And don't forget the wraiths," Eddie said. He joined us, still looking pale but not quite as exhausted as before. "We could really use that turtle right now."

"No, really, people. What is that?"

I whipped toward Osvald, ready to yell at him to quit interrupting. But I saw it too. It was a cloudiness in the air. A slight opacity that hadn't been there before. I squinted. "He's right. There's something there."

Eddie groaned. "She's coming back. I knew that was too easy."

My eyes went wide. *Easy?* What world did he live in where he thought being slashed near to pieces by flying hearts was easy?

Sebille walked over and poked the cloudy air with a fingertip. Energy flared in a spark and she jumped. "Ow!" She sucked the tip of her finger. "Whatever it is, there's an energy charge to it."

Something about the sight niggled in my brain. I joined Sebille, squinting at the apparition. It was rounded at the top and bottom, long and slender. It reminded me of something...

"Naida, you're leaking," Osvald said.

I tilted my head and narrowed my eyes even more. *What was it?*

Sebille poked one of my arms. Hard.

"Hey! Ouch," I complained, rubbing my arm. "What's the deal?"

"Osvald's right. You're leaking." She grimaced. "And sprouting."

I looked down at my jeans in horror. Had I peed myself in the chaos? Surely not. Though, now that I thought about it, I did kind of have to pee. I tightened my thighs against the thought.

Kegel, kegel, kegel, I thought frantically until the moment passed. Then I noticed the silvery magic sifting from my fingertips. *Keeper magic?* I frowned. *But why?*

Sebille turned to my uncle. "Archie?"

He shook his head. "It's not a void. Maybe it's some kind of portal."

I reached toward the thickening air. *Unless...* My finger touched the spot. Pain ripped through my core as my magic was torn violently from me. Energy flooded the cloudy spot on the air but stayed within the oval-shaped parameters.

I screamed, doubling over as the magic seared my cells on its way out.

Almost as quickly as it started, the magic

siphoning stopped. My knees buckled and I hit the ground, taking deep, calming mouthfuls of air into my lungs.

"That's the mirror," Sebille finally said. She reached out again, shoving her hand into the center of the object hanging unsupported about a foot above the ground.

I looked up and saw what looked like the back of the wooden communication mirror in the artifact library at Croakies. I shoved painfully to my feet, my body feeling like it had been bludgeoned.

The space between the aged wood frame was gray, as it was when it was opening for a new communication. Something shifted at the bottom of the mirror. I grabbed Sebille's arm and tugged her backward. "Watch out!"

We took a step back and the mirror cleared.

A small, gray shape with a snapping tail and irate orange eyes jumped through the mirror. "Meow!"

"Mr. Wicked!" I scooped him up and held him close, kissing the top of his soft head. "What in the world?"

He bit my cheek. "Ouch!"

Wicked shoved against me with his tiny feet and earned his freedom. He stalked back to the mirror and stopped, looking back at us over his angrily whipping tail. Then he turned back to the mirror and jumped through. Disappearing from sight.

"A portal it is," Archie said, sounding relieved.

Without another word, my uncle followed Wicked through the mirror.

The rest of us went quickly through after him.

As I stepped onto the cool, concrete floor of the artifact library, the first thing I noticed was the horrible sulfuric stench.

Then I noticed the sounds of crashing and thumping beyond the dividing door.

But it was the blood-curdling screams that finally started me running.

Eddie reached the door first. He threw it open, and a sliver of metal slashed through the air, mere inches from his head. The tiny arrow embedded itself into the wood of Shakespeare's desk behind Eddie and quivered there.

Eddie ducked sideways and ran toward the book-shelves.

"Watch out!" Lea screamed.

Shimmery green energy flashed past me as I ducked through the door.

The sprite cannonballed past in her bug form. She immediately started firing energy at the fat little attackers divebombing everyone in the room.

Meow! Wicked ran past me, leaped onto Slimy's terrarium and sliced his claws at any cherubs that got too close.

Inside his glass home, Slimy hunkered near his sunning rock looking bug-eyed.

So, basically normal for him.

I flung a ribbon of Keeper magic into the air, the energy coiling rapidly toward the library.

Eddie lifted his arms and flapped his hands together like discordant wings. Energy flared away from his hands and flapped across the room, growing as it moved and spinning like strange whirligigs.

Two cherubs divebombed Narina. She flung up both arms and fired powerful gusts of wind at them, sending them butt-over-belly across the room to smash into the wall.

The exterior door opened as they hit the wall. Several more cherubs flew through.

There looked to be dozens of the nasty things in the bookstore. And there were arrows flying everywhere.

I spotted Lea hunkered down in the center aisle of the bookshelves. She was covered in a shimmery aura of magic, and there was a pile of arrows on the floor around her and sticking from the wooden shelves and books. Her cat Hex, Wicked's littermate, was perched on top of the bookshelf nearest Lea, slashing at cherubs like her brother.

The air behind me sighed and I threw up my hand, catching Blackbeard's sword as it barreled toward me. The hilt of the magical sword softened and warmed beneath my palm, fitting itself to my hand as the magic it carried worked its way through my system.

Three cherubs with hate-filled eyes descended from the ceiling and they were on me, almost too fast for me to respond. But the sword knew its work. It rose to meet the attack, my body settling into a familiar fighting stance. The blade flashed—slash, slash, slash—quicker than the eye could follow.

Three cherubs burst into dust and I spun to meet three more.

The room was cloudy with the leavings of spent energy and cherub dust. It clogged my nose and stung my eyes. But I barely noticed. I was lost in the dance of the blade.

Slash, slice, lunge, sweep, sweep, sweep. Two arrows clanged against the blade and dropped to the carpet.

A ragged form barreled into the room, dropping red and green feathers on my head and along the floor as he burst clumsily into the battle.

"Argh! Rough seas and demon'd skies. The diapered curs have swords that fly." SB flapped his wings and squawked as arrows flashed in his direction. Quick as a wink, he shot forward and stabbed the nearest cherub with his beak, snagging another one out of the air as the first one turned to dust. He swung the screaming cherub in his steely claws and flung it onto my blade.

Poof! Dust filtered to the ground.

SB fluffed his feathers and danced proudly on the air. "Bwawk! Ye bilge-sucking dog of a wicked mum, whose pride for ye be small, ye'll succumb to Blackbeard's mighty bird, 'fore yer mum's tears of shame can fall."

Energy flared and burst all around me. The floor was littered with dust, my shoes kicking it up all around me as I fought.

Finally, the bookstore was free of cherubs. We collapsed into exhausted, boneless piles on the dust-covered carpet, panting.

Lea dropped her shield and staggered toward me. "I thought you'd never get here."

"Sorry. We ran into some trouble." How was that for an understatement?

"Did you get the serum?" Lea asked, her expression grim.

Sebille lifted the chain with the vial off her neck, handing it to Lea.

Lea frowned. "Is this all of it?"

"No," I admitted. "But hopefully it will be enough?"

Lea sighed. "Yeah, hopefully. Come on." She motioned toward the dividing door. "We need to call Whom right away. Hobs is in really bad shape."

22

IT'S BAD, NAIDA

Sebille and I sat on the couch, perched on the edge in tense silence as we watched Doctor Whom bending over Hobs on my bed. The sprite had healed all my weird rose-growing cuts. We'd sent Lea downstairs with Florence Nightingale's first aid kit to help the rest of our group with their battle wounds.

Narina and Eddie had poked their heads into the apartment several minutes later, and I'd gone out to tell them what was going on.

Narina had hugged me. In my exhausted, emotional state, the action brought tears to my eyes. She'd tucked a strand of my dusty hair behind one ear and told me they'd be in touch.

Eddie hugged me too. "I'll see you soon, sis."

"Thanks for your help today," I told them, wiping at tears. If I wasn't so scared and miserable about

Hobs, I'd have been grinning like an idiot to have my family back.

I watched them leave and went back inside, dropping back down on the couch again. There was nothing left to do but wait and watch.

I chewed the inside of my lips at the sight of my hobgoblin. He was so pale that even the light blue of his eyes looked dark by contrast.

Mr. Wicked and Slimy were on the pillow next to Hobs. Slimy's dark eyes were fixed on the little hobgoblin, his throat rhythmically working. *There's a dirty red aura over him*, the frog said. *It's bad, Naida.*

Sebille and I shared a look. Her lips were pinched, and the freckles on her face stood out against the chalky pallor of her skin.

Wicked's gaze was fixed on Whom. He watched the doctor as if he didn't completely trust him with his friend.

Hobs' skinny chest barely rose and fell under the sheets. He shuddered violently every few seconds. He was literally dying from a broken heart. And I hadn't even known he was in love.

I frowned, wanting to kick myself for neglecting the little guy. I should have paid more attention. I should have known he was in trouble before it got so far.

Sebille glowered at me as if hearing my thoughts. "This happened fast, Naida. We were busy with the signing. It's not our fault."

"Our" fault, she'd said. As if she was wading along the same treacherous thought process as I was. I supposed she probably was. Sebille and I were like co-parents for Hobs. We were responsible for him. We'd somehow failed.

But she was wrong. We *should* have known. Hobs was more important than some stupid book signing.

Whom had taken the vial of serum from Sebille when he arrived and had disappeared to do his thing. He'd only just emerged from his little travel house with a new gob of owl puke in his hand, which he'd proclaimed was the antidote to the love serum. He'd pressed the mess onto Hob's chalky chest, right over his heart. While he waited for it to work, Whom had used the stethoscope nestled in the feathers of his cloak to check Hobs' vitals. He'd then pinched a tiny yellow bead in front of Hobs' nose. The bead had burst, sending a flare of golden energy into the little guy's nostrils. Then he'd pulled a second bead from another pocket. The second bead had been bigger, colored a pale cream, and he'd pinched it into Hobs' mouth.

Finally, Whom had pinched two pink beads into Hobs' oversized ears. He'd glanced at us. "Healing supplements."

We nodded.

Then the good doctor sat back on his haunches, looking for all the world as if he was perching on a tree branch, and jotted notes into a journal while we waited for the medicine to work.

The minutes ticked past. I shifted nervously on the couch. Sebille got up and paced. But the minutes didn't bring Hobs back to us. In fact, he seemed to get worse. The hobgoblin's color changed from chalky white to gray, and a film seemed to cover his fixed, pale blue gaze.

He looked as if he were already dead.

My heart slowed and my breathing turned shallow as I clung desperately to hope. Even as despair tried to rip all hope away.

"Doctor Whom?"

The owlish physician looked over at me, blinking his oversized eyes.

I opened my mouth to ask him what else we could try.

Something crashed heavily to the floor downstairs. The distinctive sound of shattering glass followed the crash.

Doctor Whom's beakish mouth opened. "Whooo?"

Sebille and I jumped to our feet and ran to the landing outside my apartment door. Confused by what I was seeing, I looked down at the communicating mirror we'd used to travel back from the black castle in The Enchanted Forest.

A woman stood at the bottom of the steps, her back to us as she perused the shattered mirror. She was dressed in a red cape, a hood covering her hair and much of her face. Only her delicate nose and a slash of one pale cheek showed, telling me it wasn't a man.

I grabbed Sebille's wrist, squeezing as I leaned in and whispered. "You never told me what happened to Dacara."

Sebille frowned. "She was in a state of suspended animation on a bed of thorny roses." She shook her head. "Even Dacara couldn't have gotten out of that without help."

I winced, narrowing my gaze on the woman below. "Would she have woken up when we banished Desiree?"

The first signs of panic slashed through Sebille's gaze. That was all the answer I needed.

As if she heard our urgent whispering, the woman down below turned her beautiful face up to us, a pleased smile curving her lush lips.

It wasn't Dacara.

"It was very helpful of you to leave the portal open and your mirror unveiled," she told us. "It's such a shame I broke it." She shrugged. "But it doesn't matter anyway. I don't need a portal to return home." She tugged her cape closer to her side and I realized the voluminous cloak had been hiding something on the ground.

My eyes went wide.

A delicate creature lay on the ground behind her.

She was dressed in a brown tunic and cream-colored tights, with brown shoes on her tiny feet. A pretty crown of flowers rested in her shiny brown hair and a plain, brown leather tool belt encircled her waist, the handles of a variety of household tools sticking up from the pockets. Twin arcs of thick mahogany lashes lay on her pink cheeks and her lips were slightly open as if something had startled her before she'd fallen.

A memory of a playful, dancing gaze and gleeful laughter assailed me. I realized I was looking at my intruder from downstairs.

Suddenly all the unexplained repairs made sense.

"She is lovely, isn't she?" Desiree said in a cold voice. "It's no wonder your little hobgoblin is dying from a broken heart over her." The demon's smile widened, showing perfect white teeth. "It'll be a shame when she's gone. He'll be beyond saving then."

"What are you talking about, demon?" Sebille barked out. Her bony frame was rigid with anger. But that wasn't all. I knew the sprite well enough to recognize stark terror when I saw it. Terror for Hobs. "He's already sick. Why would this brownie's fate affect him at all?"

Desiree looked smug. She patted the place on her chest where the tiny vial had been. "It's really too bad about that serum you stole from me. The poison is called Obsession." She gave a short laugh. "It works very well. So well, in fact that I carry that antidote with me when I'm working with it." She shook her head.

All the color fled from my face and I had to grab the railing to keep from falling.

Her smile widened. "What? You thought you were creating an antidote? What you did was create an antidote for the antidote." Her laughter trilled through the room, cold and malevolent. "Such a shame. You might have saved him. Now, the poor thing doesn't have a chance. I'm afraid he'll die of a broken heart without the object of his love." She glanced down at the sleeping brownie. Despite her words, her expression was filled with delight at the prospect of Hobs' despair and death.

Sebille growled, wild energy spitting around her and her eyes glowing feral green.

I grabbed her wrist to keep her from attacking. Desiree could be gone in a blip and we'd have no way to save Hobs. "What do you want?" I asked the demon princess, my tone throbbing with anger.

She widened her eyes. "Want? Why, what everyone wants, my dear Keeper. Love."

Her features pinching into an evil glower, she reached down and slid a deceptively delicate arm around the brownie's waist, pulling her off the floor. "I would have taken the serum. But since you've proven yourself unfit to the task of finding it, you have until Midnight to bring me the shifter's child. If you fail, the brownie and the hobgoblin will both die."

"Yowl, hsssss!" Wicked flew past me, claws extended.

Desiree smiled wickedly and popped away, brownie and all.

My cat landed in the empty spot where she'd been, every hair on his body sticking straight up and his tail whipping the air. He hissed again, clawing the air as if he thought he could still reach her. "She's gone, buddy. But hold that thought in case she comes back."

Wicked ran back up the stairs ahead and dove back through the apartment door. I followed, my footsteps heavy. If Desiree had been telling us the truth, I'd as good as killed Hobs myself. Tears burned my eyes. "I thought it was love serum," I mumbled, my heart breaking.

Sebille didn't speak. She was stiff with rage. But she reached out and touched my arm. "We'll fix this, Naida."

I nodded because I had to believe it was true. Unfortunately, I was terrified it wasn't.

Whom stood in the doorway blinking slowly. "Whooo?" he asked.

I sniffed, scrubbing my wet face with my sleeve. "A very evil princess." My gaze lifted to his. "Is she right? Is Hobs going to die?"

The doctor's beakish face pinched until it looked even more pointed. "I'm afraid she was. Your little friend is in real danger of dying." He returned to the bed and peered down at Hobs, a ripple running through the feathery cloak.

"How do we stop it?" Sebille asked, moving to stand protectively over the little hobgoblin.

"We need an antidote," Whom said as if it were the simplest thing in the world.

A thought occurred and I grabbed his arm. "We gave you the serum. Can't you use what's left of that?"

He shrugged narrow, sloped shoulders, making the cloak he wore shift like ruffling feathers. "I performed the ritual to create an antidote for love serum, believing that was what you gave me. Unfortunately, the contents of the vial have been compromised by that ritual." He frowned, dense feathery brows lowering over his enormous eyes. "Obsession is a highly invasive poison. The sooner you get a sample of the poison to me, the sooner I can make the antidote, and the better it will be for him."

We all looked down at the pale, shuddering creature that used to be my fun-loving hobgoblin. Tears burned my eyes. "What are his chances, doc?" I hadn't meant to ask the question because I really didn't want the answer. But it spilled out before I could stop it.

Whom sighed. "If you can get me the serum

within a few hours, he'll have a sixty percent chance of surviving."

My heart tightened painfully. *Only sixty percent.* I swallowed a lump in my throat, struck mute and immobile with guilt and grief.

"What are we looking for?" Sebille asked Whom.

"Obsession is a byproduct of love. But unlike true love, it's a twisted strand, providing more harm than good. You must look to where love begins and follow the strands as they twist into something ugly." He shook his head. "I wish I could be more specific. But this poison is of the demonic realm." He sniffed. "I don't care for demons."

Join the club, I thought.

Sebille grabbed my arm, giving me a tug. "Come on. We need to move."

I fought her grip, not willing to leave Hobs alone.

Whom caught my gaze, his huge eyes warm with compassion. "I'll stay with him, child." He reached down and tugged a feather from his cloak, handing it to me. "Dip the quill into the substance when you find it and release the feather. It will make its way back to me."

I took the feather, scraping tears from my cheeks with the back of my hand. "Thanks."

He inclined his head and sat in a chair, where he proceeded to close his owlish eyes and fall immediately into sleep.

Sebille tugged my arm again. I let her lead me

from the apartment, closing the door softly behind us.

"I have no idea where to start," I told the sprite, my voice filled with hopelessness.

"That's easy," she told me, jogging down the stairs.

I plodded after her, too depressed to jog.

By the time I reached the bottom of the stairs, she'd already called up a book on Obsession. The magical aura had barely faded when she opened it.

Amazing myself, I was disappointed when Osvald's head didn't rise from the pages.

The sprite flipped quickly through the pages, frowning as she skimmed the chapter heads looking for something that would help.

She stopped, her finger running over a picture on the page. "Loveland," she muttered, frowning.

The name startled me out of my funk. "What?"

Sebille showed me the picture. "This says Obsession grows on a small island where life still thrives in the famed cupid city. It's called Loveland."

I grabbed the book, recognizing the broken lines of the city that Lovelace had taken me to. "I've been here!" But it hadn't been an island and nothing was thriving there. *What if we were too late?*

Sebille grabbed it back. "When?"

"Lovelace took me there when he kidnapped me."

"We need to go there," Sebille said, eyeing the

picture as if it would give her a clue how to get to it. Her head snapped up. "Call Lovelace."

"I don't know how to do that," I argued.

"Think, Naida!" her gruff command told me how worried she was about Hobs, better than any of her other words or actions had. Sebille usually took refuge in action when faced with a challenge. I tended to sink into self-pity and despair for a bit before clawing my way out and determining to fight.

I shook my head. "I'm sorry. I just don't know. He didn't give me any way to get in touch."

Sebille's expression was beyond angry. I spun away, heading into the bookstore. I couldn't do anything about her being mad. It was how she coped. But I had an idea. I found my phone and quickly dialed Grym. He answered on the fourth ring, when I was about to hang up. "Naida? I'm kind of busy."

"You're still fighting cherubs?"

"Dealing with the aftermath. What do you need?"

"Hobs is dying."

Silence met my statement, and I thought I heard a muttered curse on the other end. He sighed. "What can I do?"

"I need to reach Lovelace. We need to go to the cupid city to find the poison so Doctor Whom can make an antidote."

"Okay."

"Have you, by any chance, captured any of the cherubs that you can question? Or did they all poof away?"

"Hold on a sec," he said. "Sampson! Is that one still alive?"

I couldn't hear the response, but Grym came back online a minute later. "We have one. What do you want me to do with it?"

Sebille showed up with the book of pages, handing it to me. "Where are you," I asked him, taking the book.

"Enchanted General Hospital. Neonatal wing. Why?"

"Stay there. We'll be right over."

23

THEY LOOK LIKE ALIENS

The pages flicked past, quick and jerky, hesitating occasionally and then starting up again as the book waited for me to give it direction. I called up a vision of Enchanted General Hospital. I had no idea what the maternity ward looked like, but I just pictured babies swathed in blue and pink blankets.

The magic swirled out of the book, a clear wash of energy dappled with multi-hued sparkles that swirled overhead and then slid down our bodies to the floor. Without warning, the energy tightened, squeezing us in a relentless grip, and began to twist. The world whipped past in a dizzying rush. My vision turned wonky. My stomach roiled until I closed my eyes against the resulting vertigo. Though I was expecting it, I sucked in a startled gasp when I was yanked off my feet and dragged inside the book.

Moments later, the magic dropped us in a corridor that smelled like baby powder and disinfectant and then sifted away. The book popped into its travel size, and I shoved it into my pocket, patting it for good measure.

I glanced at Sebille, who was shoving her long, red braid over one shoulder. "I don't think I'll ever get used to that," she complained, her eyes looking slightly crossed.

Glancing around, I noticed that we were standing in front of the window overlooking the nursery. Beyond the glass were row upon row of clear bassinets, many of them occupied with tiny figures wrapped tightly in pastel-hued blankets with matching caps on their heads.

Tiny puckered faces showed in the midst of the cloth wrappings, most of them asleep.

"Aw," I said, moving closer to the glass.

"They look like aliens," Sebille groused.

But I saw the wistful expression softening her face before she ruthlessly squelched it.

"Hey," said a familiar deep voice.

I turned to find Grym striding my way.

"You got here fast," he said, offering me a smile.

"We used the book," I said, looking around. The area looked clean and calm, though I noticed the lack of medical personnel. "Is everybody okay?"

Grym sighed. "Yeah. We took the non-magics into a private room for deprogramming." He grimaced as he said it. Like me, Grym apparently didn't enjoy the idea of messing with other people's memories. "Tell me what's going on."

I told him. He listened intently as Sebille stared through the large viewing window at the little sleepers behind it.

"So this brownie, you think she's the creature who captured Hobs' heart?"

"Yes. But it's much worse than missing love serum. He's been poisoned with Obsession."

Grym whistled. "That's bad, Naida."

My stomach twisted with pain, but I nodded. "I know. The sooner we do what Desiree is asking, the sooner we can get Whom the poison so he can make an antidote."

Grym paled. "Hold on. You're not seriously considering taking her a baby."

Of course I wasn't. "She wants Devin's pregnant wife."

Something that looked like guilt slid over Grym's handsome face. I narrowed my gaze on him. "What?"

Grym continued to avoid my gaze for another minute. Finally, I grabbed his hand. "Tell me."

He sighed. "I just found out something important. I wanted to tell you but..." He sighed. "It's not my story to tell." When I braced to argue, he held up a finger. "Hold on." Grym dialed a number and spoke into the phone. "I need you for a minute," he told the person on the phone. "I'm at the viewing window." He hesitated a beat and then nodded. "Good. I'll wait."

Grym disconnected and looked at us. "He's on his way."

"Who?" I asked, losing patience with the delay.

"Me," said a husky voice I remembered from the mall.

I turned to see Devin Sampson striding toward us. Something was different about him. Something I couldn't identify, except that he seemed taller, with an aura of power I hadn't noticed before.

He nodded at me and then at Sebille. "Ladies. What can I help you with?"

"You tell me," I said. "Grym thought you needed to be here."

The gargoyle sighed. "They got a visit from Desiree."

Sampson's face tightened. An angry light filled his gaze. "I'm sure that was pleasant."

In the interests of time, I decided not to dance around the issue. "She's demanding that we bring your wife to her, or my friend Hobs is going to die." I decided not to mention the brownie, who I assumed was in as much trouble as Hobs, because I didn't want to spend time trying to explain her involvement.

The shifter didn't look surprised. Scrubbing a

big hand over his mouth, he asked, "What poison did she give him?"

"Obsession," Sebille said. "Why am I getting the feeling you know Desiree personally?"

Sampson looked surprised by Sebille's directness. He turned toward the viewing window. Something soft came into his eyes when he looked at the babies. It didn't last long. His jaw tensed a beat later. "She's my sister."

Dimpled cherub cheeks! I hadn't seen that coming. "Your...sister?" I narrowed my gaze. "You're Denzel? Brother of Desiree and Lovelace?"

Devin...or Denzel...sighed. "Unfortunately." When he saw how we were looking at him, Sampson shook his head. "Look, it's not what you think. I had nothing to do with those nasty cherubs. They did belong to me once..."

I bristled and he hurried on.

"But I left all that behind." He frowned. "I'm done with that life. I'm done with the cancer that infects the place."

I threw Grym a glower. He'd known about Sampson and he hadn't told me.

His handsome face creased in a frown.

"What cancer?" I asked, my voice too soft. My throat was tight as the pieces started to come together in my mind.

"Power, control, greed." Sampson's look was pleading. He really seemed to want us to understand.

"Love isn't supposed to be controlling. It isn't supposed to be domineering. But after millennia of learning how effectively love works to control and subjugate, my people have gone bad. Lovelace isn't completely gone yet. He still tries to maintain a level of care for his *subjects*." He said the word as if it left a bad taste in his mouth. "But Desiree..." Sampson scraped a hand through his hair, leaving it standing up in tufts all over his head. "She was always a handful. As a little girl, she was very demanding and needed everyone to love her. That's only gotten worse over the centuries."

"Why does Desiree want your wife?" Grym asked.

Sampson looked at the cop as if he'd forgotten Grym was there. He frowned. "Desiree wants a child so badly. But she can't have one of her own. I think it's because her nature is too poisonous. A child couldn't survive in that environment. So she wants the next best thing."

"Your baby," I said, nodding. "Couldn't she pay someone to be a surrogate mother?" I asked, curious.

His smile was angry. "That's what she's trying to do with my wife. Though, in her usual fashion, she cares little if the surrogate or the father agree to the bargain."

"Why *your* baby, though," Grym said. "Not that I'd wish that on any child, but why not steal someone else's baby? She has to know you'll fight her."

"Actually, until she sent her cherubs down to look for me, she had no idea where I'd gone. I'd recreated myself as a shifter. Shifter magic is a perfect cloaking device against cupid magics. But her spies found Nina, and they recognized the magic signature of our child. She won't stop until she takes our baby. And Nina won't survive the process."

Another piece of the puzzle fell into place. "So that's why they've been attacking? They were trying to draw you out?"

Sampson nodded.

"We need to get to Loveland," I told him. "We need to save Hobs, and it sounds like you need to confront your sister."

"You're not sacrificing my wife and child," Sampson said, his face dark with anger and his hands fisted. "I'll kill you if you try."

I held up a hand. "I have no desire to hurt your wife. I have another idea. But we *will* need your help. Can we count on you?"

"Of course," Sampson said. "I'm going to have to fight this battle anyway. I'll take all the help I can get." He frowned. "But we're not taking my wife to Loveland. There has to be another way."

"There is, I think. I just need to go see someone to make sure. And..." I grimaced. "I might need some of your wife's hair."

P roving how bombproof my bestie had become from hanging around with my crew and me, Lea barely twitched when Sebille and I popped out of thin air inside her closed shop, *Herbal Remedies with Mystical Properties.*

She arched a single light brown brow at me and closed the book she'd been reading. Coming out from behind the long, glass counter, Lea crossed her arms over her chest and looked a question at me. I closed the Book of Pages and tried a guilty smile. "Sorry for barging in."

"The door works," she told us. "And there's this little thing called knocking."

"I know. I'm sorry. But Hobs is dying and we really need your help."

Her pretty face paled with alarm. "What happened?" Moving behind the counter again, she started pulling down jars of herbs. "What's wrong with him? I have some fenugreek for toxins. Clove is an anti-microbial," She stretched toward the highest shelf, wiggling her fingers so a jar filled with pale green leaves floated down to her. "Sage is a good antibiotic..."

I shook my head. "None of those will help, Lea. He's been poisoned with Obsession."

She stopped and turned. "What? How is that possible?"

"It's a long story. But he's in really bad shape."

"Doctor Whom..."

"He's with him now. But he needs us to bring a sample of the poison to him so he can create the antidote."

Lea wrapped her arms around the big jar of sage and nodded. "Okay. I'm with you so far."

"We need to go to Loveland in the demon realm," Sebille said.

Lea blinked. Then she laughed. "That's funny. I thought I heard you say you were going into the demon realm."

Sebille and I stared back at her. She paled. "Festering Frog flatulence! Seriously? That's like a death sentence."

"We'll have someone to help us," I said. "Someone who knows his way around the place. Someone who's from there."

"Brock?"

Brock was a friend of ours from nearby Illusion City. He was a demon, but he was a good one. Though, in his ten-foot-tall demon form with enormous bat-like wings, he was a little scary. I shook my head. Getting Brock's help wasn't a bad idea. Unfortunately, we didn't have time to hunt him down and pitch it to him. "No. One of the cupid princes is coming. His sister, Princess Desiree, is behind all these cherub attacks. And it turns out she's been hunting for him. Or, actually, his pregnant wife."

Lea's brows lowered as she tried to decipher my poorly-told story. "Long story short," I said impatiently. "She wants the baby. Denzel knows he needs to confront her about it. But I'm afraid Desiree will just blow the place up if we don't show up with the pregnant wife."

Lea's mouth fell open. "Oh no. We're not giving an innocent baby to this monster."

"No, we're not. But I was hoping Nina Sampson could make an appearance. Or, maybe somebody who looks just like her?"

Lea blinked. Then blinked again. Finally, she said, "You're thinking four-dimensional glamour?"

"Yes."

She turned around and started putting jars back into their spots on the shelves. As she wiggled her fingers again to send the sage skyward, Sebille and I shared a look.

Sebille, whose patience had never been a snake with a long tail, said. "Lea, we need to hurry. Hobs might not have much longer."

My bestie made an impatient sound. "I'm working as fast as I can," she said, pulling another jar from the shelves and opening it to scoop lacy green leaves into a bowl. "You have hair?"

I found myself grinning in relief. "I do." I handed her the hair. "Can we help?"

Lea nodded. "Sebille, get the Bilberry extract out of the fridge and make me a tea with it. Use lavender and basil for the base. Naida, go to my closet and find something that looks like the type of clothes this woman would wear."

My steps lighter than they'd felt in hours, I hurried up the stairs at the back of Lea's shop to do as she'd asked.

24

NOT HAPPENING, GARGOYLE

An hour later, we exited Lea's place to find Grym and Sampson waiting for us on the sidewalk. Lea locked up and turned to a flummoxed Sampson. He stared at Lea, his expression filled with wonder. "That's amazing." He eyed the rounded belly. "You look just like my wife. Is there a baby in there?"

Lea flinched. "No. Just a pillow." But she kept rubbing the bump as if she did have a little bundle of joy in there.

"You even sound like her," Sampson said, poking a finger at the pillow "baby".

"It's a four-dimensional glamour," I told the shifter as Lea smacked his finger away.

"This is why you wanted Nina's hair?" He asked.

"Yes." I frowned. "Can we get moving please?" I

couldn't shake the feeling that we were frittering Hobs' and the little brownie's lives away standing there.

"Yeah, sorry," Sampson said, giving me a tight smile. "We can go."

"Where?" Grym asked. "How do we get to Loveland?"

"Lovelace just popped me over," I said.

Sampson winced. "Yeah, I can't do that. I've been away from there too long. I've lost my intrinsic connection to the place."

"Then how?" Sebille asked.

"Through a portal," he said. "The ogres have the closest one."

Sebille and I shared a horrified look. "There has to be another way," I said.

"Not if you want to do this in the minimum amount of time," Sampson assured us.

Grym gave us a crooked grin. "Hey, while we're there, you two could go see the naked ogre on the throne and ask to see the fine print in that contract you signed."

"Not happening, gargoyle," I said on a growl. I lifted my brows. "And you're not my favorite person right now, so you might want to button it."

Grym chuckled at the look on Sampson's face. "Long story. I'll tell you later."

"You will not!" Sebille and I both said at once.

Fighting a grin, Sampson pointed toward an old-fashioned, panel-sided car that was parked in front of the herbal store. It looked a little like a hearse. I really hoped that wasn't prescient. "We can drive to the boundary of King Rhorr's land in my car. We'll have to walk from there."

We piled inside and Sampson drove out of the lot. "It's a fifteen-minute drive to the border. Then it should take us another fifteen to the portal. Assuming we don't get waylaid."

My brows rose to my hairline. "Waylaid?"

Sampson made a dismissive sound. "You know ogres."

Yeah, I did. Which was why my stomach was churning from his words.

We drove in silence through a lush, green landscape with gently rolling hills that got sharper and larger in the distance. The foothills rolled toward a range of perpetually snow-capped mountains that bordered and then eventually cut through The Enchanted Forest.

It was a beautiful drive. Until it wasn't.

One minute the landscape was lush and green. The next it was brown and rocky. Sampson pulled off the road and drove across a dusty patch of ground bordered on three sides by smaller rocks built into a low wall. It was clearly a parking lot built by ogres. Sampson stopped the car in the middle of the space and killed the engine.

We all sat looking across the land in front of us,

seeing the broken towers and archways that I remembered from when Sebille and I had been there before.

Huge chunks of rock dotted the space, like squat, gray trees with no branches. Every gust of wind carried whirls of dust across the barren acreage.

We all filed out of the car.

Sampson pointed toward a tiny archway in the distance, next to a small pond with muddy looking water. "That's the portal we need."

"How can you tell?" Grym asked. "There are dozens of them."

Sampson nodded. "I don't have a strong connection to the place anymore. But I can still see its aura. There's a glossy red aura over that portal. It will take us to Loveland."

We started walking.

After a few steps, Sampson jerked to a stop and turned to Lea in her Nina glamour. He gave her an apologetic look. "I need to treat you like you're Nina," he said. "Desiree might have spies around the portal."

Lea nodded and let him take her arm.

We managed to make it nearly to the portal before we saw the ogre. In fact, we got within fifteen feet of it.

So close.

A bald, purple mountain stepped out from behind a boulder, the ogre's heavy features fixed in a murderous expression. He was holding a club that might have weighed as much as I did, and his thick, hairy arms were too muscular to fall straight at his sides. He had no hair on his head, but he had a coarse, rectangular patch of hair hanging from below his lips. The rough beard was cut straight across at the bottom and flexed as he snarled a warning to us. "Who goes there?"

"Who writes this guy's dialogue?" I murmured to Sebille. She snorted in response.

Sampson lifted one fist in the air and then smacked it hard against his chest. He spoke a few words in a guttural language that I didn't understand. But I recognized it as the language Rick and Maxine had spoken with the naked ogre.

The mountain with the club didn't respond except to narrow his small blue eyes.

"This is Prince Denzel of Loveland," Grym said. "I'm Detective Grym of the Enchanted Police Department." He pointed to me. "That's the Keeper of the Artifacts, Naida Griffith and that," he jerked a thumb toward Sebille, "Is Princess Sebille of the fae."

The ogre's gaze slid to Lea-Nina and he grunted.

"My wife," Sampson said. He reached down and placed a big hand over Lea's belly and said, "Our unborn child."

The ogre pursed his lips thoughtfully.

Sebille leaned close to whisper. "Ogres love babies."

I nodded. Good to know.

The creature's small eyes softened for a beat as he stared at Nina-Lea, and then he threw back his head and laughed, a sound like boulders tumbling down a mountainside. The strong scent of roses wafted over me as he bent double and slapped his thick, hairy knees. "We fight," he said, his eyes alight. He straightened and jerked a thumb toward Sampson and then Grym. "For women and child. Winner takes all."

Okay, the baby thing had definitely backfired.

Grym shook his head. "That's not going to happen. I demand an audience with King Rhorr."

The ogre shook his head and slammed the club on the ground. Twenty feet away, a chunk of an enormous column of rock cracked away from the top and slammed to the ground.

Fluttering ferret farts! He was going to kill Grym and Sampson with that thing. I stepped forward. "Listen, you. We're not prizes to be won or lost. Now just step aside and you can get back to your business." I grimaced. "Whatever that is."

The ogre blinked, his dark brows lowering as he thought about my demand. He slammed the club down again. "We fight!" he roared. The sound rumbled across the land like a boom of thunder, echoing against the distant hills.

Without warning, he lumbered toward Grym, swinging the massive club across his middle.

Grym barely managed to suck backward in time to avoid being struck, but I knew it would only take one direct strike in the wrong place to kill him.

Unless...

In a flash of light, Grym transformed into his gargoyle shape.

Gently shoving Lea-Nina aside, Sampson followed suit. In the blink of an eye, he became the giant wolf I remembered from the mall. Both men attacked at once, driving the massive creature back with a rapid-fire array of slashes, snapping jaws, and club-like pounding from Grym's rocky fists.

But the ogre didn't stay on the defensive for long. He raised the club above his head and slammed it into Grym. It only grazed his arm, but the impact was enough to drive Grym to his knees.

Before the ogre could wind up again, Sampson leaped onto his back, fangs bared and claws raking the ogre's thick skin.

The massive claws barely scratched the ogre's flesh.

"We have to do something," Lea said in Nina Sampson's voice.

"You think?" Sebille said. "But what?"

"I'll blast him," Lea said, lifting her hands to start weaving a spell. A single spark fizzed at her fingertips and then died. "Hot diggity dangit!" she exclaimed in frustration. "I can't use magic in this glamour."

Sebille popped into her sprite form. "I'll see if I can help."

I threw out my keeper magic and waited, but nothing came. I frowned. There were certainly artifacts in that place. We'd seen one of them.

"The ogres lock their artifacts down with special earth magic," Lea-Nina said. She sighed. "Where's the king when you need him?"

My eyes went wide. "The king!" I said, turning on my heel.

"Where are you going?" Lea yelled after me.

I was running toward the largest archway in the distance. "To see a naked ogre." He was the closest thing to an ogre king I knew of. Maybe he could help.

"This really isn't the time, Naida," she replied.

I couldn't argue with that. There was really no good time to see a naked ogre. And yet, it seemed I was making a habit of it.

I ran toward the archway I thought was the right one. The meaty sound of flesh striking flesh and the occasional snarl from the shifter dogged my steps. I felt my will lagging as I approached the portal. What if it was the wrong one? Maybe I needed to go through with an ogre, or I'd be fried by magic. What if the naked ogre had dropped something and was bending over to get it when I barged inside?

Ew, ew, ew, ew, ewwwwww!

I shut my thoughts down and forced myself to keep running. "Not good, not good, not good..." I chanted as I ran.

And then suddenly I was there and had no more time to talk myself out of it. I closed my eyes and plunged into the portal before I could change my mind.

As before, the magic enveloped me in a weird, gelatinous embrace that tugged against my skin, slowing down my passage even as I fought to move more quickly through.

Despite feeling that the more I pushed, the slower I went, I managed to shove my way through the portal a beat later. The magic released me with a soft burp of air.

I stumbled a few steps forward, pinwheeling my arms to keep from falling as the uneven rock floor threatened to pitch me onto my face. Digging my heels in, I stopped mere inches away from the enormous throne I remembered.

It was empty.

No, no, no, no! I didn't have time to search for the wise man or whatever he was. I needed to find the king immediately.

I heard something that sounded like an old woman in sneakers shuffling over a hard floor. Gazing frantically around, I determined that the sound was coming from a passageway behind the throne.

I suddenly realized I had nothing to defend myself with if I was attacked. Would my meager defensive magic work on an ogre? Unlikely.

I was pretty sure the ogres' bladders could withstand a shot of my defensive magics. Also, having met a few of them already, I figured they'd just view kinky hair as a new fashion statement to be celebrated.

Nevertheless, as the shuffling grew closer, I yanked my magic forward and let it sizzle in my palms.

A beat later, the naked ogre shuffled out of the passage and jerked to a stop, a massive sandwich drooping from his hands and a smear of something that looked like mustard decorating his cheek. He fixed his dark, bead-like eyes on me, surprise turning to delight as he no-doubt recognized me. The wild mop of white hair looked even woolier than the last time, sticking out around his broad face like the aura around a star, and the bulbous red nose twitched above the mustard-glazed lips.

"Argh!" I screamed and covered my eyes.

A deep rumbling sound filled the cavern. I peeked between two fingers as the naked ogre lumbered closer, still clutching his sandwich.

"Hello, Keeper. It's so nice to see you again."

I quickly covered my eyes again as he trundled around the throne. "Ah!"

But then I recognized the soft swish of fabric and risked a look. Thank the goddess! He was wearing a purple robe trimmed in white fur. "I need your help. We're trying to get to a portal because Desiree is trying to steal her brother's baby and my friend Hobs is dying and I need to save him from Obsession and his brownie is going to die too but your ogre is clubbing my friends to death and I don't mean clubbing like dancing and drinking fruity drinks..." I pantomimed dancing and drinking in case he didn't get it and his black eyes sparkled. He swiped a long tongue out and lapped up the mustard and then motioned for me to go on.

"...And this big bald ogre is trying to kill my friends and take the women and the baby well me and my two friends Sebille you met Sebille remember and Le...a...Nina...and we can't we don't have time because Hobs is dying did I mention that..." I stuttered to a stop when he held up a mustard-painted hand.

"You wish me to stop my ogre from killing your friends?"

I panted from not breathing and nodded.

Carefully placing the sandwich on the arm of the stone throne, the ogre stood. He patted me on the shoulder with a big hand, practically flinging me to the ground, and started walking me toward the portal.

The sour smell of mustard wafted up to my nose. I looked down, grimacing at the wide stripe of the stuff painting my shirt. "I really appreciate your help," I said as we plunged into the clutching magic of the portal.

When we popped out on the other side, he said. "It's my pleasure." He squeezed the shoulder he was still holding. My knees buckled under the pain. I was pretty sure my bones were rubbing together from the compression. "I mean, we're practically family, amiright?"

I was nodding before his words registered. "Huh?" I said, a beat too late.

The naked ogre whistled, long and shrill.

In the distance, the bald ogre jerked to a halt. He had Grym in a stranglehold in one hand and was sweeping Sampson off his back with the other. His big head turned our way.

The naked ogre lifted an arm, his fist punching the air.

The bald ogre dropped Grym and Sampson and turned away. He picked up his club and lumbered back behind his rock.

Sometimes-naked ogre smiled down at me. "There you go." He swiped at the mustard he'd left on my shirt, smearing it over a larger area. "Say hello to Sebille for me. We'll see you soon. We have much planning to do."

"Uh...er...a...yeah. See ya." I gave him a wave and took off running.

I had no idea what he was talking about, but I didn't like the sound of it. I really hoped there wasn't something in the small print wayyyy down at the... er...bottom...that the sprite and I were going to live to regret.

But, I was pretty sure there was.

25

LET'S GET THIS SHOW ON THE ROAD

We stood near the fountain I recognized from my previous visit to Loveland. The same creatures who'd been climbing all over the castle at the end of the avenue the last time I'd been there were still scurrying back and forth, leaving a slightly cleaner wall behind them wherever they'd been.

Still, much of the structure was covered in a gray to black film that looked like mold. Whatever was poisoning Loveland, the hard-working cleaners were barely keeping ahead of its debilitating effects.

"Where will the Obsession be?" I asked Sampson. He stood next to Lea-Nina, his expression sad as he stared at the distant castle. His dark hair stood up in spots where blood had hardened the strands together. Though the wounds had closed when he'd shifted back to human form, the deep bruises along his jaw and over his shoulder, which were visible beneath his torn clothing, had still not healed.

Grym didn't look much better. His clothing was torn and flapping around his arms and legs from changing into his much bigger gargoyle form without stripping first. His hair was a mess and his face was battered and bruised. Dried blood formed a thin trail down his throat, and there was a smear of it across his forehead.

That ogre had beaten the stuffing out of the two men.

Thank the goddess, the almost-naked ogre had stopped it before they'd been killed.

Grym turned and caught me staring at him. He gave me a smile that made my belly tighten. I was still mad at him for not telling me about Sampson, but I'd learned my lesson. I'd give him a chance to explain, and we'd take it from there.

"I can't believe you got Rhorr to stop that fight." Grym shook his head. "He must really like you."

I winced. I didn't tell him I hadn't known the naked ogre was the king. For now, I'd just let him think I had powerful friends. Then I remembered what the king had said about my being part of the family. Did he know something I didn't? What if I was part ogre? It wasn't like anybody would have told me if I was. I'd had to force what little I knew about my family out of Archie. And I still didn't know most of what happened back when I'd been a toddler that had made my entire family leave, sticking me in the care of a surly troll who'd pretended she was my grandmother.

For all I knew, I had an ogre somewhere in my family tree.

Frowning, I determined to browbeat Archie into telling me more about my family. I could definitely threaten him with a painfully full bladder and kinky hair.

"...garden she keeps gated and locked. Nobody's allowed in there except her and the gardener."

I refocused my attention on Sampson.

"How do we get the key?" Sebille asked.

Sampson shook his head. "Our best bet is to find the gardener."

"What about Desiree?" Lea asked. "What's the plan there?"

Sampson's face turned hard. "You let me deal with my sister. You all just get what you need and get out of here. Make sure you're gone within our time-frame of twenty minutes though, or you might get stuck here."

"What are you going to do?" I asked.

"I'm going to remove her ability to leave this place." He grimaced as he glanced around at the dilapidated homes and the rotting fountain. "She's destroyed this place. Let her live with what she's done."

Silence pulsed between us for a beat as everyone

grieved what had probably once been a beautiful and thriving land. I scanned a look skyward and saw an overcast sky, layer upon layer of gray clouds hanging low as if trapped there by Loveland's poison.

At the end of the lane, the wooden doors of the castle opened, and a single figure descended the steps and started toward us. I recognized the tall, lanky figure of Lovelace Cupid, his figure looking even more skeletal than the last time I'd seen him.

Lovelace didn't appear to hurry toward us, but his strides somehow ate up the distance. Within only a couple of minutes, he was mere yards away. I looked him over, judging him even less healthy than the last time I'd seen him. His pallor was gray, his face even more wizened than before, and silvered strands turned his unkempt hair gray at the temples and threaded the rest more liberally than before.

The man inclined his head to me. "Keeper," and gave Grym and Sebille a cursory glance, dismissing them without interest.

He didn't appear surprised to see his brother, but his gaze fell on Lea-Nina and his smile was sad. "Hello, my dear. You're just as lovely as I thought you'd be."

A consummate actress, Lea turned to Sampson. He tucked his arm through hers, pulling her against his body. "This is my brother, Lovelace, Nina love," Sampson said.

She smiled. "It's a pleasure."

Lovelace seemed flustered. His gaze kept slipping to her belly. "We must get you off your feet." He motioned toward the castle. "Come. I've set out tea. I'm so happy you're here. There's been no joy in this castle for decades. It's about time we had tiny feet pattering around again."

It took Lovelace several steps to realize we weren't following. He stopped and turned back, one brow lifting in question.

Sampson stepped forward, taking a protective stance in front of Lea-Nina. "We aren't staying, Lovelace. Stop pretending this is anything but extortion. She'll kill me and, once the baby's born, she'll kill Nina. You know this. Desiree won't wish to share the child's affection with anyone."

Lovelace dithered, his long fingers twitching together and apart and then winding together again. "She's not as bad as you believe, brother..."

"Isn't she?" Sampson asked. "Look around you, Lovelace. She's destroyed everything. Why do you stay and let her destroy your life too?"

"I can't leave her alone!" Lovelace said, clearly appalled.

"It's what she's brought on herself," Sampson said, his voice filled with passion. "Come with us, brother. You have a family she's keeping you from. Be my brother again. And let Desiree choose her own path. You don't owe her your life."

More dithering and twitching ensued. Lovelace clearly didn't know how to respond. I sort of understood. Change was hard. And Lovelace had found a certain level of comfort in his life, despite how dreary it was. But he was slowly but surely shriveling up under his sister's tyranny.

Lea reached a hand toward Lovelace. He looked at it, his face filled with awe. Finally, he clasped her fingers and lifted them to his lips. She smiled. "Come with us, Lovelace. Be an uncle to our child. Live again."

Lovelace stared at the bump he believed contained a child. He moved closer, holding a palm above Lea-Nina's belly. He glanced at her. "May I?"

Sampson opened his mouth to deny his brother, but Lea shook her head. "Let him, darling. It won't do any harm."

Sampson stared at her as if to ask if she was sure. Lea nodded. She reached for Lovelace's hand and placed it over her stomach. A beat later he jumped, his eyes alight, and grinned from ear to ear. "It moved!"

Lea-Nina laughed. "He's very active."

"Please, brother. I need your help," Sampson said, wrapping a grateful arm around Lea's shoulders.

Lovelace reluctantly took his hand away. I watched as he pulled himself upright, straightening his shoulders. Above us, a ray of sunlight bathed the ground where we stood. Just a flash of light, but the warmth felt delicious in the moist cold of the place.

He nodded. "What do you need from me?"

Sampson looked relieved. "Help me keep Nina safe. I'll try to talk reason to Desiree, but if she doesn't relent, we'll need to exile her in Loveland."

Lovelace flinched, taking a small step back in horror.

I was afraid we were going to lose him at that point. But he swallowed hard and nodded. "You mean to engage the power threshold?"

"Yes. Will you stand with me, brother? It will take the power of two to perform the rite."

Lovelace sent another lingering look toward Lea's fake but apparently moving belly and sighed. "Yes. In truth, I'm relieved. I've known for a long time that she was out of her mind. But she kept to herself, so I let it be. But now..." The gray cast to his skin deepened. "She's hurting people. And I know you're right. She'll hurt you. She'll hurt Nina. And, in the long run, she'll harm that precious child. I can't have that on my conscience."

"All right then," Sebille said, weary of delay. "Let's get this show on the road. We have a very sick hobgoblin to save."

Lovelace spared her a quick glance, and something lit his eyes for a beat. "What do you need from me?"

"We need to find Obsession and get a sample to

send to our physician. Can you help with that?" I asked.

"I can. Come."

I had to nearly run to keep up with the long-legged man. Despite his unhealthy looks, he didn't seem feeble in any way. He led us to a gate that was set off a ways from the castle. Black metal fencing, thickly interwoven with dense green vines that had one-inch-long thorns on them, ran as far as the eye could see in both directions. The vining was too dense to see through the intricate balusters to the garden beyond.

The gate was topped with a beautiful heart scroll. Hearts were also spun into the metal of the elegant balusters. If the metal hadn't been chipped and rusty on nearly every spike and baluster, it would have been beautiful.

Lovelace laid a hand on the uppermost heart and screamed at the top of his voice, "Aelfsvald. Aelfsvald. Aelfsvald." He gave us a smile. "I do apologize for yelling. Poor creature's deaf as a post."

We waited for a long moment, until a loud whirring noise warned us the gardener was coming.

Lovelace looked at Sebille. "You're a fairy, right?"

She frowned and then nodded. I could tell from the expression on her face that she wondered how he knew. He shook his head. "I'm familiar with the Keeper's acquaintances." He jerked his chin toward the whirring sound.

"Aelfsvald is loyal to Desiree. He'll protect her with his life from anything he feels might endanger her." The whirring was mere yards away. Lovelace lowered his head toward Sebille and spoke softly. "You know how to induce sleep?"

Sebille blinked in confusion. Then understanding lit her face. She nodded.

"Good. I don't wish him harmed. But he'll try to stop you."

The whirring stopped, and a rusty voice came through the vining. "Yes, Master Lovelace?"

"Aelfsvald. We have guests at the palace. Denzel has returned to us and brought his lovely wife. They are with child."

The latch on the gate lifted. The heavy iron moved slowly inward.

A small, stout figure stood in the opening, his back stooped and a gnarled walking stick in one knotted hand. The fairy leaned heavily on the stick. He eyed each of us in turn, his gaze dark and his features pinched. Aelfsvald's gaze stopped on Sebille and the shaggy brows lifted. "Ah. Hello, mistress fairy."

Sebille inclined her head. "It's not often I meet a garden fairy who enjoys being of the larger world."

I was pretty sure she was commenting on the fact that he'd left his fairy form to become human-sized-ish. He was about the size of your average little person.

He nodded. "I am a solitary fairy," he explained a bit sourly. "It is less lonely this way."

Sebille nodded. "I mostly just like to eat their food."

He jerked, his wrinkled lips puckering as his round body seemed to convulse. A strange choking sound emerged from him.

I took a step closer, thinking he might need the Heimlich or something. "Are you okay?"

Lovelace chuckled. "He's not used to laughing. He's a bit rusty at it." Lovelace leaned closer to the old fairy and yelled, "Isn't that so, Aelfsvald?"

The fairy jerked and stopped the choking sounds to glare up at the much taller man. "You needn't scream in my face, master."

Lovelace winked at Lea-Nina, as if to say, the poor fool doesn't even know he's deaf. "Well, I'll leave you to our guests. They would like to see the garden. I believe they have a particular interest in one of our special plants. Perhaps you wouldn't mind playing at being a tour guide."

Aelfsvald waved a hand as if shooing Lovelace away. "We'll be fine, master. Go on with your business."

"Lovely." Lovelace smiled at Sampson and Lea. "Shall we go speak to Desiree?"

"Absolutely, brother."

Grym looked at Sampson. "If you don't need me..."

"We'll be fine," Sampson gave Grym a telling look. "But Nina may be bored with our business discussions..." he arched a brow. "Maybe you could stay nearby so she can join you in a few minutes? I'm sure she'd like to walk the gardens too."

"Understood," Grym said.

I understood too. Sampson wanted to present his "wife" as proof that he'd done as Desiree demanded, and then he wanted Grym to get her out of there with the rest of us.

"I'll wait near the front door," Grym said. He sent me a look, and I nodded. As soon as I got the sample, we were all going to book it back to the portal together.

We watched the four of them head for the castle. Lea turned once to find me watching her leave. I must not have been as good at hiding my worry as I'd hoped. She gave me a smile and a little wave. It was a reminder that I wasn't to underestimate her. She was a witch, after all. One who was powerful enough to make herself look and sound like another woman. She could even make a pillow move like an unborn baby beneath a demigod's hand.

Yeah. She'd be okay.

"Come along then," the gardener said. "Which plant is it you wish to see?"

Sebille strode past him and into the garden, forcing him to follow. I closed the gate behind us and stood there a moment, looking around at the vibrant plumage of what would have been considered a lush garden anywhere in the universe. That it existed in so devastated a spot as Loveland was more than surprising.

A small island where life still thrives in the famed cupid city.

Desiree clearly put most of her magical energy into making the garden thrive.

"I don't know where to start," Sebille said in a falsely bright voice.

I forced a smile as I glanced around. "It's beautiful."

"Okay, first, tell us what Princess Desiree uses to keep her skin so soft and radiant," Sebille said in a half-whisper as if sharing a guilty secret.

Choking sounds emerged from the diminutive form of the fairy gardener again. "Now, now, miss. You don't expect me to give away the mistress's secrets now, do ye?" Without warning, the old fairy lifted his walking stick, and magic flared from it in waves of green sparkles.

When the magic cleared, he was holding a deadly-looking sword in his small hands. He sliced the air where Sebille had been, but she'd popped into sprite form and was buzzing around him, trying to avoid the lethal blade in his hand.

"Go, Naida!" she screamed, and then she sent a wash of energy over the blade, turning it to a snake that coiled in on itself in the blink of an eye and struck at Aelfsvald. He quickly dropped the snake, and it transformed back to a sword before it hit the ground.

And then, somehow, it was back in his hand.

"Do ye think me so old and daft I'd fall for that, *Princess* Sebille?"

Oops! Apparently, he'd recognized her.

"Go!" Sebille screamed again. She dove sideways as the fairy's blade transformed into a rapidly coiling knife, like a magical corkscrew, and drilled the air where she'd been.

I forced myself to leave her behind, trusting that she could take care of herself.

26

GET YOUR FOOL HEAD OUT OF YOUR BACKSIDE

I was looking for a white flower about the size of my head, with enormous dark green leaves. From what Sebille and I had read before we left, Obsession's leaves were covered in pale green hairs, prickly, like the hair on an elephant. The hairs stuck in the skin and caused painful blisters and potentially death.

Fun. No wonder Desiree kept an antidote around her neck.

I hurried through the labyrinthine garden, trying to peer over one row of plants to see the rest. But everything in the garden was huge. Water dripped in a constant refrain from the enormous leaves, and the flower heads were all oversized. The combined scent from the variety of blossoms was so heavy it actually started to make me sick after a while.

I'd turned several corners, run along several pathways, and been tripped up by a few vines snaking between raised flower beds by the time I ended up in the center of the space. It was a circular area, with a small marble fountain featuring a delicate fairy dumping water from a petal--shaped bucket.

I knew the fountain well. I'd already ended up there several times in my attempt to navigate the garden. I dropped, panting onto a stone bench, and wished I had Sebille's wings so I could get an aerial view of the place. The Obsession plant had to be nearby. If only I could find it.

Wings buzzed up behind me. I sucked air and said, "Finally! I thought you'd never get here. Is he asleep?"

I started to turn, catching the glint of light off a slender blade just before it pierced my throat. "Ah!" I threw myself off the bench and army-crawled beneath it.

"No, young lady," Aelfsvald growled out. "I am decidedly *not* asleep."

Crusty crab cankles! The fairy was getting on my last nerve. "What did you do to Sebille?"

He hovered just above the ground and shoved the blade toward my thigh.

I shot energy toward the thing as he lunged and managed to push it off course. The slender blade slid into the wooden leg of the bench and stuck.

The fairy's wings buzzed frantically as he tried to pull it free.

"Ha!" I exclaimed, untangling a leg from the encroaching vines and slamming the bottom of my foot into the stupid fairy.

He yelped in pain as he shot backward and crashed into the fairy in the fountain. His tiny form went boneless and slid down the marble figure, landing in the flower bucket with a soft splash.

Crawling out of my hidey-hole, I stood and yanked the sword out of the bench, carrying it with me to check him out. I prodded him gently with the sword, but he didn't move.

"Good," I said. "Take that!"

More buzzing ensued.

My nerves all aflutter, I swung around and lunged.

Sebille had a glower on her face, a truly colorful black eye, and energy dancing around her fists. "Go ahead," she said. "Make my day."

I sighed, lowering the sword. It promptly turned back into the walking stick, the head of which, I noticed, was a dark silver cat. "Awe," I said. "It looks like Wicked." The thing whipped around and slashed at my hand, drawing blood, and then settled back into immobility.

Sebille laughed. "It acts like him too."

"Har," I said, glaring at her.

"Come on. The Obsession plant is over here,"

she told me. "I saw it when I was flying over to rescue you." She took off and I trudged after her.

"Who rescued whom?" I asked, feeling cranky.

The plant was nestled in a dark corner of the garden, under an overarching trellis that was covered in flowering vines. The flowers on the vines smelled like cat urine and had thorns on their stalks the size of my little fingers.

Sebille hovered several feet away from the trellis. "I don't know what this vine is, but I get the feeling it's guarding the Obsession. Try not to touch it."

"Ya think?" I said, easing past while trying to make myself small—an impossible feat. I really needed to get back to the salads since the giant, salad eating dinosaur named Tildy was gone. The time-traveling tortoise had certainly taken us on a few adventures. But she would mostly be remembered for the fact that she kept eating my lunch.

The space beneath the trellis was shadowed, the air icy and thick with magic. Every time I moved, an invisible energy skittered over my skin, bringing gooseflesh up on my arms and forming ice along my spine. "I don't like the feeling of this place," I told the sprite.

She buzzed over the trellis and behind it. "Weird."

My gaze shot in her direction. "What's weird?"

More buzzing and more frantic movement ensued. "Um, Naida..."

I reached for the feather Whom had given me, anxious to get the job done and get out of there. "I'm hurrying."

The bulbous white flower had long petals that folded up from the sides, their tips tucked into the top, making it resemble a white orange. As I stood there, the petals quivered and started to open, emitting a delightful floral scent that sifted along my pebbled skin, soothing it. A smile tugged at my lips, even as alarm bells went off in my head. The opening petals revealed a quivering pool of silvery liquid at the blossom's center. The poison? I didn't know, but it seemed likely.

"Naida, you need to get out of there!" Sebille said. Her tone was hushed but taut with urgency.

I reached the tip of the feather toward the sweet-smelling blossom. A sense of warmth and love filled me. A sparkling wash of energy rose up off the flower and embraced me in delight.

My hand that was holding the feather paused. I fought to remember what I was doing there.

Birds sang in my head. Sunshine bathed me in golden light, and I looked around at a meadow that spread as far as the eye could see in every direction.

Naida!

Why did Sebille sound so frantic?

I looked down at the feather in my hand. My gaze lifted to a sea of Obsidian flowers, each one opening slowly to the sun.

The scent coming off the blooms was heady, like the finest wine, imbued with love.

The smile on my face turned giddy. My fingers began to open. The feather started to slip away. I eyed the lush green grass beneath my feet and thought it would be nice to lay down for a while, let the sun coat me in warmth as I breathed in all that delicious fragrance around me.

Naida! Get your fool head out of your backside!

Well. That wasn't very nice. That Sebille was such a buzzkill...

Whack! Pain burned in my jaw like fire.

Whomp! Agony ripped through my middle.

The feather slipped from my fingers.

Argh!!!!

What *was* that infernal buzzing?

Kaboom!

I jerked, my eyes shooting open as explosions ripped through the peaceful garden.

I stared with glossy eyes at the feather down by my feet. What was I doing?

"Naida! What in the name of the goddess's favorite protein bar are you doing? Get the sample and let's get out of here!"

I blinked, glancing up at the sky above me. Two fairies fought with flashing blades and colorful energy blasts. Smoke filled the lush garden and the ground rumbled as fairy energy blasted and something exploded not far from where I stood.

Oh. Yeah. The poison. I bent down and reached for the feather just as a particularly powerful blast shook the ground beneath my feet and caused the trellis to wobble.

The flower's poisonous hairs barely missed my arm. I jerked away from them, the last of the muzziness draining from my brain.

I grabbed the feather and quickly dipped its tip into the glossy pool of liquid in the center of the bloom.

"Ugh!" A foul gust of black mist shot up from the flower as the poison clung to the feather. The nasty mist stung my face and eyes and I stumbled back.

"Naida!" Sebille screamed again.

The feather wobbled in my fingers, trying to escape my grip. I held on. "I'm coming!"

I turned to leave the trellis. I didn't make it. On the heels of another concussive blast, the entire structure wobbled sideways and fell on top of me.

I screamed as the poisonous thorns of the vining pierced my skin.

The feather jerked violently and flew out of my grip, floating skyward.

"No!" I tried to grab it, but the thing was too fast.

"Naida?" Grym's voice said, filled with worry. "Are you okay?"

Other than several seriously burning holes in my arm and shoulder, stinging eyes, and a general feeling that I was going to collapse, I felt great. "I'm fine. Help me out of here, will you?"

Lea came running down the path, her glamour gone and her hair flying out behind her. "We need to get out of here. Sampson and Lovelace are barely holding her off." I spared her a quick glance and saw the little brownie running along behind her.

Good. That was good.

Grym grabbed my hand and yanked me to my feet. Agony slithered through the entire left side of my body and my leg buckled out from under me.

"Naida?"

My stomach clenched in sizzling pain. Nausea burned and Fire scalded along my flesh. Something acidic oozed from the thorn holes and scorched its way down my arm. I was pretty sure I could feel blisters forming in its path.

Grym tried to haul me off my feet.

"Don't touch the poison!" I screamed, suddenly sure I'd make him sick too.

Energy exploded around him, the light burning my eyes and making me stumble back. He wrapped a hard, muscular arm around my middle and threw me over his rock-like shoulder.

He'd transformed again. His gargoyle form was impervious to most poisons.

"Good idea," I mumbled as my world turned charcoal at the edges.

"Come on!" Sebille screamed. The last thing I heard before the world fell away was the sound of fairy wings beating Hades out of that horrible garden.

27

YOU'RE INVITED TO ATTEND A SPECIAL EVENT

I woke sometime later and jerked upright. "Hobs!" My gaze shot around the room. I was relieved to see I was in my apartment. In my own bed. Something eased in my chest.

But Hobs wasn't where we'd left him. And Doctor Whom's traveling birdhouse was gone.

I shoved at the blankets and stood, nearly hitting the floor again as dizziness swamped me. I eased myself back onto the mattress, breathing through the woozy feeling.

Sebille's voice rang out loud and clear in the Make Me a Magic Muffin song. The sprite opened the bathroom door a minute later. She looked at me and frowned. "What are you doing?"

I squinted. "Right at this moment, I'm trying to whittle two Sebilles down to one," I told her.

Both sprites gave me a crooked grin. "That's

probably from the poison. Nasty stuff. Whom almost couldn't save you."

She didn't have to be so cheerful about it.

Blood fled my face in a wave. "How long have I been out?"

Sebille shrugged. "Long enough to annoy the hobgoblin out of here."

Relief washed through me. "He's okay?"

"Right as rain. The feather with the Obsession sample arrived here shortly after you dropped it and Whom set to work right away healing the little runt." Her eyes sparkled. "That's the good news. The bad news is that he's in Lurve."

I shoved at the covers, scooting back with the intention of laying down again. "The brownie?"

She nodded. "I'll let him tell you. You want tea?"

"Yes! Please." My stomach gurgled. "And some toast?"

She rolled her eyes, clearly feeling put upon. But at least my double vision had resolved and there was only one of her. The thought of two Sebilles nearly finished what the poison had started.

I shoved my feet back under the covers. My toes met warm fur. Something squeaked, and I yelped, jerking my feet back.

A tiny white mouse clambered out from beneath the covers, ears and whiskers twitching with pique. Another followed on its tail and another. The entire "nest" encompassed six of the irritated little rodents. "What the?"

Sebille turned away from the teapot. "Your medicine. They're hiding from the cat."

I sighed. One of the downsides of using Doctor Whom was that he gave out mice as medicine. It probably seemed reasonable to him, being an owl and all, but for the rest of us, it was an exercise in frustration. I certainly wasn't going to gobble the little guys. But I couldn't just put them out on the street either. I had no idea if they knew how to fend for themselves out there.

I patted the covers on my lap and the tiny critters filed over and curled up again, settling back to sleep with a chorus of tiny sighs.

I grinned. "We'll have to find homes for them, or Wicked and Hex will drive them crazy." I'd had the "talk" with Wicked about eating my medicine more than once. But he had a cat's instincts and didn't seem able to keep himself from chasing them.

Sebille handed me a steaming mug of tea and set the plate of toast down on the bedside table. I grabbed the heavily buttered slice and took a big bite.

"I'm going back to the store. We've had a steady line of Ben E. Nigma fans pouring over the stock since we got back. There was a line around the block." She shook her head. "Thank the Universe for Baca. She's been a goddess-send."

"Baca?" I asked, crumbs spewing from my mouth.

Sebille ignored my question, stepping through the door.

"Bring me back a cookie!" I yelled after her. She ignored me, and I lay back on the pillow with a sigh, closing my eyes.

I dozed. Waking up only when the mice all squeaked in alarm and dove back under the covers. I sat bolt upright, ready to grab Wicked if he jumped onto the bed to stalk them.

But it wasn't my cat. Hobs stood in the doorway holding a plate. He fixed me with a pale blue gaze filled with guilt. "Miss. I brought you cookies."

I patted the bed next to me. "Thanks. Sit. I think we need to talk."

He dragged himself over to me, looking miserable. I took the plate from him and set it on the bedside table next to the cold remains of the toast.

Hobs stood beside the bed, eyes downcast and long fingers nervously twining. The little shock of light brown hair between his big ears lay limp against his pale skin, mirroring his dejected attitude.

I couldn't bear to see him so upset. Taking a deep breath, I got right to the point. "You stole the love serum, didn't you?"

He frowned, his gaze still not meeting mine. He pulled a hand out from behind his back and handed me the serum. It was in a small bottle, only three inches tall and rounded at the bottom with a narrow neck.

I looked it over, noting the broken wooden stopper that seemed to have been glued back together.

Just like that, a lightbulb lit in my brain and I knew.

"No," I said, shaking my head. "That's not right. You *didn't* take the serum. The brownie took it, didn't she?"

"It's not her fault, Miss. That mean lady was in the vault. She was breaking everything. She didn't see the bottle fall and the lid crack. Baca grabbed it and ran to hide until the noisy came on and the lady popped out of there." His eyes glistened with unshed tears. "She only wanted to fix the lid, Miss."

I stared at the tiny bottle, wondering how something so small could cause so much trouble. I needed to make Hobs understand how important it was for him not to mess with the artifacts. I didn't know how to start. Finally, I just started with the first question that popped into my mind.

"Why?" I'd get to the rest after he told me why he'd broken my trust and endangered us all.

"Baca's my friend, Miss. I didn't want you to make her leave."

I bit back a sigh. He obviously thought I was horrible. "This is not a playground, Hobs. Messing with artifacts is dangerous. In this case, people were hurt. You almost died. This is serious."

Then I remembered his little tux, and I asked, "Did you take some of this serum?"

He shook his head. "Not on purpose. When she showed me I..." His chin dropped even lower. "I think some got on my finger."

Closing my eyes, I couldn't believe the mess of accidents and coincidences that had occurred to bring the whole Cupid thing to boiling point. My eyes popped open again when I realized, if Baca and Hobs hadn't taken the serum, Desiree might have gotten her hands on it. And she'd have done much worse things with it.

An ugly thought occurred on the heels of that one. What if the brownie had intentionally left some serum residue on the bottle when she'd given it to Hobs? If she had, she needed to leave immediately. In the meantime, I had to make Hobs understand that he didn't need magic to be loved. "Hobs, people should love you just because you're you. If you need magic to create love, then it's not really love. You know that, right?"

He nodded, but he hesitated just long enough that I doubted he really did understand.

I reached out and took his hand. It was warm, and the skin was baby-soft. "You're very loveable," I told him. "I love you. Sebille loves you. If Baca's the right girl for you, she'll love you too."

He sighed, his chin dipping lower. "I messed up, Miss. I'm sorry."

On an impulse, I pulled him closer and gave him a hug. "Yes. You did. Because you should have brought it to me right away. Sebille and I have been looking all over for that serum."

"I know, Miss. I was going to bring it. But then I started feeling all funny inside and I...I forgot."

"I know it's hard for you to resist using the artifacts," I told him in a quiet but firm voice. "But you can't live here unless you do. You know that, right?"

He sighed, tears glistening in his eyes. "Yes, miss." He stood up. "I'll leave."

I reached out and snagged his hand before he could get away from me. "No. I'll talk to Sebille and Grym. They need to agree to give you a second chance..." Sebille because she worked with me at Croakies and I trusted her judgment. Grym because, technically, misuse of magical artifacts was against supernormal law.

Hobs' hopeful gaze lifted to mine. "Really, Miss?"

I nodded and then laughed when he threw himself at me. "I'm sure they'll be fine with it," I said. "But no more messing with the artifacts."

"Yes, Miss!" He turned toward the door, stringy muscles bunching to sprint away.

"Hobs?"

He skidded to a halt. "Yes, Miss?"

"How did Baca come to Croakies?" I wasn't

surprised that, once she'd gotten inside, Sebille and I hadn't seen her. Brownies did their work at night while others slept, cleaning and fixing things in the places where they lived.

His smile fell away. "She was sleeping outside, Miss. In a box. I had to help her."

I sighed again. Thinking about that beautiful creature living on the street broke my heart. But I couldn't let him keep bringing in strays. We'd be overrun, and the artifacts would be at risk.

"I'll have Grym look into her past. She can stay in the bookstore only...for a while. But I'm not making any promises. If Grym thinks she's untrustworthy, she'll have to leave."

His smile returned. "Thank you, Miss! Baca wants to pay her way. She's fixed lots of things with her tool belt."

I looked up at the spot on my ceiling where there'd always been a water stain. The stain was gone. "Yeah," I said, realizing she had.

Archie was coming through the door as Hobs shot out. My uncle jerked back with a laugh. "Whoa, there, son. Slow down."

He shook his head and then glanced at me. "Well, you look better. Sebille told me you were awake."

The void sorcerer was in his street clothes. "You've been signing books?"

He nodded. "We just closed up. My fingers are

cramping."

I laughed. Who would have ever thought my boring, bookish uncle would become a famous cozy mystery author.

He reached into thin air and pulled two steaming cups of tea from a void. Grinning, he handed one to me.

"You have your own personal void?" I asked.

He nodded. "A necessity now that I'm doing two jobs. Three if I count helping you." We shared a grin and sipped. "The boy looks good," Archie said.

"Hobs is much better." I frowned, thinking of the pretty brownie. "I'm afraid he's going to get his heart broken, though."

"It happens to all of us, Naida. He'll be fine." He crossed his hands in front of him, cocking his head at me. "Sounds like you had quite the adventure."

I drank tea and sighed at the warm feeling in my belly. "Did Grym tell you how it all turned out?"

"He did. Apparently, Princess Desiree is now inextricably bound to her family's lands, unable to leave until her two brothers return and release her. Uncle Lovelace will be living with Nina and Denzel for a while, and by all accounts, is buying out toy stores for baby gifts."

I grinned, feeling only slightly sorry for Desiree. She pretty much deserved her fate. "Lea and Grym are okay?"

"They're fine." Archie's eyes sparkled. "In fact, I

was wondering if you were up to coming downstairs. You have visitors."

Grym! Excitement had me shoving blankets aside to get up. "Just give me five minutes."

Archie stood, the sparkle flaring brighter. "Brilliant! I'll see you downstairs."

I quickly visited the bathroom, brushed my teeth and hair, and dressed in clean jeans and a feminine white blouse. I looked longingly at the cookies Hobs had brought me, my stomach rumbling, but decided I didn't want to take the time to eat them.

Then I bounced down the stairs, anxious to hear what had happened after I'd been poisoned and passed out.

I hit the dividing door at a run and opened it without slowing very much.

And screeched to a stop with my mouth hanging open.

Grym was there as I'd hoped. But he didn't look happy. He was standing near the tea counter. His arms were crossed over his broad chest, and he had a bunch of red roses gripped in one hand. He was clutching them so tightly, he'd broken the long stems and they were drooping.

Sebille stood a few feet away from him, her long, freckled face the color of chalk. She was holding a rolled-up document of some kind in one hand, and the other was stretched out in front of her as if she was considering blasting our visitors.

The ogres we'd met on our first visit to King Rhorr's lands were standing just inside Croakies' front door, which, I was relieved to see, was locked behind them, the *Closed* sign turned to the window.

The ogres were also carrying flowers, and they were smiling.

"What's going on here?" I asked, sending a worried look toward Maxine and Rick.

Sebille handed me a scroll made of creamy parchment. I unrolled it and squinted at the abundance of teeny tiny characters written in the same language as the rental agreement we'd deciphered in the void. Across the top was a single short sentence, written in English, in large, black letters.

King Rhorr Invites You to Attend a Special Event.

"What's this?" I asked Sebille.

She continued to stare at the two ogres, mute and clearly astonished.

I looked at Grym.

He gave me a frustrated look and growled out. "It's an engagement party."

"Whose engagement?" I asked, confused. Had this been what Rhorr meant after he'd called off the ogre with the club?

Sebille finally turned to me, her iridescent green gaze wide in her face. She tried to talk, but the words wouldn't come. She swallowed hard and tried again. "*Our* co-engagement." She jerked a thumb toward

Maxine and Rick. "We're apparently marrying them."

My knees went soft beneath me. "Huh?"

Archie cleared his throat.

Grym sighed. "At least we now know the contents of the small print at the end of that contract you two signed."

Sebille made a choking noise and dropped into a chair.

I looked at my uncle. "But I thought you went to find out what it was about. You didn't know?"

His grin widened. "Rhorr wouldn't see us. We decided to deal with it after we cleared up this Cupid mess." I stared at him for a long moment, remembering Archie saying we were committed to something worse than giving away our firstborn child.

And they'd never even seen the fine print. "That was mean," I told him, frowning.

He laughed gaily. "You deserved it. Who signs a contract with the ogres without reading the fine print?"

Rick and Maxine nodded.

Relief filled me. I laughed. "So this..." I swept an arm to indicate the two flower-carrying ogres. "You're all just messing with us, right? To teach us a lesson?"

Grym turned a glare on me.

Archie laughed. "Not at all. You've made quite a mess for yourselves."

I stumbled over to sit at the table with Sebille, the world spinning wildly around me. "Goddess on a thigh master. What have we done?"

"Apparently, you've gotten engaged," Archie said, succumbing to hilarity that was entirely inappropriate.

I turned a glare on him. "It's not funny."

Grym finally gave in and laughed too. "It's a little funny."

I shook my head, returning my gaze to the twosome at the door. I wondered if anybody had noticed that one of them was a girl. I paled, suddenly wondering which one I was supposed to marry.

I didn't wonder for long.

Maxine winked and blew me a noisy kiss.

The End

DON'T MISS OUT

Stay up on all Sam's news by joining her newsletter, and get a copy of a fun mystery just for signing up!

SIGN UP HERE: https://samcheever.com/newsletter

READ MORE ENCHANTING INQUIRIES

If you enjoyed **Love Croakies**, you might want to check out the rest of the series: https://samcheever.com/books/#enchanting

Enjoy this taste of Book 12: Piped Croakies:

The Pied Piper shall lead them all astray...A captured audience helpless to its sway. The pipe's infectious music bids them come...and come they will...two by two or one by one.

Just when I thought my life couldn't get any weirder, life upped the strangeness quota to a never-before-seen level.

When a long line of critters, dazed and seemingly oblivious, marched past Croakies, I knew we had a *situation* on our hands.

Actually...if you counted being unwillingly affianced to a big old pink ogre...I had more than one situation.

Le sigh.

Then someone died. A king declared war on Enchanted. And my situation became a *crisis*. It would be up to me to find the perpetrator and bring him to justice while wrangling the rogue pipe artifact he used for his nefarious deeds.

Buffalo buttocks! I really do need a vacation.

PIPED CROAKIES

Prestidigitation, Legalese, and Larceny

"We need an anti-ogre ward on the front door," Sebille growled before flinging two garment bags onto Shakespeare's desk, where I was studying ogre law.

I frowned at the bags. "What are these?"

Rather than respond, she reached over and unzipped the one on top, pulling it open to show me something from a fashion nightmare.

I shook my head, widening my eyes at her. "A really ugly dress? Where did it come from?"

"Where do you think, Naida!" she screamed, surprising even herself if the excessive blinking was any indication. She scrubbed a hand over her face, her hand shaking. "Sorry. This stupid wedding thing has me twisted in knots."

I could certainly understand that. I was spending ten hours a day, to the detriment of all my other work, trying to find a loophole in the contract we'd signed.

"These are supposed to be our wedding dresses." She grimaced. "I'm not marrying that ogre," she told me, her tone seeming to imply that I thought she should.

I raised my hands in self-defense. "I'm with you. We're not going to marry them. Even if we need to take a really long vacation on another dimension to avoid it."

She nodded, appearing mollified.

I tugged the bag away from the fluffy pink, black, and white dress, grimacing at the abundance of tule puffing out through the middle and over the hips. The dress seemed custom-made for ensuring its wearer looked thirty pounds heavier than she was. I forced my lips to uncurl and held it in front of Sebille. "At least you have the figure to make the most of this," I told her, earning a sour look in response.

"That's *your* dress, Naida."

I was pretty sure all the color drained from my face. "What? No. It can't be."

She showed me the card that had been shoved into a small pocket near the hanger. My name was scrawled over the cream-colored square in heavy black ink.

Whatever blood I had left in my face fled south. My five-foot-eight-inch, slightly fluffy frame would look terrible in the dress. "I can't wear this! I'll look like a really big piece of ugli fruit."

Sebille snorted. "You will. Thank goodness mine is more tasteful."

I cast a jaundiced blue eye over her current outfit of a short-sleeved forest green dress with hot pink polka dots, which she wore over striped pink and purple socks that disappeared beneath the flounce which landed below her knees and were tucked into her usual shiny red Wicked Witch of the West shoes. At least the shoes matched her fire-engine-red hair.

As usual, her fashion choices literally hurt the eyes and were an assault on good taste. "You don't say?" I responded.

Sebille rolled her eyes. "You're just jealous."

I flapped my lips, not sure what direction to go, and then gave up, shoving the nightmare in tulle toward the bag. "If I wasn't already determined to avoid this wedding, that dress would be enough to do it."

Sebille flopped down into Casanova's chair, twitched unhappily as the over-sexed furniture pinched her left buttock, and then reached down to smack the velvet seat hard enough to make the chair jump and try to scurry away. The sprite flung an immobility spell at the unfortunate thing, and it screeched to a halt on the concrete. Finally, the horrid piece of perverted furniture had met its match.

The door dividing the bookstore from the artifact library opened, and a tiny face peeked through. "Miss?" Hobs, our resident hobgoblin, said. "Something's wrong."

I closed my eyes, striving for calm. Something was always wrong. Casanova's chair creaked as Sebille stood up. "I'll go," she said crankily. "You keep looking for that loophole."

Sighing, I shoved the garment bags aside and bent over my book again. *Prestidigitation, Legalese, and Larceny in Ogrish Law: How to Maneuver around the Rocklike Obstinance of an Ogre King's Law* wasn't exactly compelling reading. Nor was it particularly helpful. My uncle Archibald Pudsnecker, a.k.a. Pudsy, told me the hard-to-read tome was my best chance to find a way out of the contract Sebille and I had signed without reading the small print.

In our defense...and I believed it was a really good defense...the contract had been written on the wide, pudgy back of the ogre king. It was a long contract, and the part that got us into trouble was located in the nether regions. And I mean that literally.

I'd closed my eyes and slashed the pen over my

side of the posterior parchment without studying the last paragraph of the diabolical contract.

I'd know better next time. Fool me once; shame on you. Fool me twice, and I'd put holes in your posterior paper with a quill pen.

The door opened again. Sebille's head poked through. "Um, Naida."

I dropped my forehead onto the book, pounding it a few times against the aged pages. My long, brown hair flew around my head from the repeated blows.

She ignored my tantrum. "You're going to want to see this."

I lay there another beat and then sat up with a sigh. "I'm coming."

When I came through the door, I frowned at the sight in front of me. Mr. Wicked, Fenwald, Mr. Slimy, Hobs, and our newest member of the Croakies household, Baca the brownie, were all lined up along the windowsill, staring at something on the street.

What was really strange wasn't so much that they were lined up there. It was the way they all sat, so completely still, that seemed unnatural enough to give me pause.

Especially Hobs. He rarely sat still at all, let alone for any length of time.

I glanced at Sebille. "What's wrong with them?"

"Huh?" She frowned at me. "Not them, Naida." She motioned for me to follow her to the window.

Not a single one of my housemates looked up when Sebille and I joined them. I looked out at the scene in the street and felt my eyes go wide. "That's..."

I fell into a kind of daze, watching the parade on the street with uncommon focus.

A long line of animals, lined up as far as I could see in both directions, moved quickly past without so much as a glance from side to side.

Cats walked in front of dogs. Dogs walked in front of ferrets. Ferrets walked in front of bunnies. Bunnies hopped in front of squirrels. Birds flew above frogs, and frogs hopped in front of ducks.

It took me a moment to yank myself out of the light trance the sight had dropped me into. I literally shook it off and stepped away from the window, feeling dread tightening my chest. "What's that about?"

No response. I glanced at Sebille and discovered that she was enthralled as I'd been. "Sebille?"

Silence.

I reached over and poked her shoulder with a finger. She blinked and frowned. "Ouch, Naida."

"You were in a trance."

She rolled her eyes. "Of course I wasn't."

I shook my head. She had been. "Do you have any idea what's going on out there?"

"Not a clue. I tried to go outside, but the door wouldn't open."

"What do you mean, the door wouldn't open?"

"I mean, it wouldn't open. It was like there was some kind of spell holding it closed."

I hurried over to the door and turned the knob, pulling it open. Giving my assistant a look, I arched a brow.

"I'm not lying, Naida," she snapped. "It wouldn't open before."

I stepped outside and looked around. The street was empty. "Where'd they all go?"

"Naida?"

I turned at the familiar voice of my friend Leandra. Lea was an earth witch, and she had an herbal shop next to Croakies. She was standing on the sidewalk outside *Herbal Remedies with Mystical Properties*, looking slightly dazed. Mr. Wicked's littermate, Hex, was clutched tightly in her arms. "Did you see that?"

I frowned down the street. "They were just here. Did you see where they went?"

Lea looked more spooked than I'd ever seen her. And that was saying something because she and I had been in some really weird situations together. "I was tugging on the door, trying to get out here. I couldn't open it. And then it suddenly..." She stared at her hand, her voice trailing off.

Sebille hit the sidewalk, all three cats and Slimy in her wake.

I threw a panicked look at the shop, but she shook her head. "I told Hobs and Baca they needed to stay out of sight."

"Good." The last thing we needed was for the humans in the neighborhood to see a hobgoblin and a brownie standing on the street.

Lea walked over and placed Hex on the sidewalk next to the other cats. The three of them immediately started twining together like some kind of furry, three-looped infinity symbol.

Something bad is coming, Slimy said inside my head. I nodded, knowing he was right. Residual energy bit along my arms, and a sulfurous stench still clung to the air. I looked at Sebille. "Talk to your mom. Maybe she can read the energy signature and tell us what that was."

For once, Sebille didn't argue. She strode away toward the enormous greenhouse behind Lea's shop. Her mother, Queen Sindra of the Enchanted fae, was currently living in the huge space, paying Lea for her hospitality by making her garden grow. The queen had recently been making noises about moving to one of the magical forests nearby. But, so far, she hadn't made any serious movement in that direction. Lea...and even though she'd never admitted it, Sebille...were hoping she didn't. I had to agree. The queen was powerful. But more importantly, she was experienced in the ways of the magical community. She'd been a vital ally for us on many occasions.

"Did you hear the music?" Lea asked.

Ripped from my thoughts, I turned a blank look in her direction. "Huh?"

"The music? It wasn't like anything I'd ever heard. It was strangely..." She frowned. "I'm not sure how to describe it." She placed a hand over her belly. "It felt like fingers grabbing my guts and tugging me forward."

I hadn't felt that. Had I? "I didn't hear any music," I told her, hoping I wasn't lying. I had a vague feeling that I might have heard something, but I didn't think it was music.

"It didn't sound like music," said a voice from the street.

Lea and I looked up to find our friend Rustin striding toward us. Sadie, his tiny amalgamate dragon, was perched on his shoulder, her rainbow-hued wings lifting and falling with every step. The usually cheerful little dragon appeared subdued.

Rustin was a little older than me, in his late twenties, with a strong jaw, a piercing blue gaze, thick black hair, and the cutest pair of wire-rimmed spectacles sitting on his classically perfect nose.

"Hey," I greeted my friend.

He stepped onto the sidewalk, and Sadie flew off his shoulder as he stopped. She joined the cats and the frog on the sidewalk behind us. "It was more like a hollow chiming sound," Rustin said. He frowned, rubbing his temple almost absently with two fingers. "It gave me the devil of a headache."

Sadie rose off the concrete, giving him a little trill as she fluttered around us with almost manic excitement.

He nodded. "Sadie says it was a lullaby. Like her mother used to sing to her."

I looked at Lea, lifting a brow in question.

Still rubbing her stomach as if it pained her, the witch seemed to be considering her response to my unspoken question. "I'm not sure. I have a vague impression of a specific memory. I was sitting around a campfire at Enchanted Lake with a bunch of my friends. Somebody was singing. It was a beautiful, haunting melody. That's what I heard."

"Odd," Rustin said. He shoved his glasses up his nose. His piercing blue gaze was contemplative. "It's definitely some kind of magic."

"But focused on animals?" I asked, shaking my head. "I've never seen anything like that before."

"It's a spell of some kind," Lea said. "I'd stake my store on it."

Judging by the sulfurous stench it had left behind, I tended to agree. I settled a speculative gaze on the small group of our animals, which had grown bored and were heading back into the store to see what trouble they could get into. "We need to find out what that was. If it was an artifact, I need to wrangle it. The potential for it being used for bad things is monumental."

"I agree," Rustin and Lea said in unison.

Lea nodded toward the disappearing backside of my mentor's black cat. "What's Fenny doing here?"

I sighed. "Alice showed up with him last night. Apparently, she's going to be island hopping for the next month. She's in search of a magical pitcher of Margaritas." I peaked my brows as Lea laughed.

"Margaritas, huh?" Rustin said, grinning. "The cat doesn't like Margaritas?"

"Fenwald tends to chunder when Alice moves around too much. At least that's what she keeps insisting." I shrugged. "I don't mind. I've actually come really close to telling her to just leave him here. Being around the other cats is good for him. And he's good company."

"That's a great idea," Lea said. "She can come for visits whenever she misses him."

I grimaced. "Way to talk me out of it," I told her.

"I'm going to go research music-based spells," my friend told me. "I'll let you know what I find out."

"Thanks," I told her. "We're getting Sindra's opinion too. And I'll research possible artifacts."

I turned to Rustin as Lea headed back into her shop. He was staring off down the street, tension evident in the way he was holding himself. "What?" I asked my friend.

He gave a little twitch and turned to me. "Huh?"

"What's got you so bothered?"

"I have a really bad feeling about this, Naida."

I couldn't agree more. "Slimy thinks it portends bad things."

"I agree." He pointed toward Croakies. "Do you mind if Sadie has a play date today? I'm going to do some research too. Between all of us, we should be able to figure this out."

"It's fine. I'm sure they're all in the artifact library by now. Wicked is probably leading them on a dust bunny adventure."

Rustin's smile was tight. "Great. I'll let you know what I figure out."

———————

Read the rest of the book: https://samcheever.com/books/piped-croakies/

ALSO BY SAM CHEEVER

If you enjoyed **Love Croakies**, you might also enjoy these other fun mystery series by Sam. To find out more, visit the **BOOKS** page at www. samcheever.com:

Enchanting Inquiries Paranormal Mysteries - **For more fun adventures with Naida, Sebille, and Wicked!**
Reluctant Familiar Paranormal Mysteries
Yesterday's Paranormal Mysteries
Gainfully Employed Mysteries
Silver Hills Cozy Mysteries
Country Cousin Mysteries
And More...

ABOUT THE AUTHOR

USA Today and WSJ Bestselling Author Sam Cheever writes contemporary and paranormal mystery and suspense, creating stories that draw you in and keep you eagerly turning pages. Known for writing great characters, snappy dialogue, and unique and exhilarating stories, Sam is the award-winning author of 80+ books.

To learn more about Sam and her work, visit her at one of her online hotspots:
www.samcheever.com
samcheever@samcheever.com